Why did she fear Brennig?
Ellen asked herself.

"Brennig..." she murmured sleepily. Then, with a start, she remembered the man who was waiting for her back home. "Brent..." Their names were so similar, but the two men were so very different.

Weren't they? Or did Brennig remind her a little of Brent, and was that why she was drawn to him? It was so confusing. One moment she thought they were alike, moved alike, laughed alike, and then it became more and more difficult to see Brent's face in her thoughts, difficult to remember his voice. Difficult to remember the little things about him...

Echoes of the dream-glazed and heart-turning day throbbed around her. That awful surge of loneliness she had felt on the bridge swayed around her in the darkness.

The curse of Wrenn's Oak bridge...

How could it be?

But how could it *not* be?

Dear Reader,

Winter is truly here, so you'll really need to bundle up as you read our newest Shadows, because both the weather and fear will have you shivering if you're not careful.

Regan Forest takes you to Wales in *Bridge Across Forever,* an eerie tale that combines a touch of the past with the present to create a story unlike any you've ever read before. This one has an ending that will truly surprise you.

New author Carrie Peterson checks in with *The Secrets of Sebastian Beaumont,* a marriage of convenience tale with a scary twist. You'll never think of the traditional plot line in the same way again.

In months to come, look for more spooky reading from such great authors as Helen R. Myers and Lindsay McKenna here in the shadows— Silhouette Shadows.

Yours,

Leslie Wainger
Senior Editor and Editorial Coordinator

REGAN FOREST

BRIDGE ACROSS FOREVER

SILHOUETTE® Shadows™

Published by Silhouette Books
America's Publisher of Contemporary Romance

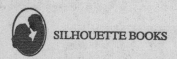 SILHOUETTE BOOKS

ISBN 0-373-27021-6

BRIDGE ACROSS FOREVER

Printed in U.S.A.

REGAN FOREST

grew up in western Nebraska's sandhills and spent her early years close to nature, indulging thousands of fantasies of faraway, enchanted places. A world traveler, she also spent many years overseas, pursuing such adventures as picking wild berries in the Black Forest, tromping through the African bush and walking the icy halls of medieval castles—accompanied by the resident ghosts, of course!

She actually wrote her *first* novel at the tender but precocious age of eleven, and today she is published by Harlequin Books, as well as Silhouette Shadows. She lives in the Southwest now, with her husband, kids—and dogs—and is constantly inspired by the magnificent Arizona sunsets. She counts herself blessed, since she is doing exactly what she'd always wanted to do most: writing romances, which are the world's best place for the touching and sharing of dreams.

To Bill, with love

PROLOGUE

Floodwaters clawed at the bridge, licking the long skirts of a witch who stood with arms outstretched over storm-crazed waves. Lightning cracked over an adjacent churchyard, flashing white on the just-laid tombstone of the only man she would ever love...a man who had died by her hand because he refused to love her in return.

A man whose surname—Cole—she had cursed for eternity.

Now she must search for him in death.

Rain pounded the swollen shores of the river and beat the water relentlessly. Nesta's cloak flapped like raven's wings against her reaching arms. Her angry cries caught on a wail of the wind, harmonizing with the moans of ancient water spirits inhabiting the river Lugg—evil spirits guarding the border between Wales and England, who were coaxing her toward their watery lair.

When she jumped into the black, writhing waves, a terrible lightning spear slashed her scream; shards of her howling lament fell over her, to be swallowed by the river.

The storm sighed into silence.

No trace of Nesta was ever found, but from her mysterious disappearance, a legend grew, an obscure tale of a woman's face appearing in the shivering water near the bridge. Not many know the legend or see the macabre specter—only those who still possess the name—and therefore the curse—of their murdered ancestor.

Persons whose veins carry even the smallest ember of his fiery blood cannot cross the Wrenn's Oak Bridge without walking into despair—unknowingly, for the only one who knew of the curse was the witch's original victim, Brennig Cole. And he had never made it to the other side, either in life or in death.

CHAPTER ONE

Present

A pair of swans moved leisurely through the shallows. On the medieval bridge in Wrenn's Oak that connected Wales to England, an American in blue jeans stood gazing out over the river and the hills beyond, breathing in the beauty around her and thinking, *I'm really in Wales, walking the same paths my ancestors walked. At last.* Ellen Cole smiled at the sight of a distant castle ruin and long-tailed sheep grazing sleepily on the slopes. The red slate roofs and chimneys of the houses on the other side were picture perfect.

During her first hour in Wrenn's Oak, exploring the village, Ellen had been drawn from the churchyard by the beauty of the bridge, with its lazily moving water and reedy shores darkened by shadows of overhanging willows. Squinting as the sun's rays tangled in the flowing ripples below her, she could hear a sound that was almost like the river breathing.

Suddenly the water began to shudder near the bridge. Out of the tiny waves appeared the face of a woman with eyes formed of deep, drowned shadows, and long, dark hair that floated and flowed on the ripples.

Shock gave way to fear. Ellen gripped the stone rails, unable to look away from the evil shadow-eyes. The diabolical thing in the water didn't fade when she blinked; it remained fixed in the water's spasms. A strange breeze shivered through the willows and brushed her forehead with a damp, cold gust that blew off as quickly as it came.

Horrified, she backed away from the railing. *A hundred thousand others have walked this medieval bridge... how many have looked down and seen a woman's face?*

When she dared look back, the face was no longer there. It was only the odd way the water had rippled, she told herself fiercely. It had only been an illusion.

An illusion? At the center of the bridge, standing with one foot in England and the other in Wales, Ellen suddenly felt an overwhelming, dark sorrow enter her body. Coldness, left by the chilling breeze, moved through and then lodged uncomfortably in her heart along with the strange remorse of having just lost something. The despair of aloneness was so powerful, she couldn't move. Something stopped her from stepping into England.

However dazed, she knew instinctively that what she had seen was not her imagination. The phantom that had writhed in the spangled water had to be the cause of the awful darkness assailing her senses. For some reason the thing had shown itself to her. Horrified, she turned her back on England, retracing her steps to the safety of the Welsh side of the village from where she'd come. Her knees trembled. Her heart pounded. That face in the water...with flowing hair that became ripples...what could it be?

The steeple of the Wrenn's Oak church cast its pointed four o'clock shadow over the old graveyard that sloped to the mossy riverbanks. Crossing its thin shadow, Ellen hurried away from the bridge, looking over her shoulder, half-afraid the evil thing she'd glimpsed might follow her.

The graveyard lay in silence. There seemed no order to the placement of the few scattered stones; perhaps many were missing. Chipped or broken, some leaning, some fallen, the stones basked in the sun like tired old soldiers whose battles were fought too long ago for anyone who walked among them now to remember. Or care.

Ellen cared. Her ancestors might lie beneath these stones. In fact, she had come to search for fading names when the music of the river and the old stone bridge had distracted her. From where she stood now, this short distance away, the swans still swam in peaceful shade; there were no warning signs of an evil presence lurking in the water.

Trying to will away the lingering fear, Ellen turned her attention to the graves, studying each one, looking for an ancestor's name.

The sun, moving westward, reflected on the stained-glass window of the chapel, sending rays of color over the grass, effecting an illusion of life. In the pink splash of such a ray, she found it.

The gravestone leaned west, away from the bridge. It was thick and square, showing the wear of centuries. The worn letters were just visible: BRENNIG COLE BORN 1607 DIED 1631. The blacksmith's grave! Ellen reached out to touch the aged stone. It felt so cold even in the sun.

Her great-grandfather had described the tombstone of a Cole ancestor, a blacksmith in this village. A strong and handsome man, legend had it that he had discouraged bandits from the village by stabbing three of them to death. Later, his wife had been sentenced to hang for murdering him—for reasons no one ever knew. This hanging was recorded fact. But no documentation of her execution or her grave had ever been found.

In the silence of the churchyard, Ellen stood transfixed before the time-battered stone, imagining that day in 1631 when the grave was open to receive a young man's body. Were there mourners' tears on his coffin? Sobs of farewell? Flowers on the freshly turned earth? That day the sun would have reflected on the stained-glass window just as it did now, and the murmuring song of the river would have been the same song she was hearing now.... And the shadow of the steeple would have darkened this ribbon of grass just as it did now....

That day three and a half centuries ago... was the summer air clotted with whispers of murder?

A large yellow butterfly lit on the tombstone, moving its wings to invite color from the sunlight. When Ellen reached toward it, the butterfly flew to her wrist. Its touch, light as mist, somehow thawed the chill inside her. Her knees ceased their trembling for the first time since the bridge.

She began to walk, strolling from the churchyard onto the crooked road. The butterfly glided along, hovering weightless on the air, following her.

"Look," she offered. "Why don't *I* follow *you?* Since I don't know my way around here and you do."

In this village of her ancestors, Ellen walked past a few small houses, crossed the narrow business street and strolled along a lane where the residences grew farther apart. The butterfly led the way—a little quiver of gold darting and flitting around her head.

There were massive trees in this part of town, and the homes were very old. Some had thatched roofs, most had dormer windows, all closed by shutters. The village was much as she had pictured it. More charming, though, with the river running through and the view of the medieval castle high on a hill.

The butterfly lit on the rail of an iron gate, fluttering its wings as it had done on the tombstone. Ellen halted in front of a cottage with a To Let By Week Or Month sign in the window.

Such a charming old house! Why hadn't she thought of letting a cottage? With a sense of excitement, she opened the gate and walked the short flower-lined path to the door. It was easy to picture herself throwing open the east shutters to the morning sun, and walking in the garden.

There would have to be a garden, she reasoned, following the stone path around to the back where a taller gate stood open. Inside the stone wall, Ellen drew a delighted sigh at the sight of a wild garden, prolific and overgrown and filled with color. She recognized plants and flowers of the Welsh hills. Cowslips and primroses and parsley ferns hugged the outer stone walls. Bright Welsh poppies bloomed along rocks, and purple orchids grew in the shade of overhanging oak and willow branches.

Movement in the shadows caught her eye. From a tangle of ivy that completely covered a wooden back gate, a man carrying garden shears stepped out, rustling leaves with the brush of his arms. Huskily built in jeans and a short-sleeved shirt, he halted and stared.

Ellen moved off the path. "Pardon me . . . I saw the To Let sign. . . ."

He walked toward her, under the flickering dapples of sunlight filtering through the trees. When he stopped at a blackthorn shrub in a bright slash of light, Ellen was hit by vertigo, a quick spin of fear, for his eyes in direct light appeared as pale as glass, without pupils. Then he moved his head and the bright arrow of sun shifted, and color flooded into his eyes like the reflection of the sky.

The yellow butterfly, still with her, swung in the air between them.

"Brimstone," the man said in a voice deep and heavily burred.

"What?" She blinked, trying not to stare at the shifting shades of color in his strange eyes and wondering if she should turn and run.

"The butterfly. A brimstone, it's called." He cleared his throat. His slow Welsh accent was very thick. "A male. The female brimstone is white." He smiled then, showing even, white teeth.

The butterfly vanished into a cluster of yellow poppies.

Accepting the welcome in his smile, Ellen asked, "Is it your house?"

"The owner is Mrs. Jenkins, who lives just...there." He pointed to the house across the street. "Are you of a mind to stay?"

Ellen was mesmerized by his voice. It was as if she had heard it before somewhere...or knew somebody with a voice like that, without the accent. "Yes, I think so," she answered. "For a few weeks."

"It's a fine cottage."

Shading her eyes, Ellen gazed up at the dormer window. "It looks very old."

"Over three centuries old. Like many of the buildings around here."

Her heart stirred. The old, old house humbled her, excited her, invited her.... "I think I'll see if Mrs. Jenkins is at home."

"She is. But knock loudly because her hearing is not good."

"Thanks. Are you a friend of hers?"

His ice blue eyes reflected the shadows of the moving leaves. "No. I'm just working the garden. Mrs. Jenkins will be happy to see you. The cottage has been empty for some time."

Ellen made her way back along the stone path, noting the quiet of the neighborhood. Two children were riding bicycles at the far end of the street, and a woman was walking her dog. There was a feeling of peace here.

An elderly woman wearing a pale blue apron answered her knock.

"Mrs. Jenkins? I was told you're the person to contact about renting the cottage."

"Aye, that I am." This response came with a happy smile from which a tooth was missing. "I'm asking fifty pounds per week, or a hundred seventy-five per month, which is a savings of twenty-five pounds."

"I'd like it for a month, then."

The smile broadened. Mrs. Jenkins wiped her hands on her apron. "Surely you want to have a look at it first."

Ellen turned and glanced back at the cottage. It stood in hushed seclusion, so oblivious to time, at peace with the runaway growth of flowers that hugged its walls. The yellow butterfly had led her here. Yellow butterflies were lucky; she'd always thought so. Never mind that her guide was called brimstone. "I'm sure it will do fine."

"Excellent, then." Mrs. Jenkins untied her apron and tossed it onto a bench in the foyer, taking a key from the single drawer of a lamp table. "Let me show you about."

Walking with a cane and a limp, she led the way across the street, asking in her musical voice, "Are you American or Canadian?"

"American. My name is Ellen Cole. My ancestors were from this area and I wanted to see for myself the places my grandfather talked about with that distant look of longing in his eyes. Wrenn's Oak is even more beautiful than I'd imagined."

"Cole, you say? A fine Welsh name. Aye, there are Coles living in the valley." She studied the young woman curiously. "Americans usually hurry through, if they come at all to our wee village."

"I have a month's vacation and I decided one must stay in a place to know it. I'd like to write some stories about Wrenn's Oak someday, record some of the legends my grandfather loved." It was also true that she couldn't afford to tour all over Britain, even if she'd wanted to.

Mrs. Jenkins unlatched the low wrought-iron gate and held it open for her.

They entered a small, dark foyer from which a staircase led to the upper floor. On one side was the parlor, furnished in provincial antiques, with flowered drapes and a floral-patterned rug. On the left was a dining room, where a massive oak hutch displayed a collection of stoneware pitchers. Across the back, the spacious kitchen was painted blue and white, with a stone fireplace and a sturdy oak table and chairs. Ellen pictured a seventeenth century family gathered around this kitchen fireplace on icy winter nights.

"You see the modern stove," Mrs. Jenkins said proudly. "Small but efficient, with an oven. You will find a supply of firewood on the back porch. The nights can get chilly."

Dishes were stacked neatly behind glass cupboard doors. French windows looked out on the garden with its vine-covered walls and trees filled with bird songs. If the gardener was still out there, Ellen couldn't see him. She drew her gaze back. "It's a lovely kitchen."

"Aye, isn't it?" The old woman leaned on her cane. "Forgive me, I cannot easily climb the stairs to show you the bedrooms. One is comfortably large. There are quilts. I shall make up the bed with fresh linens."

"There's no need for you to climb the stairs," Ellen said. "Just leave the linens on the landing, and I'll make up the bed after I go to the hotel for my bags. I checked into the hotel earlier today, thinking I would look for a bed-and-breakfast somewhere in the environs. But then I saw this house just by chance when I was walking around. Lucky for me. I love it."

Mrs. Jenkins, who wore a dark skirt and a crisp white blouse, brushed a wisp of gray hair from her forehead. She smiled. "Just by chance? My dear, nothing happens just by chance in this life. Have you heavy bags to carry from the hotel?"

"I have a car. A college friend who lives in London loaned me hers. She's spending the summer in Italy, so I drove up from London. Is there a place to park?"

"The back alley is wide enough for parking." Mrs. Jenkins handed her tenant the key on a little chain. "I hope you will be very comfortable here. You are welcome to use my washing machine. If there is anything else you need, please let me know. I'll leave the linens and check tomorrow to see if everything is all right."

"Thanks. I'll cash some traveler's cheques in the morning and give you the month's rent in cash tomorrow, if I may." As they walked to the door, she asked, "Why does no one live in such a lovely house, Mrs. Jenkins?"

"I bought it for a song after the widow Gleani Cole, who lived here, passed away. I could sell it, I suppose, but I haven't the inclination to do so. I rather like letting it. One meets interesting people."

Ellen opened the front gate for her, and as soon as her landlady had gone, she walked to the back garden. The young man wasn't there. Flitting among a mass of bugle-shaped purple flowers was an orange-and-black butterfly. Not a brimstone. Her butterfly should have been in the garden waiting for her, but it wasn't.

From the parking area, she carried her bags through the ivy-covered back garden gate and unlocked the kitchen door. On the table Mrs. Jenkins had left neatly folded white-and-pink flowered bed sheets, a stack of four pink towels, a canister of tea and a plate of fresh pastries.

Pleased with herself for having discovered this sweet, quaint cottage, Ellen headed up the stairs with her bags. The stairway was dark and narrow. Antiques and flowered curtains furnished the two bedrooms upstairs. The larger room held two twin beds with comforters of dusty rose. The wallpaper was pale pink with silver stripes and clusters of lavender and pink flowers. The house felt stuffy, yet everything was freshly dusted. She opened the window and stood looking down on a view of the back garden. Branches of an elm tree reached the sill. Below, primrose grew in a copse of velvet green. A thrush was singing a wistful, dusky song.

For a moment, Ellen thought she saw the shadow of the gardener move across the copse, against the stone wall, yet there was no sign of the man down there, only the deepening shadows of twilight. A cool breeze blew from the distant hills, down across the river and through the shallow valley.

A rumble in her stomach reminded her of the pastries on the kitchen table. Quickly she made up one of the twin beds with the fresh-smelling sheets.

Five minutes later, waiting for the water to boil for tea, Ellen was assailed by a sensation that she was not alone. Turning, she thought she caught movement in the hallway, but only the pale, soft shadows of the kitchen were visible. It had to be a carryover reaction from her horrible experience on the bridge, she told herself—the sight of that face combined with the teasing of the hotel proprietor when she'd gone to collect her bags.

"It's called the Afan House," he had said good-naturedly. "Aye, I know the cottage. I've not darkened its doors myself, lass. It's haunted, that one. If you wonder why it's vacant, that's because of its ghosts."

"Haunted?" she had repeated. "Ghosts?"

She had wanted the man to smile, but he hadn't. "I cannot say firsthand. Cannot say I know of a specific sighting. But everybody says the house is haunted."

"Well, I suppose it would be—a centuries-old house."

"Would you be changing your mind, then, lass?"

Ellen had laughed and replied sincerely, "Not on your life! It's exciting! What's to be afraid of? Ghosts don't go around hurting people, they just...haunt."

Now, in the gloaming, as the kitchen filled with somber shadows, she caught herself looking over her shoulder as she had done on the bridge. Sitting at the table with her journal, she sipped tea and nibbled raspberry-filled biscuits. From somewhere in the depths of the house came a sound like footsteps. As night descended, the creaks and groans of the house were growing louder.

She swallowed hard and listened. It came from above, as if someone were walking around upstairs. Ellen's heart beat fast with excitement more than fear. It might be the elm branches hitting the window, or a shutter banging in the mild breeze. Or maybe a ghost? Spirits didn't harm people. If there was one in this house, it might have been here for a very long time.

It was nothing. She would ignore it. Scribbling in her journal, she studied the name Afan House. Did the word have any special meaning? Tomorrow she must ask. She'd ask that gardener with the pale eyes and the deep Welsh voice, and the tight jeans.

Morning seemed a long way off—on the other side of a night of eerie noises and a growing conviction that she was not alone in this house. Not a comfortable feeling, yet it stopped short of fear. Fear was what she'd felt on the bridge; the chill had reached all the way to her toes and had rendered her temporarily immobile. After that, a few creaks and things going bump were little threat. All the more to write about, and to make this cottage intriguing. The sense of adventure was growing with each passing moment.

Mrs. Jenkins would have warned her if there was anything to be warned about. Maybe the guy in the garden would have, too. Why couldn't she get him out of her head?

"Guilt," she said aloud. "Guilt! My first day here and I'm thinking about another man. Damn." She sat back, wondering if the night would get cold enough to justify a fire. "You're thinking about me right now, Brent, I know you are. And I'm here in a house with ghostly footsteps sounding upstairs, thinking about the smile of a stranger in my mysterious garden. The man with the baffling eyes..."

Gazing at the turquoise ring Brent had given her for Christmas, Ellen wallowed in her guilt. Brent had been so nice to her this past month, and she had been too preoccupied with her trip plans to appreciate it. But he should have come... he should be here... after all, his ancestors had been here, too.

The fact they had the same last name was what had brought Brent Cole into her life. That was chance. But he didn't share her interest in what was probably a common heritage.

Nothing happens by chance, Mrs. Jenkins had said with conviction and a long life of experience behind her words.

Ellen sighed and gazed out the window. Silver shadows cloaked the garden. The rooms around her seemed darker than they should. Again she heard the sound of someone moving upstairs, when there couldn't be anyone else in the house. Gooseflesh formed on her arms.

"My adventure..." she muttered in fixed resolve, this time in only a whisper, as if fearing someone could hear her talking to herself. "There can't be danger in this lovely cottage. Any old spirits who live here only add to the atmosphere."

Even so, it would be very nice if Brent was with her tonight. Sensitive man that he was, he'd be assuring her they were alone in the house whether he believed it or not. "You should be here!" she told him. "I think this whole village is haunted, Brent. All the hills are haunted. The river is haunted, and the bridge..."

What time would it be in Arizona, anyhow? Would Brent be on the patio working? Trying to ignore the sounds of the house and the trees whispering outside, Ellen pulled up thoughts of a very different garden, Brent's oasis in the desert, where she would probably be right now if something hadn't drawn her to Wales. Something she thought she'd understood before she came, but now she wasn't quite so sure.

It seemed both right and wrong to be here. Scary and not scary at the same time. Lonely and not lonely.

When she closed her eyes, it wasn't the face of the handsome gardener that came. It was Brent's face, with the love and the sadness she had seen by the pool that night....

CHAPTER TWO

Two weeks earlier...

The rugged slopes of the Santa Catalina Mountains reflected the pink and orange hues of the Arizona sunset. Giant saguaros reached up their arms to catch the cooling breeze of a summer evening; their shadows sketched dark slashes against the slopes of the foothills.

Ellen climbed out of the pool onto the tiled deck, wrapped herself in a towel and poured another gin and tonic. The desert air was balmy. A dove called wistfully from somewhere beyond the adobe patio walls, where a group of wild javelina rooted about; she caught the musky smell of the wild pigs and heard their soft snorts.

Nearly dark, and Brent wasn't here yet. Stretching out on a chaise longue she herself had designed, Ellen watched the lights of Tucson sparkling like jewels in the valley below. Her gaze moved up past a pale sliver of moon to Venus, rising bright in the western sky. Her thoughts wafted back and forth, sometimes spinning between anticipation of Wales and Brent's talk about the future. It was easy to picture herself living in this lovely house of his. Yet something held her back. Something seemed missing from her life. Adventure. Travel. She just wasn't ready to marry yet and move in here with him, as much as she loved this place. As much as she loved him.

The faint crunch of tires on gravel announced Brent's arrival. Ellen smiled. It would take him six minutes exactly to get changed into his swim trunks and greet her at the pool with a kiss. Predictable Brent. One could set a clock by him, except this evening. Even knowing she would be here waiting for him, he was an hour late getting home.

Palm leaves, slivered by patio lights, rustled softly overhead. A tiny bat swooped over the pool. The outside lights went on and Brent's well-proportioned frame appeared at the bedroom's sliding glass door. His rubber thongs flapped as he made his way across the tiles. He bent down to kiss her. "Sorry I'm late. I've been talked into coaching another would-be Olympic swimmer."

She smiled up at him. Reflections of the sunset bronzed his hair. "He must be good or you wouldn't have agreed to coach him."

Brent shrugged. "The potential seems to be there. The kid's a strong swimmer, but has never had any coaching." He was mixing himself a drink at his adobe brick outdoor bar. "I explained to the father that I can take these kids only so far, and after that he'll have to find a professional coach, not somebody like me who just does it for a hobby."

He gulped back half the liquid, set down his glass and dived into the pool. Ellen watched him glide gracefully through the water with the style of the collegiate champion he had been once. Brent had never competed after college because he had had other ideas of what to do with his life. One never got rich racing back and forth down swim lanes, he had said. Now, at thirty-one, builder of some of the finest custom homes in the Tucson valley, he had already cleared his first million. His own home was the best advertisement for his creative designs in Southwest architecture.

Ellen knew she was lucky. She was envied for being Brent Cole's girlfriend. But they had differences. Brent played the differences down. She couldn't. After several laps, he climbed out and sat beside her, drying his face with a towel.

"Some clients of yours came to my store today," Ellen said. "They thought I was your wife."

"Why wouldn't they, when our names are the same? It's a problem you convinced me not to worry about. Does it bother you suddenly?"

"No," she lied. It probably wouldn't be fair to admit to it, although it had begun to bother her—now that she and Brent were so close—that she should be taken for his wife, never having been a bride.

Brent finished his drink and touched her hair affectionately. "You're restless lately, honey. You're thinking about your trip, I'll bet."

"Every minute. I wish you were coming with me."

"We've been over that," he said mildly. "I can't leave my work for a month to sit on a dot on the map that no one except your grandfather ever heard of."

A few yards away, a small, deep pond lined with mica-splashed rocks reflected silver light. Brent walked to the pond and switched on an underwater bulb so he could watch the goldfish glide about.

Ellen stood beside him, gazing down at the fish. "You could come with me if you really wanted to. Tucson weather has been over a hundred degrees for weeks and the monsoons will begin any day. You won't be starting construction on any new homes during the rainy season, will you?"

"There is more than enough work on homes already underway. I can't get too far behind schedule. And I've got three swimmers counting on me."

"You just don't want to go to Wales."

"No, honey, I don't. I don't share your interest in the obscure past of our ancestors."

"But it's all so fascinating! I might even discover how you and I are related . . . if I can go back far enough."

"Ah, that's pretty farfetched," he said. "There are a lot of people named Cole. I can't be related to them all."

Ellen smiled. "People with the same surname *are* distantly related, somehow. And you did have some ancestors from Wales and England both, so they might well have lived near the border, like mine."

The day two years ago, when she'd met Brent Cole at a party, was as clear in her mind as if it had happened only moments before.

"Brent Cole, the architect? I've heard of you," Ellen had said. "Who hasn't? Your homes are well-known."

"And I've heard of you," he had answered. "You're half of Bishop-Cole Gardens."

She had nodded, raising her drink with a mischievous smile. "Designer of the highest quality patio furniture in the Southwest. And I have it on good authority that you refer all of your clients to our competitor, Patios Plus. I've thought very seriously of looking you up and asking you why—when my designs are superior quality and more original by far, for your famously original gardens."

The young builder had studied her with intelligent, sensitive eyes and answered, "It's your last name. Cole. People would assume we're related and that I'm conjuring up family business. Conflict of interest. Bad image."

His reason was incredulous. "You've ignored me just because we have the same last name? That's the most unfair thing I've ever heard! You don't even know my work. My custom outdoor furniture is especially designed for

Arizona living, like your homes. You're cheating your clients by not recommending me, and some of them are discovering your mistake." She'd gulped at her drink for courage, but there! It was out. She'd been wanting to meet this guy and have her say for a long time.

Brent had looked down at her from what had seemed a very great height, with neither anger nor amusement in his soft hazel eyes. "Are you really that good?"

"Check for yourself."

"Okay, Miss Cole. I don't like being accused of unfairness, especially when the accuser might be right. So I *will* check you out. You can furnish my own patio. I have imported Mexican tiles in an alcove where the Jacuzzi is and there's a space for outside seating, also in a covered area where the wind whips in leaves and causes a constant mess. Do you want to see what you can do?"

"Absolutely! Thanks for the challenge." Ellen had known that evening that more was going to come of this than a contract for furniture. She had looked into Brent Cole's eyes and he had looked into hers, and they had known....

Now, two years later, with the fish pond added and plans for a fountain, Ellen felt more at home in Brent's beautiful home than in her own town house closer to town. Brent had mastered the desert environment.

Brent had fallen into silence, watching the colors in the western sky. Ellen said, "They delivered some stones a little while ago, for your fountain."

"Good," he said, smiling, "I've drawn up a new design for it. The rocks will appear to be a natural formation, with the short palms around them, and water will splash down into the pond. We'll have the sound of splashing water day and night."

His enthusiasm was clear. "You've planted your own roots deep in the desert," she said.

"Yeah." He led her back to the edge of the pool and began mixing them each another drink. "I've put down roots and you haven't."

"I don't have to. I was born here. I don't want roots anywhere. I want to fly free."

"Which is the difference between us," he said sadly.

"A big difference, Brent, but I hope we're not a hopeless cause."

"So do I." He proceeded to slice a lime and squeeze the slices into their drinks. "Some of our values are different. But I love you."

"I love you, too." She accepted the glass. "Even if you prefer nesting to adventure . . . to mystery. Ah, mystery's the thing!" The mystery of the past, she thought. And of places she had never been.

Brent clinked the ice in his glass slowly. "I can't offer you mystery. I can offer you a hell of a lot, but not that."

She lowered her eyes. "And I can't offer you the peace you want in your life."

A warm desert breeze rustled through the garden. "I'll miss you while you're away."

"You could join me later. Oh, would you, Brent? You could fly over and spend the last few days with me and I could share with you what I've learned and show you around and we could have a wonderful time. Won't you?"

"It sounds like a great idea. Sure. By that time, I'll be missing you so much I won't care whether you show me around the countryside or not."

Ellen hugged him. "You will come? For sure?"

"Yeah. We're going to work on compromises, honey. I want to share some of your interests and, hell, maybe I'll even like exploring some crumbling castles."

He kissed her and lowered the straps of her swimsuit. "Let's turn off the pool lights and go into the water, shall we?"

In the distance a coyote howled. Palm branches rustled overhead. Ellen felt the cool of the water and the warmth of Brent and the comfort of being in his arms.

It was so good here with him, she thought. Why did another part of her have to drag her away? There was a pull from the dark of old centuries reaching up and tickling her senses. There was a whispering, mysterious world out beyond Brent's patio walls. If only he could understand. The past was pulling her to Wrenn's Oak.

Here in Tucson, the just-delivered stones for his fountain were from the desert floor, and they served as symbols to weigh Brent down to the earth. But she...she wanted to fly.

CHAPTER THREE

Footsteps again. The echo jolted Ellen from her reverie. Vivid images of a Tucson night with its hissing cicadas and coyote wails dropped away and the Welsh cottage became reality again.

She sat up straight; a shiver moved down her legs. The stairs were creaking as if from heavy feet descending. Someone *was* in the house! It couldn't be Mrs. Jenkins— not on the steps. There was no sound of her cane, and she wouldn't just walk in without knocking, anyway. Earlier Ellen had managed to convince herself that the footsteps were only imagination, or else they belonged to the ghost rumored to live here. But the creaking on the stairs was changing to footsteps in the hallway, coming nearer....

With every nerve tensed, Ellen sensed a presence behind her. Unable to take a breath, she slowly turned her head.

The gardener was standing in the kitchen.

Gasping surprise, she stepped back. The teacup rattled in its saucer as her knee hit the table leg.

"I'm sorry," his deep voice said. "I didn't mean to startle you."

Her trembling hand moved involuntarily over her heart. "I had no idea you were in the house!" Her voice was so thin it sounded as though it belonged to someone else. "Why *are* you in the house?"

"I came in from the garden some time ago," he said as if this were an explanation.

Something was wrong here. The guy just walked in at will? "Do you want something?"

"I thought I'd make myself a cup of tea if I'm not in your way. I don't want to get in your way." He moved toward the stove. "I see you've already filled the teapot."

Ellen stood frozen. The man's accent was so thick she had to listen carefully when he spoke, but it was clear enough that he was making himself at home in the cottage she'd rented. What nerve!

"I've leased the cottage for a month," she said, her lips pressed tightly. His voice was friendly enough, but the trembling in her knees wouldn't stop. Something was very strange about this man who seemed to think it was all right to just walk in and help himself to tea.

"For a month? Mrs. Jenkins must be pleased." He lifted the lid of the teapot. Steam poured out. "May I pour you another cup, and perhaps be so brazen as to help myself? There seems plenty here."

Ellen felt the warmth of anger rise from her neck and cause her cheeks to flush. "Do you just walk into this house whenever you feel like it? No matter who is living here?"

The man's pale eyes darkened as if a shadow had crossed in front of them. "Mrs. Jenkins didn't tell you? I stay here, also—I have the loft room."

"*What?* You *stay* here? But that's impossible! Mrs. Jenkins would have told me if there was a man living in the house."

His plan to pour tea was forgotten. He leaned against the counter, rubbing his chin, looking worried. "I assumed so, yes, and that it was all right with you. Perhaps she was afraid you wouldn't take the cottage if you knew.

Maude Jenkins is a widow. She depends on this cottage to supplement her small income and it has been empty too much of the time. She probably didn't want to frighten you away."

Ellen shook her head, trying not to show her agitation. "She knew I'd find out soon enough!"

"Aye, so. But she knew also you would find me a very quiet tenant. I won't bother you. Except to use the kitchen occasionally and the water closet upstairs. I won't get in your way."

Ellen began to pace. It had all seemed so perfect. And now her privacy had suddenly vanished. She had wanted to see the attractive gardener again, had even looked for him. But this! He was living in the house? The situation was impossible!

"This situation is...very uncomfortable," she told him. "You live here all the time?"

"No, no. I have come from Shrewsbury for a few weeks of idleness." He gazed about the room. "I enjoy being in this cottage. It belonged to my family many years ago, which, I suppose, is why I like to stay here. The truth is, I can afford only the loft, in exchange for doing some work in the garden. It needs work... the garden does."

The sadness in his eyes was so evident he must have been aware of it, because he didn't look at her as he spoke. There was such an uncertainty about him, Ellen thought. He must be embarrassed that Mrs. Jenkins hadn't told her he was there. It was awkward for both of them, although the idea of a man and a woman—two strangers—sharing one small cottage didn't seem to bother him, or their landlady. Maybe this sort of thing was commonly done. Odd, she hadn't thought of the third-story room when she was upstairs, even though she had noticed the small window under the eaves when she first saw the house.

"I'm not sure about this," she said.

He hesitated, then offered, "If you are too uncomfortable with my being here, I'll find another place."

"That wouldn't be fair to you. You were here first. If anyone leaves, it should be me."

"No," he said.

She looked at him, at his pale eyes and a face so handsome it was distracting. It was his looks as much as anything that caused her discomfort. "You're concerned about Mrs. Jenkins. About the money."

He nodded, frowning, and finally poured himself a cup of tea and carried it to the table and sat down across from her. He tasted the tea and looked thoughtful, even doubtful, like a kid tasting spinach for the first time.

"Is the tea all right?" she asked.

"Fine." It sounded like a polite lie.

"I like it rather weak."

"It's fine." He took another slow sip. "Look, we might give it a try. I won't be in your way, I promise. I haven't even introduced myself." He held out his hand. "My name is Brennig Cole."

Ellen paled. A ripple of fright passed through her. *"Brennig Cole?"*

"Is something wrong?"

"It's...the name on one of the tombstones in the churchyard!"

The man grinned, showing a set of perfect teeth. "That would be my ancestor. Brennig is a family name, has been for generations. My father had the name and his father before him." He took a swallow of his tea. "You were looking at tombstones?"

"Yes, and that particular one. Brennig Cole is an ancestor of mine...on my father's side."

"Ah, now there's a coincidence! You're American, aye?"

She nodded. "My name is Ellen Cole."

"Hmm. That means some of the clan got themselves to America at some point in time. Have you traced an ancestor's arrival in America to any specific dates?"

"My great-grandfather was born somewhere near Wrenn's Oak. His name was Thomas Colwyn Cole, and his father's name was also Thomas."

The man smiled. "You might know more of your forebears than I know of mine. Most members of my family left Wrenn's Oak a long time ago."

"But the house. You know about it."

"Aye. It was built in 1625. The man whose tomb you saw was the blacksmith who built this house, lived here, was murdered here."

Here? In this house? Her heart pounded with rising excitement; the coincidence was startling. She tried to calm herself. "My grandfather talked about this blacksmith. Do you know anything about his life?"

"Aye." He met her disbelieving eyes. "I've heard the story many times."

She pushed the plate of pastries toward him. "Have a cookie with your tea."

He grinned. "Is this a gesture of friendship, then? A way of saying you intend to stay? Or is it a bribe?"

Ellen laughed. "It's a bribe. I've got to hear that story. But it's also a gesture of friendship." She reached for a biscuit herself. "I'll make you an offer, Brennig Cole. In exchange for stories about this village and the Coles who lived here, I'll cook some evening meals for us."

His eyes brightened. "I like this offer. I will purchase wine."

She sat back and stretched her arms. "Super! My research has landed squarely in my lap in the form of a magnificent-looking cousin."

"Cousin?"

"You'd have to be. A cousin generations removed!" She thought, every man I meet is named Cole! What is this? Some kind of weird curse? "Tell me about yourself, Brennig. I assume you're not married?"

"My wife is dead," he said in a tone of finality that did not encourage further questions.

Ellen didn't like the look in his eyes when he spoke of his wife. Hurt was there, and something more, something questioning. His self-protective shield made her suspect his wife had died fairly recently; at the mention of her his shoulders moved and a strange look came into his eyes.

"I'm sorry," she offered. "She must have been young."

"Aye, she was." His reluctance to talk about this was evident, but he seemed to feel he had to explain something to her. "I was...I was hurt...and then she...my wife...was gone." He blinked, as if to blink away a bad memory. "She loved gardens and sea gulls. She loved to walk up to the castle on the hill."

Ellen asked gently, "Have you come to forget?"

"No. I have come to remember."

"She was here, then."

"For a time. Once."

Ellen studied him, certain he was holding some secret close to his heart...something to do with his wife. What have I agreed to? she asked herself. Just because this man was named Brennig Cole didn't mean she could trust him. A dark side of him lurked in his silence, but there was another side she could almost pity. He seemed strangely lost.

"You said you were hurt, and that you've come to rest. Will my being in this house interfere with your peace of mind?"

"To the contrary. Your presence is like a salve to an aloneness I haven't got used to. When I saw you in the garden, I was hoping you would stay."

Ellon gazed at him and made a quick decision to divulge the secret of how she got here, whether it sounded weird to him or not. "The butterfly... the one you called a brimstone. It was in the churchyard, at Brennig Cole's tombstone, and it followed me and then I followed it, and it led me to this cottage. To the house he lived in. I find that coincidence absolutely incredible."

"There is no such thing as coincidence," Brennig said.

She swallowed. No one in this town seemed to believe in chance. "Are you saying I was meant to find this house?"

"You're here, are you not? Where you wanted to be."

"I didn't even know about it." She looked about, at the beamed ceiling and the shadows in the small alcove by the back door. A breeze was swaying the branches outside the windows. Was the brimstone butterfly still out there, hiding amid the flowers?

The silver light of evening shone in the stranger's mysterious pale eyes. Sometimes, in fleeting moments, his eyes frightened her. She said, "I was told it's called Afan House."

"Aye. The house of the wild raspberries. So named because of wild raspberries growing in the garden. They are still growing there. They bloom year after year without tending."

"I was also told it's haunted."

"Who told you it is haunted?"

"The proprietor at the hotel. It's such an old house, I thought it ought to have picked up a ghost or two during its thousand dark nights. His ghost, perhaps? The man who was murdered here?''

Brennig smiled softly. "Do you believe in such things?"

"I've never known what to believe about haunted houses. When I heard footsteps earlier, I thought it might be a ghost, but it must have been you. Have you seen anything ghostly here?"

"Nothing to be afraid of. Sometimes there are mischievous brownies about."

Her head jerked up. "Brownies? You're joking, aren't you?"

Brennig looked confused for a moment. "Joking about the brownies? No. Perhaps there aren't as many as there used to be, but they are still hiding about the old places."

She pulled a face. "What are they?"

"You don't know?"

"Little creatures who run around in the night?"

"Aye." Brennig seemed not to comprehend her disbelief. He shrugged and then came a slow smile. "Don't worry. I've not seen a brownie, and if there is a spirit haunting Afan House, it means no harm to you."

"How can you know that?"

"I know the house."

She leaned closer, no longer caring whether he was teasing her about the brownies. "There is a ghost here, isn't there?"

"Perhaps," he said in a voice so soft she could barely hear. "Does that frighten you?"

"No. It intrigues me. What have you seen?"

"I haven't seen a ghost." His gaze shifted to the wooden-cased clock on the wall. "I think I must get to the shop before it closes. There is no jam for breakfast."

Ellen got quickly to her feet. "Nor bread."

"I shall buy bread when the bakery opens early in the morning."

Oh, Lord, Ellen thought. We're making plans for breakfast, this stranger and I! What the devil have I gotten myself into? On the one hand, it was very exciting—meeting a distant cousin in an ancestral home. On the other, it was coincidental enough to be frightening. Even the man's quick acceptance of her was a little frightening. He knew even less about her than she knew of him, and didn't seem very curious. He had agreed to tell her the old stories, though, and that promise was so powerful she shrugged off all the doubts. It was too great a deal to turn down.

Brennig was saying, "The village pub serves fine meals at reasonable prices. If you like, I'll take you there tonight."

His smile steadied her qualms—wariness that came and went like an out-of-control yo-yo. Ellen was as drawn to him as she was uneasy about him, and she knew it. "The pub sounds fine," she heard herself say.

In moments he was gone.

Ellen stood alone in the pleasant oak-and-brick kitchen, bewildered. Brennig Cole—a direct descendant of the murdered blacksmith—acted as though it were the most natural thing in the world for them to be in this house together, just the two of them. Only her intellect told her it was unwise; her heart reacted quite differently. In her heart, she felt she had known him for a long time and he was a friend. The truth was, he was not a friend and the whole situation was bizarre, and she ought to proceed with caution.

Caution was not one of Ellen's strong tendencies. It was more natural to see a lonely man—a somewhat lost man—who wanted her company. He *had* said he'd come here for rest. It was for convalescence, she decided. He must be trying to recover his physical health after some kind of accident that had killed his young wife. An accident he didn't want to talk about, perhaps a car crash. That must be it. It would explain the shadows of sadness in his eyes.

Gathering the towels, she went upstairs with her mind forming questions. Where had the murder taken place? In the dark shadows of her bedroom? Had Brennig Cole been murdered in the room where she was sleeping?

Brennig evidently knew. She would ask him tonight.

CHAPTER FOUR

Freshly showered and dressed in a tweed skirt and sweater, Ellen found Brennig waiting in the kitchen. He was still wearing his jeans but had changed his shirt. She was as startled as the first time at his unusual good looks.

"Fine night for a walk," he said. If you like, we can walk the long way round.

"Would that be by the bridge?" she asked carefully.

"Ach, not the bridge. It's best to stay away from the bridge. There is danger there." He was filling a glass at the kitchen tap. She waited for him to continue, but he didn't.

"What danger?" Remembering with a shudder the face in the river and the awful sensations of sadness she had felt, she watched his Adam's apple move as he drained the glass of water.

"There is a curse on the bridge," he answered. "The bridge is haunted by a spirit who has put a curse on it."

She shivered. A spirit? That face...? Should she tell him what she had seen? "People cross back and forth over the bridge all the time, Brennig. What's the danger? I mean, other than seeing *her?*"

Brennig turned swiftly. His pale eyes shone as they stared. Ellen couldn't tell what message was in his gaze but she felt fright when the question came at her like an arrow. "You saw her?"

"I saw the face of a woman in the water below the bridge. It terrified me. What was it? Have you seen it, too?"

He nodded, still staring at her, but did not answer further.

She reached out, frustrated, and stopped just short of touching his arm. "Brennig? You've seen that face? What *is* it?"

"Most people can't see it," he muttered. "Only those affected by the witch's curse see it. Only those of a certain family blood." He ran his fingers through his thick, dark hair. "If you saw the spirit of the witch, it means you are right about being a descendant of the blacksmith Brennig Cole."

Ellen's stomach was churning with dread. "What curse?" she prodded.

Now he wouldn't look at her. He turned toward the window and stared out at the gray twilight.

Obviously he didn't want to tell her. Could it be that bad? Visualizing the hideous sight in the water, reliving the overpowering sense of loneliness, Ellen knew the curse was bad, knew that she had already felt its tendrils. She swallowed and braced herself.

"Brennig?" she said to his back.

"It might be better if you didn't know."

"It would not be better! I've already crossed the damn bridge! Is all this real, Brennig, or just local superstition? No, not superstition. I did see the face of a woman. A witch, you said?"

He finally turned to face her. His face had gone extremely pale. He still wouldn't look directly into her eyes. "The spirit's name is Nesta," he answered. "And she is evil. She cursed Brennig Cole, whom she loved, because he did not love her. And she cursed his children and all the descendants of those children. Anyone who carries a single drop of his blood in their veins and who crosses over that bridge will lose his or her true love. Forever."

Ellen took a step back, stunned. A vivid picture of Brent's face with his hair tousled and the morning sun-mist behind him formed in her mind. For a moment she could feel his touch, warm and good and reassuring. A pain stabbed at her heart. Lose him? Oh, God... Her voice came out on an exhaled breath. "It can't be true!"

"I believe it is true," Brennig said, studying her reaction with a cock of his head and his eyes squinting.

Her head swam. She saw Brent by the fish pond with the silver-lighted water reflecting on his sweet face, and her heart went heavier than lead. *It can't be true.* Then, in an unexpected flash, she remembered that Brennig's wife had died. Did he believe her death was caused by the curse? Was it the curse?

Dear Lord. The emptiness, the loneliness, she had felt on the bridge... what did it mean? Had the curse already doomed her? A wave of that same gray loneliness swept over her yet again.

"Are you all right?" Brennig asked.

"No. I'm trying like hell not to believe what you're telling me. It's just legend, Brennig. Just superstition."

He looked at her sadly. "I wish that were so. But Nesta is quite real. You saw her yourself."

"And you think it...*she*...is dangerous."

"I know so, Ellen."

She looked at him long and hard, at his handsome face, his haunting eyes. "I can't help but wonder what's really happening here, Brennig. Ever since I arrived in Wrenn's Oak it's been one unexplainable thing after another. The face, finding the tombstone, and then being led to this cottage by a butterfly, meeting you...and now you tell me I'm probably the victim of an ancient curse."

The mysterious Welshman didn't smile. "Strange forces are at work in this village. Evil spirits of the Dark Ages have gripped onto the waning tide of each century and ridden their way into the next. They conceal their secrets behind the hush of sunny summer afternoons like today. But their presence is felt."

Ellen shuddered. "Are you trying to say that ancient evil spirits are responsible for my being led to this cottage?"

"No. I was referring to the curse. Not all the forces here are evil. Something did lead you to Afan House, but it had nothing to do with Nesta."

Mystery hung in the air, clammy and unreal. "How do you know this? How do you know so much about this witch, Nesta?"

"She is part of Wrenn's Oak's history," he replied simply, and then, "Are you ready to go?"

When they reached the front gate, Brennig took her arm protectively. His touch startled her. It was like the touch in a dream when the colors are too vivid and music can be seen by the eyes, and warmth comes too hot from the first sun of morning, cold coming from the light of a rising moon. It was surreal, being with a man who bore the name of an ancestor. The world she had ventured into felt comfortable and uncomfortable at the same time, and she was unable to decide from moment to moment which was which—whether she was where she belonged or whether she ought to get out of this weird place as fast as possible.

Being attracted to the Welshman made it worse. But what woman wouldn't be attracted to a male who looked like him? His perfect features, his easy smile, his strange, dangerous eyes, his naturally sensual body language... Being attracted to him made her extremely sensitive to his moods. His pain was so close to the surface he couldn't hide it, even though—she thought—he tried. There was an anxiety about him that bothered her, something on his mind he wasn't talking about. Did it have anything to do with the accident that had injured him and killed his wife? Or was he secretly bothered by her being in the house, even though he claimed to be happy about it?

Ellen was taken aback by a wave of helplessness that caught her when Brennig Cole took her arm at the gate— as if by his touch he had taken some sort of control over her. Yet his touch was curiously gentle and so were his eyes when he smiled.

"It's a beautiful setting," she remarked for the sake of conversation. "What flowers are giving off that wonderful fragrance?"

He hesitated and frowned. "I don't know."

"The air's filled with the perfume. You smell it, don't you?"

Brennig raised his head and closed his eyes as if he were trying. "Lilies of the valley, perhaps?"

It was a question, not a statement. Odd, he wouldn't know. "I'm not very good about plants," she confessed. "Except cacti that grow in my native desert. I really like the wild, green garden behind this cottage."

Sighing distantly, Brennig said, "It is said he liked it, too—the blacksmith, I mean. He died in the garden."

He had answered her question even before she asked it, and the answer was a surprise. "He was murdered in the *garden?*"

"Aye, so the legend goes."

"Oh, tell me!" Ellen pleaded. "Brennig! Instead of walking, let's go sit in the garden, where it actually happened, and you can tell me the legend. Will you? Please?"

He laughed. "You are not anxious to get to the pub for some dinner?"

"Oh, you're hungry. Well, we can—"

"I'm not hungry," he interrupted. "If you want to sit in the garden, sure, we'll do that. I've some claret in the kitchen. We'll open the wine and sit in the garden. It won't get completely dark until ten-thirty or so. There's a bench under a willow. I'll fetch the wine and goblets and meet you there."

Ellen followed the stone path around the side of the house, to the garden. The fragrance came stronger under the overhanging greens. Ivy vines covered the high walls. The garden was gnarled and out of control. Bushes crowded one another and flowers competed for space.

Where? she wondered, pausing at the bench where willow branches swung golden over a space of mossy grass. Where in this garden had a woman murdered her husband? And how had she killed him? And why?

Brennig emerged through the kitchen door carrying an open bottle, with two goblets tucked under his arm.

"I know what you're thinking," he said. "That this garden needs a bloody lot of work."

"I wasn't thinking that. I was thinking about the murder. It was such a long time ago. Do people still talk about it?"

He sat down beside her and poured the claret. "Aye, in such a small village a murder accompanied by a sordid scandal lasts centuries. The story gets passed down and embellished."

She accepted the wine. "Your presence here must fan the flames of the legend because of your name."

"These people don't know me. I don't live here."

"Right. You live in Shrewsbury. I assumed you lived here in your youth."

"My grandparents lived here. I never met them. I've visited Wrenn's Oak as a lad, and later my wife and I stayed here. It is a strange hamlet, Ellen. Once you get to know it, you won't want to stay long."

She eyed him quizzically. Brennig raised his glass.

Ellen raised hers in response. "To coincidence," she said.

"And to memories." His glass clinked against hers.

"To memories," she agreed, and only afterward thought, memories? What memories?

Brennig tasted the wine, frowned slightly, and then tasted once again as he had tasted the tea earlier, like a curious foreigner. Wasn't *she* supposed to be the curious foreigner?

Sipping the wine, she asked, "Are you familiar with all the details of the legend, then?"

"Aye," he answered huskily, staring down into the goblet.

"Great! What luck! Start at the very beginning."

He leaned against the rough back of the old wooden bench, ignoring a gold leaf that floated down and landed on his arm. He seemed deep in thought, trying to pull up the details of a story he had been told long ago.

"In the early sixteen hundreds, when he was still a youth, this man—my namesake—fell in love with a beautiful dark-haired girl whose father was the village judge."

Ellen sat back, very aware her shoulder was touching his. "There's a love story in this legend?"

"A love story... aye, definitely so."

"What was her name? The girl he fell in love with?"

"The judge's daughter was called Nesta." As he said her name, Brennig's voice went harsh and his shoulder stiffened. "As I mentioned earlier, it was Nesta's face you saw in the river beneath the bridge."

"My God!" She blinked. "But the face I saw was so evil, Brennig!"

He nodded. "And the young blacksmith knew it, but not at first. Not when he thought he loved her."

Ellen closed her eyes and forced herself not to think about the beautiful, evil thing she had seen. "Did Brennig and Nesta sit together on quiet nights in this garden?"

"No. The house was not yet built. They met on the riverbank where the willows hung almost to the ground and the grass was as green as emeralds."

Eyes closed, Ellen imagined the murmur of the river. Breathing in the fragrance of lilies and honeysuckle, she listened to the music of birds in the high branches above them, music in the hush of twilight. She had dreamed of finding the rest of her grandfather's legend, but had pictured herself seated in a dreary library, nosing through musty-smelling books.

This was beyond her dreams . . . sitting in the very garden where the blacksmith had died, and with a man—a distant cousin, no less, who carried his name. Maybe she was dreaming. . . .

But no, the place where Brennig's shoulder touched hers felt hot and tingling on her skin, even though his shoulder had been as cool as leaves at first. His voice, deep and burred, was the voice of Wales itself, recalling its past. The picture he painted was so vivid, she could think back on her first look at the wide, soft riverbanks where wild gooseberries grew along low walls and yellow flowers dotted the grass, and it was easy to imagine two lovers sprawled there on the grass in seventeenth century clothes.

The girl in Ellen's mind smoothed her long skirts as she and her lover watched the swans floating. To Ellen's horror, though, the face in the water rushed to the forefront of her image. Nesta's face. The young man she pictured as the Brennig Cole who sat beside her now.

With her eyes closed and her ears tuned to her memory of the river's song, Ellen could see the shadows forming in that young man's eyes as Brennig spoke....

CHAPTER FIVE

The year 1626

Nesta arranged the folds of her full, velvet skirt over the grass while she sipped wild gooseberry wine and watched the swans glide through the shallows of the river Lugg. Beside her, Brennig rested on his elbow, teasing her long dark curls with his fingertips.

"Rumors of our coming marriage have spread through the village like mayweed," she said happily, dipping a finger into her wine.

"How can that be," he asked, "when everyone knows your father will never approve our marriage?"

Nesta licked her finger provocatively. "Oh, aye, he will! The rumors please me, Brennig. All the girls are so envious, for I shall have the most handsome husband within a thousand miles . . . and the bravest hero."

The young man shook his head. "If there truly are marriage rumors, then I must speak to your father without any further delay. I shall put forth my best efforts, Nesta, but it will be for naught. The only daughter of a judge does not marry a blacksmith, whether he has slain three highway bandits or a hundred." He looked at her sadly. "Do not keep thinking about a wedding. You are making things up in your mind, just as someone made up the bruit about us."

She laughed. "It is I responsible for the tittle-tattle. And why not? Their envy warms me to the bone. You are mine, and about this there shall be no argument from anyone."

He shook his head again.

She would not be discouraged. "Oh, aye, do the formality of asking my father for my hand. Not today, though. I need a wee bit of time. Tomorrow. He will give his permission tomorrow."

"He will not."

She ran her fingers along Brennig's cheek and his neck, looking deeply into his pale blue eyes. "He will. And he will honor you with my dowry and give us a fine wedding, and the townspeople will come and they will talk of our wedding for years to come."

He started to answer, but she clasped a finger gently over his lips. "Father will do as I ask. He will not go against my wishes." She laughed. "My sweet, your eyes grow wide with surprise to hear me speak so. My father knows he would be very, very sorry if he tries to keep my true love away from me."

"Such disrespect toward your father is not a matter even for jest," he said, straightening.

"Jest? Hardly. I could . . . and would make the judge's life quite miserable, and he knows it. He is a wise man, wise enough to understand my power." Nesta rose suddenly and flung her arms wide, and twirled in a dance of joy, her skirt swirling, the red satin bodice catching the glow of sunlight, her dark hair bouncing. "As your bride I shall wear sweet briar in my hair and we shall walk on rose petals!"

With sunlight in his eyes, nineteen-year-old Brennig watched her from his place on the grass until she stopped to question his long silence. She stood looking down at him. Her hair had pulled out of a wide ribbon that held it and blew gently around her face. "So quiet, my sweet lad?"

He did not smile. "What power are you talking about?"

Her red lips formed a slow smirk. "Why, my power of persuasion."

"What power?" Brennig repeated, his voice softer than before. "You speak shockingly about your father. What reprisals would a father dread from a daughter's demands? What manner of threat, Nesta?"

"Whatever I decide it shall be," she answered gaily, reaching down for another sip of the wine that had already loosened her tongue.

The man she had chosen for her husband-to-be stared at her coldly, as though he were seeing her for the first time. He was, indeed, catching a glimpse of her soul—for the first time. His jaw was tight. "The power of the Evil Eye?"

She circled him playfully, her steps unsteady from the effects of the potent wine.

"That's impossible," Brennig said. "I've known you all your life. I would know if you posses the Evil Eye."

"I happen to have loved you all my life," she answered. "If I had hated you instead, you would not doubt it."

He studied her eyes, trying to see into her soul, remembering the carefree days of their youth. He thought of girls who competed with Nesta's beauty, how they would develop warts or blotches on their faces. He thought of boys who teased her, how so often they would find themselves in poison oak. He remembered nettles where they should not be and candles falling, spilling hot wax on Nesta's enemies. How could it be true? And how could it *not* be true, when she was standing before him drinking and gaily confessing that it was.

The Evil Eye.

Sensations of horror shot through Brennig's young heart and left it empty and hard.

She continued to lay on her effervescent plans for their future. "Oh Brennig, do you not see? Do you not see that we can have *whatever* we wish? My father cannot stop us! No one can!"

"And I?" he challenged in a voice like ice. "What happens when *I* have wishes contrary to yours?"

She reached out to touch his cheek, choosing not to notice that he flinched. "That could never happen. My love for you is eternal. I shall be the best wife a man like you could ask for."

"I will not marry a witch!" he blurted in a voice like the bleak, deep winter.

Stunned, she gazed at him, her eyes flashing yellow in the sun. He had never before noticed the yellow shine of her eyes.

He turned away. "You wreak revenge and pain on those who do not please you, even your father, who loves you."

Breathlessly she shouted, "My power is a divine gift!"

"Your power is evil. I see that now." Brennig sat with arms clasped around his knees, gazing out at the river with grim anger darkening his eyes.

Nesta was silent.

"Are there others?" he asked.

"Others?"

"Shall I attempt to be polite and call them friends?"

She squinted at him threateningly, a look he had never seen. "Aye, there *are* others like me and we meet in moonlight in the grove of enchanter's nightshade on the moors."

"Where the ravens nest in January," he said, teeth clenched.

His implied meaning was clear. The raven's chicks hatched in the violent storms of breaking winter, symbols of the evil storms that claimed newborn lambs. The raven was a witch's bird, each sought out the other. The heat of Brennig's eyes mingled with the cold of hers. "You should not have started the premature rumors of a wedding, Nesta. The mother of my children will not be a witch."

Her eyes flashed, but her voice remained eerily calm. "You would not leave me. You love me! You have loved me since my fifteenth summer."

"I thought I did. I never believed you were a soft and gentle woman—which I always would have preferred—but I loved your laughter and your clever, quick mind, and I thought becoming a wife and mother would tame your wild eyes. I saw mischief in your eyes, but I did not see the evil, until now. I see it now."

Her face flushed. "You cannot humiliate me by casting out my love! I will not allow it!"

Brennig rose to his feet. "I have no wish to humiliate you. If you like, bruit a tale that your father refused to give his permission. Or say it was you who rejected me because of my humble birth. It is of no importance to me what you say. But leave me in peace, Nesta."

Her lips quivered with rage.

He repeated, "I am warning you to leave me in peace."

"Never!" she vowed, flinging wine from her goblet, staining his shirt with bloodred spots. "Never! If you refuse to marry me you will never again know the meaning of peace! You will regret it forever!"

CHAPTER SIX

In the garden Brennig's voice dropped into silence. He sat in the gloaming, pulling his gaze away from the lens of time. A twentieth-century breeze blew rich in the high trees. He shifted on the bench and set his empty wine goblet on the flagstone walk.

"Good Lord," Ellen said. "The original fatal attraction."

"The what?"

"It's an American film about a woman obsessed with a lover. She tried to kill him and everyone he loved. Nesta did the same thing, didn't she?"

"Aye, with the powers of her witchcraft."

Three blackbirds pecked and scratched in the weed-grown borders, ignoring the voices of the intruders in their garden. Shadows of evening crept down the garden walls and along the curtains of ivy. A chill moved in the shadows. Ellen thought suddenly, There is someone else here, someone besides Brennig and me...

She glanced about the garden, but there was only the rustle of leaves and the stiff, indifferent moves of the blackbirds.

"Is something the matter?" Brennig asked.

"Do you think this garden could be haunted? By him?"

He frowned. "Why would you think so?"

"I can't explain. I feel something wrong out here, as if someone is listening or watching us."

Brennig smiled patiently. "There is nothing to be afraid of. Not in this garden, or the house."

"The way you say that seems to imply there is something to be frightened of elsewhere!"

He rubbed his chin thoughtfully and didn't answer.

"Brennig? What? Tell me!"

He seemed hesitant to answer. "The bridge is not a good place for you to be."

"Why? Are you saying Nesta is still dangerous? And to me?"

"Nesta appeared to you in the water, which means she is aware you are here. If you ask what could she do? I don't know, Ellen."

She looked at him skeptically, wondering if he was serious about his fears for her, or if he was too caught up in the legend. Still, she *had* seen that hideous thing. "Do you believe in witchcraft?"

"Of course. One can see dark forces at work everywhere. When people invite the darkness into their souls, we name them witches."

"Nesta must have eventually convinced Brennig to marry him, since he was murdered by his wife."

"No," Brennig answered. "He married a village girl named Eira."

"Eira..." It seemed to Ellen she had heard the name somewhere. "Why did Eira kill him?"

Brennig picked up his goblet and rose to his feet. "Eira didn't. Aren't you getting hungry? I will continue the story—the worst of the story—after we've had some dinner. You must be getting hungry." He offered his hand and they made their way along the moss-covered stones to the street.

"Was Eira as beautiful as Nesta?" Ellen asked as they walked.

He glanced at her, then away. "It is said she was."

"In stories it always seems important for maidens to be beautiful."

"All women are beautiful," he said.

This statement was spontaneous, from the heart. Knowing he meant it, Ellen saw the man in a new and different light.

"Some are more charming than others," he qualified, walking beside her, his shoulder brushing hers. "You, for example, are a woman who possesses such charm men must be in awe of it. I imagine yours is the kind of charm Eira possessed, because she was admired by everybody in the village."

Charm? she thought. *Me?* Was it his way of saying he was attracted to her? She knew it anyway, because of the way he looked at her—swift glances before he caught himself, penetrations into her soul. Glances like darts carefully aimed by a skilled marksman. It was unnerving trying not to transmit her own thoughts with her eyes or a twist of her head... thoughts about him... about the beauty of him... the intrigue of him...

And curious thoughts about his inability to disguise his sadness.

The pub was small and cozy, with a bar across one side, an unlit fireplace and a battered upright piano. With longing, she thought Brent would like this place. She would bring him here when he arrived. Half-a-dozen small tables with chairs were crowded into the room. Stags' horns lined the high walls. They sat at the only vacant table and Brennig ordered two mugs of a popular local ale. Curious glances and guarded greetings came spontaneously from the pub's regulars.

"Do you know any of these people?"

He shook his head.

"You haven't spent much time in the pub since you arrived?"

"I arrived only today."

"Oh! I didn't realize that." She studied him in candlelight. "You came here to recuperate? Were you badly hurt in the accident?"

The man who sat across from her looked down at the scratches in the worn tabletop. His fingertip followed one deep scar so old it had been blackened by many coats of varnish. "It is said that time mends all wounds, all pain. But it doesn't."

A waiter set their drinks in front of them and they ordered a meal—the evening special of roast beef and roast potatoes and peas, served with freshly baked bread. Ellen noted that Brennig's accent was different from that of the locals, reminding her that he, too, was a stranger in the village of his family roots. He had come "home," and yet Wrenn's Oak wasn't any more his home than it was hers.

She held up her glass. "To reunions." Not until she had taken a swallow of the ale did she ask herself with a start why she had proposed such a toast. They were strangers here, unnoticed, unrecognized, yet Ellen felt she had been here before. Could it be her grandfather's stories coming alive? Could it be because he had always wanted to come to Wrenn's Oak, and she had done it for him?

Brennig hadn't even blinked at her toast. He had merely smiled and raised his glass. The man both intrigued and frightened her, and she couldn't give a reason for either emotion. He was mysterious, and his eyes and his laughter were strange. His voice, too, had a way of losing and gaining volume, like a radio. When he became thoughtful, his voice would fade.

She watched him sip the ale with great interest; either he was unfamiliar with the brand or it had been a long time since he had tasted it. He licked his lips and took a long drink.

She asked, "Do you like it?"

"Like what?"

"The ale?"

"It's weak, but better than nothing."

"Weak? Good heavens. This makes American beer taste like soda pop."

"What is soda pop?"

Ellen laughed. "Never mind. I like the taste of your local brew, but I don't dare drink too much of this so-called weak stuff or you'll have to carry me home."

"Drink to your heart's content, then, since you are guaranteed a ride home, if on my shoulders."

"Sure. Make a fool of myself my first night. Is the food good here?"

"It was recommended by the greengrocer."

"It smells great, I'll say that."

"The food?"

She frowned. "Can't you smell the wonderful aromas every time they open the door to the kitchen?"

"Mmm," was all he said.

Cocking her head, she observed, "You don't have a very keen sense of smell, do you? You couldn't smell the flowering vines, either."

"I used to have. But not since . . . since I was hurt."

"I'm sorry. I shouldn't keep reminding you, then."

"I can remember the aromas," he said. "So I don't mind."

Cigarette smoke hung in the air. Welsh voices and laughter surrounded them. The light in the pub was dim. Ellen looked across at the features of the man, marveling at her luck in meeting a very distant cousin who knew the legends she had longed to hear.

"I like this place," she said.

"So do I."

She sipped from her mug. "Don't keep me in any more suspense, Brennig. If Brennig Cole's wife, Eira, didn't commit the murder, how was she blamed for it?"

"A few townspeople decided she was jealous because Nesta wouldn't leave her husband alone."

She rubbed her arms, chilled at the thought of a cold-blooded murder. "Did Nesta kill him for revenge?"

Brennig didn't answer. He was deep in thought.

"Brennig? Hello?"

He looked up. "I'm trying to remember the details. I've never been asked to recount the story, and I'm not sure what the local version is."

"You mean as opposed to the family version? The Cole family version?"

He nodded dully.

"Give me the family version as best you remember it. Tell me what you know about Eira. Did she love him?"

"She loved him very much. Even after he was dead."

His voice had become husky; Ellen wondered why. This story mattered to him more than a legend should. She asked, "How did he manage to get himself murdered?"

Brennig moved his fingertips over the scratches and scars on the tabletop like someone reading braille.

"Tell me!" Ellen urged, fighting down the impulse to follow the path of his fingers over the aged wood scars. "Tell me how Eira loved her husband even after he was dead. Tell me what Nesta did!"

At the mention of Nesta's name, Brennig's eyes flashed with anger, as they did every time he thought about the witch who had cursed his ancestor. From what Brennig had said, he believed the curse affected him; perhaps he blamed it for his ill luck and the loss of his wife. Whatever the reason, it was apparent he hated the sound of Nesta's name.

And so did Ellen, by now. Brennig thought they shared the longtime effects of the witch's curse, and she was beginning to believe it herself because, during these ragged, tangled hours with him, she had thought of the man she loved only in fleeting moments. Brennig held her thoughts captive. He enticed with his eyes and his voice. She almost wanted him to. It felt so incredibly strange and so incredibly comfortable being with him.

"Tell me what Nesta did," she repeated. "Tell me what happened."

Brennig inhaled with a great sigh; sadness dulled his eyes. "It is a horror story, but if you really want to hear it, I will tell you. About two years after he rejected Nesta, in the shadows of her rage, Brennig married a farmer's fairhaired daughter named Eira. Nesta appeared at the wedding ceremony all in black, and as the vows were exchanged, a fierce wind blew across the moorlands, silencing the warbling birds.

"The blacksmith built the cottage for his bride in the first spring of their marriage, 1628. They called it Afan House for the wild raspberries that crept into their sunny walled garden, and in that year Eira gave birth to a son.

"Brennig was ever wary of the witch's wrath. He noticed shadows where none should be and knew the shadows were her way of reminding him that she had sworn revenge. He heard echoes in the night, and felt particularly on edge when he and his wife attended services in the church. Nesta was always there, even at the baptism of their son, and Brennig felt stirrings of her evil presence. He knew she was in touch with dark forces.

"To counter gossip that she had lost Brennig's love, Nesta planted and fed rumors that his marriage was unhappy. Worse, through charm and sweetness she managed to befriend Eira, who was trusting of the judge's beautiful daughter and would not heed her husband's warnings. No one else in the village knew Nesta was a witch; many felt Brennig had broken her heart. To Brennig's chagrin, Nesta began calling at the Afan House, welcomed in by his young wife.''

Ellen leaned forward, touching his hand on the table. His skin felt surprisingly cool. She no longer heard the music from the piano or the voices in the pub. Brennig had a way of taking her back in time, making her feel as if she were there, those centuries ago, with these people she was coming to know. With him, the past seemed so real—too real—and becoming more so by the minute.

She said, "Nesta came to their house?"

"Always when Brennig was away. He had been closely watching Nesta from a distance, and he knew she was aligned with a witchs' coven, even though he couldn't prove it, and he knew she was dangerous. He was waiting for her to make her move. Nesta knew it and savored this power over him, so she was in no hurry to make the move he knew was coming.''

"Why did she wait so long?"

Brennig shook his head. "To show her power by threatening Brennig. She was trying to make him fear her, keep him on edge. Such was her style. Also, I suppose she didn't want any suspicion to fall on her, and it didn't." He rubbed his chin thoughtfully. "Her delay was hard for him, as Nesta planned it should be. On the ninth day of each month and the ninth month of the year, he worried about being away from Eira and his son—''

"What was significant about nine?"

"Nine is a witch's number.''

Ellen swallowed. Her grandfather had once told her the number nine was unlucky. Hearing the same conviction in Brennig's voice now, she asked, "Do you believe in witches, Brennig? Do you believe they can actually cast spells?"

The question seemed to surprise him. "Of course. I've seen what their evil can do. The spells can last for centuries."

He believed every word of the legend; this was obvious from the emotion in his voice as he spoke. He tended to easily lose the present, and to take her with him into the murky past with the magic of his voice and his eyes.

"How can you know such details?" she challenged.

He blinked. "It is the story. We have always been avid storytellers here."

Impatient to get to the actual murder, Ellen prodded, "So Nesta came to their house one day and murdered him? How?"

"Most believe it was her intention to kill his wife. Others believe her plan was carried out just as she intended."

"But she did come to the cottage?"

"On the thirty-sixth month of his marriage."

"A number divisible by nine!"

"Aye. On that autumn day Brennig went off hunting with friends, intending to stay two days in the woodlands. By then Eira had given birth to another son. She and her two babies went to her father's house outside the village to help plan the wedding of a cousin. She intended to stay at the farm overnight. But her husband returned unexpectedly..."

Ellen's heart began to beat faster. She thought of the battered old tombstone in the churchyard and her earlier vision of a funeral. Now she knew it would have been autumn and the day might have been bleak and cold in this land of early winters. Did the two women who loved him stare across at each other through tears of grief? Did the witch stand above his coffin with a satisfied smirk? Or did Nesta sob out a final goodbye? Was the word *murder* on the lips of the mourners?

"That day—" she began

"That day," Brennig interrupted as if he were reading her thoughts. "That day Nesta took her revenge...."

CHAPTER SEVEN

The year 1631

In midafternoon Brennig came limping from the wild-lands. His two-year-old son Margam, who had been play-ing with kittens in the yard, ran out to meet him. Eira followed not far behind, hampered by her long skirts and the discomfort of sixth-month pregnancy.

"Are you hurt?" she shouted long before she reached him.

Brennig picked up the breathless child and hoisted him into the air. "I turned my ankle on the scree at the foot of the bracken slope. It was no use trying to keep up with the hunt. It's swollen as a ripe apple."

Eira gave him a welcoming kiss. "Come into the house and let me wrap it for you, and have a rest."

"I've no time for a rest," he said, returning her hug with affection. "There is enough daylight left to gather in the raspberries. With this unexpected change in weather, there might be a hard frost tonight."

His wife's brow wrinkled. "I should have picked the raspberries before I came. I didn't expect a frost."

"No," he said patting the small swell of her stomach. "Bending isn't good for you. We must listen to the physi-cian and be cautious with our wee daughter."

Eira blushed. "Wee daughter, is it? No. My mother says it will be our third son." She noted his limp. "And you shouldn't walk any farther on that ankle."

"We'll borrow your father's horse cart, then."

"They'll want us to stay for supper."

"Tomorrow we'll come back with the cart and bring a basket of raspberries."

Margam ran ahead. "Why are you walking crooked?" he asked.

"Because my foot hurts," Brennig answered. "Go fetch Grandfather and tell him we wish to hitch up the horse." He knew that if he walked the rest of the way home, carrying his one-year-old, the ankle would only sustain worse injury.

When they were home in Afan House, Brennig had difficulty removing his boot, refusing to allow his wife to help.

"You'll get stains from the bramble berries on your dress," he said, gingerly inching the boot from over the swollen ankle and wincing with pain.

"You are too concerned for me," Eira said, kneeling to examine the injury in the light from the garden window.

While she was wrapping the foot and ankle, she asked, "Did you have any noonday meal?"

"No, and I'm hungry as a wolf."

"There are vegetables, and some cooked fowl. I'll heat the kettle."

Their younger son was crying, having been wakened from a nap to come home in the bumpy cart in a cloud-covered chill. "I will begin a fire and heat the kettle," he said. "And have some bread and vegetables. Then I must get out to the garden. Go tend to the children, love, and I will tend to myself."

He hurried so he could get the job finished before it was dark. The berries, growing profusely, had ripened in the autumn sun. After he had worked for fifteen or twenty minutes, Brennig began to feel dizzy. He ignored it at first, pushing off the cause to the pain in his ankle. Perspiring even in the cold, trying to keep working, he heard voices from the kitchen where a window was propped open. Nesta's voice. And Eira's.

He swore under his breath. Nesta always had a way of following his moves; she must have come believing he was still away hunting. Brennig sensed trouble. He did not want Nesta alone with Eira.

But when he attempted to go inside, the dizziness worsened until he fell to his knees, his head spinning violently. How could he have become so ill so fast? Something was very wrong. The ground under him was moving. He was unable to get up.

"Brennig!"

It was Eira's voice, but he couldn't answer her.

Met with only silence, Eira hurried out to the garden. Nesta followed after, her long, silk skirt sweeping the stone path. They found Brennig on his knees, clutching his stomach.

Eira gasped. "Brennig, what is it?" She rushed to him.

"I don't—" he began.

Nesta's shadow felt ice cold as it moved over him. She stood looking down at the man on the ground. Brennig turned his head. He saw the fear in the eyes of his wife, and then cognizance in the eyes of Nesta. Nesta's wickedness was gleaming like reflections of a moon on a dark night. But horror was there, too.

When he saw her eyes, he knew.

Nesta had taken her revenge. But he was not the intended victim.

"What is it? What's wrong?" Eira cried, brushing his hair from his eyes.

His limbs felt ice-cold. The pain in his stomach was causing violent seizures of shaking. Brennig fell back. The vision of the two women blurred through his dilated pupils. He grasped at his wife's sleeve, choking on the words he forced through his lips.

"Poison..." he muttered.

Eira shrieked in horror and panic and called his name over and over. His eyes closed and he lapsed into a coma.

"Poison!" Nesta howled. "Brennig has been poisoned! Why did you do it, Eira? *Why?*"

Eira could not hear the calculated accusation over the screams of agony coming from her own heart. She kept calling his name, trying to shake a response from her unconscious husband. He was dying in her arms.

"Help!" Nesta cried. "We must get help!" She was shaking as violently as Eira, who was sobbing into her husband's chest.

Nesta stood with tears dampening her cheeks, staring at Brennig's lifeless form.

"You killed him!" Nesta shrieked at Brennig's wife.

CHAPTER EIGHT

Sitting at the table in the pub, Ellen sucked in her breath. "Nesta tried to poison Eira and killed Brennig instead? How did she do it?"

"Deadly mushrooms were found in Eira's kitchen. The only explanation is that Nesta got into their house while Eira was at her parents' farm and put them there with some other mushrooms. She thought Eira would eat them while Brennig was away hunting, and she would have if he hadn't turned his ankle on the scree."

"The children would have eaten them, too!"

"Aye, that's so. When a witch vows revenge, there can be no limit to her evil. Brennig knew that. He knew about witches."

"But Eira got blamed."

"As I said, no one else knew Nesta was a witch, except perhaps her own father. She had already spent considerable effort spreading rumors of their unhappy marriage. Now she continued it, building lie upon lie, until the village was convinced Eira was the murderer. It was Nesta's father who sentenced Eira Cole to death by hanging, the accepted punishment for murder."

"How awful!" Ellen shuddered. "Was she executed?"

"No," Brennig replied. "In the dead of night Eira escaped with her two young sons. No one ever knew how she did it, so the talk spread that her husband's ghost came to her in the night and told her to flee, and helped her. She ran over the bridge to England. Although they searched for months, neither she nor her children were ever found."

A shiver of fear moved through Ellen as she watched Brennig's eyes. He must have been feeling, as she was, the agony of that young woman who had lived so long ago. She said, "As you pointed out, it would have been a perfect setup for Nesta to murder Brennig in a way his wife would be blamed, and that way get rid of both of them. Couldn't she have planned it from the start?"

"Possibly, but I don't think so. I think Eira was her intended victim, because her death—and probably the deaths of his children—would have caused him far more agony than dying."

She gazed at him, still puzzled by his eyes. "You've thought a lot about this story, haven't you? About how those people felt?"

"It's a legend I've known all my life, and unlike most legends, it is based on documented proof."

Ellen pushed her finished plate aside. The dinner had been a long one. She swallowed the last of her third ale. "If no trace of Eira or her children was ever found, then you—or I—couldn't be his direct descendant."

"Sure we could. Those children lived, and there would have been a third because Eira was pregnant."

"And Nesta? What became of her?"

"Nesta," he repeated with clenched teeth as if he were speaking of a personal enemy. The hate in his voice was unnerving. "Nesta fell or jumped from the bridge, either by accident or suicide. She joined other evil river spirits that have lived in these waters for centuries. After Eira escaped, Nesta called upon the dark powers to put a curse on the bridge over which she ran, and upon all who would ever carry the blood of the man who had betrayed her.

Nesta's spirit resides in the river, and as long as she is there, the curse prevails.''

A fearsome flash of light crossed Brennig's eyes. So strange was that flash that gooseflesh formed on Ellen's arms. Frightening hatred. Hate for a spirit?

She swallowed. "But I have crossed over the bridge! I've seen Nesta's face!''

He looked at her with curiosity and sadness mixed. "I'm sorry,'' was all he would say.

Brent's smile came vividly to her mind, and she thought, Oh God, what if the curse is real and I've lost Brent? Despair settled over her, a kind of knowing. Ever since she had crossed Wrenn's Oak Bridge, Brent had seemed more and more distant. Her attention had focused on this stranger, who fascinated and frightened her—as if her distraction were something she couldn't control. As if he could deliberately erase her emotions for a man he didn't know, in the same way that he pulled her into a centuries-old story and gave it life and somehow made himself—and her—a part of it.

When they were walking back to the cottage, there was still a hint of gray light in the western sky, even though the hour was approaching eleven. The air was chilly. A breeze blew thin drifts of fog between the trees and down the narrow lane, giving the illusion of ghosts. Or maybe, Ellen thought, they *were* ghosts. If there was such a thing as a haunted town, it was Wrenn's Oak. One could feel the spirits of the past everywhere, like Nesta—the dead still living.

Ellen said carefully, "You have crossed the bridge...."

"Long ago."

"And you have lost your wife...."

"Aye," he said with bitterness, and dropped into a silence that told her he was not going to talk further about the death of his wife.

He seemed to be lost in his own thoughts as they walked. Brennig watched the frail wisps of fog move along the hedgerows. When his shoulder brushed hers, Ellen felt again as though she were touched by some magic that sent her soul flying. Such a mystical feeling, and yet, oddly, Brennig didn't even seem to notice.

He asked, out of his silence, "Is there a scent of sweet briar along here?"

He *had* said he had no sense of smell. She answered, "I don't know what sweet briar smells like."

"The flowers are full of perfume and the leaves smell spicy. I recall a briar hedge . . ."

"When you lived here?"

"Aye."

"I thought you said you'd never lived here."

"Visited," he corrected. "It was a long time ago. Many things have changed, but some things haven't."

Ellen sighed and resisted the temptation to ask him more questions about his life. He had said he came here to remember, but yet it seemed painful for him to say exactly what it was he wanted to remember. Happy times with his wife, no doubt. Private things not to be shared with an American tourist.

She said softly, "I do catch the scent of flowers and spice. It's lovely."

This made him smile. "I thought you would like it." It sounded like the comment of an old friend, a man who knew her well.

But he didn't know her.

When they reached the cottage, he said a polite goodnight and disappeared up the stairs. Ellen stood at the bottom landing, listening to his footsteps echo away into the darkness.

She closed the shutters in her room to keep out the night's cold, and lay awake under a down comforter thinking about the Welshman who was sleeping upstairs in the loft. The house was so quiet and yet she was not alone. It wasn't like her to condone a situation like this, and yet, relying on her instincts as she always did, Ellen knew this man would not harm her.

If he would not harm her, then why did she fear him? What was it she feared? And, at the same time, what was it she trusted? Her own emotions baffled her. She was utterly fascinated by him; just to look at his face was mesmerizing.

"Brennig..." she whispered. "Brent..." Their names were so similar, but the two men were very different.

Weren't they? Or did Brennig remind her a little of Brent, and that was why she was so drawn to him? This was confusing. One moment she thought they were alike, moved alike, laughed alike, and then it became more and more difficult to pull up Brent's face in her thoughts, difficult to remember his voice while listening to Brennig's. Difficult to hear his laughter through the wails of wind in the high trees. Difficult to remember the little things about Brent...

Echoes of the dream-glazed and heart-turning day throbbed around her. The night washed over her like waves heavily pounding. Memories were loud in her ears. The day was too much to comprehend. That awful surge of loneliness she had felt on the bridge swayed around her in the darkness.

The curse?

How could it be? How could it *not* be?

And why would Brennig warn her about Nesta's power? If that thing in the water really had power, as Brennig believed, why would it want to harm *her?* Because she was a distant descendant of Eira? How could Brennig know that much about the ghost of Nesta?

Nesta *was* a ghost, this much Ellen knew, because she had seen her! There was no disputing what she'd seen, and Brennig, too, had seen it, didn't dispute the evil of it. Hopefully, the thing stayed in the river and couldn't get out!

Somewhere in the deepest night, Ellen was wakened by noises. Footsteps. Brennig was moving about. After waking a second time to the sound of the echoing steps, not above but below, she rose, opened the door and peered out into the hallway. The house was pitch-black.

Restless, she slipped on a robe, turned on the lights and made her way to the kitchen for a glass of milk. Brennig wasn't down here and there was no sign that he had been. He must see in the dark like a cat. There were no noises now; he must have gone back up to the loft.

Dawn came very early to the Welsh hills in summer. Even before she saw the first slits of light through the shutters, Ellen heard him stirring again. It was unnerving. Did the man never sleep?

She opened the shutters to a view of the garden turning golden in fresh sunlight, and then hurried back to bed rubbing her feet vigorously against the sheets to try to warm them. It was pleasant to lie under the down and watch the flowers on the papered walls come to life with the rising sun. Mornings brought brilliance and warmth.

She imagined Eira and Brennig Cole waking to sunlight in this very room more than three and a half centuries ago. She imagined him reaching out to her, and Eira reaching back in the dark of winter mornings. Eira, a young wife and mother whose love for a man brought unspeakable tragedy to them both. She had been dead for so long, and yet Ellen could feel her happiness in her love and her agony in watching her husband die and then running with her children for her life. Over the bridge into oblivion.

Tears welled in Ellen's eyes. It was so unfair. Brennig must have thought of those people enough to have worked up an incredible hatred for Nesta, who somehow still lived. Ellen could understand; she had begun to hate the witch, too.

For some reason, she believed Brennig when he said Nesta could be a danger to anyone who saw her ghostly face.

Lying in bed, she heard the shower running in the bathroom across the hall and Brennig singing loudly. She recognized neither the song nor the language in which he sang. It seemed to be a garbled mixture of English and Gaelic Welsh, and in that old language, the song sounded medieval. His voice was nothing less than beautiful, with a kind of echo that reminded her of Tom Jones. All Welsh people love music, she remembered. Brennig's singing was a fine beginning to a summer day. Maybe it wasn't so bad, after all, having him in the house.

In a few minutes, when all was quiet, she forced herself from the warmth of the bed. Pleased to find he had left the bathroom spotlessly clean, Ellen drew a warm bath and soaked luxuriously, with no plans for the day except to cash some travelers' cheques in town, pay Mrs. Jenkins the month's rent, and maybe, if she felt like it, lend a helping hand in the garden, and write to Brent. She wouldn't try to write the legend, it would be more exciting to tell him when he could see the gravestone and the house. Brennig hadn't said how long he was staying. He might still be here in three weeks when Brent came, so she'd better explain ahead that a Welshman was staying in the loft.

Would Brent be jealous about that? He would trust her, just as she trusted him. As pleased as she was over this adventure, she missed him in so many unguarded moments.

The kitchen smelled of burned toast and the refrigerator door was standing open. Brennig was sitting at the table scraping the black from a slice of toast.

"It smells like you've had a fire in here," Ellen said, waving away imaginary smoke.

"I'm no good in a kitchen, never was."

She closed the refrigerator. "Is the toaster not working right?"

He looked up as if he didn't know what she was talking about. "The knobs on the stove are misleading."

"You didn't use the toaster?"

"What toaster?"

"The one right here on the counter, Brennig."

"Ah, that. Well, no . . . I didn't see it."

And he probably didn't smell the bread burning, she thought, since he couldn't smell *anything*. He'd have to be blind, as well, not to see that toaster. "Here," she said. "Let me make you some toast."

"Ach, don't bother. It tastes like peat mud anyhow."

"I'm not surprised, burned like that."

He brushed crumbs from the tabletop. "I made some tea. At least I remember how to do that."

What was there to forget? Ellen wondered. He obviously was one of those guys whose wife had done everything for him and now he was helpless without her. "Is there enough?" she asked.

"I made enough for both of us."

In a moment she was sitting at the table across from him, sipping from a blue china teacup. He was showing a few signs of having been up most of the night. A shaving cut on his chin had formed a scab. Only the bottom buttons on his shirt were fastened. Either he had been in too big a rush to button the top half, or he liked to go around with his chest showing.

Not that she minded looking. His husky chest was bulging from the shirt. The guy was a pleasure to tired eyes, and from his behavior, she couldn't tell whether or not he knew it. He should know, but there was no conceit in his body language, only sensuality that constantly distracted her.

"Good tea," she complimented.

"It's difficult to ruin tea, I suppose."

"Would you like me to fix you something to eat? Some eggs, maybe?"

He thought about this for a moment before he answered. "Not now. Thank you, but I think I will go outside to the garden and do some work while the day is still cool. There is much to be done to make the garden look as it should."

Ellen smiled. "Now there's something new. A man who turns down the offer of food."

Brennig laughed and finished his tea. "Later, I'll eat. I'm not used to...to working with a full stomach." He rose with a slight bow and exited through the French doors into the sun-filled garden.

Ellen watched him for a time, through the window, as she drank her tea, thinking how pleasant it was to watch him. It would be fascinating to know in what way the two of them were distantly related, but there was probably no way to find out. Brennig didn't seem particularly interested in trying to trace it, probably because he knew they couldn't. Eira would have had three children, at least two of them sons to carry on the name. Her ancestors must be Eira and Brennig if Nesta reacted to her presence.

Ellen opened the window to air out the room and proceeded to clean up the burned crumbs and straighten the kitchen. In the bright morning, the creaks and groans of the old house seemed to have disappeared. It was a lovely day with few clouds in the sky. There were things to see.

In midafternoon, after long strolls around town and tea with her landlady, Ellen returned to Afan House, filled with a special kind of excitement. Wrenn's Oak and its environs were just as her great-grandfather had described. The cobblestoned main street with its quaint shops. The grassy common, busy with starlings and scampering rabbits on a near hillside, the flowering hedgerows, the verge of flowering red poppies along the country lanes, the sweet-flowing river meandering lazily through the shallow valley, and the dark silhouette of a ruined castle high on a hill. Even more beautiful than she had imagined, Wrenn's Oak inspired photo snapping. There was something so familiar about it because of the pictures her grandfather had painted in her mind. Ellen felt at home here; she loved it.

Brennig was still in the garden when she returned, and the result of his labors were evident. Piles of trimmings lined the alleyway, and the slats of the back gate were visible through the pruned ivy.

She entered through the open gate. "It's looking great out here, Brennig. All the flower beds weeded. Mrs. Jenkins must be very pleased."

"I'd rather you were pleased, Ellen."

"Me?" She blushed with the flattery. "Well, actually, I love this garden and I'm very pleased."

"Good." He was pushing a small wheelbarrow filled with clippings and leaves. "I like it, too."

"You've been working out here all day."

"Garden work is good for the soul. I enjoy it. And I hate to see a garden gone to weed."

Ellen closed the gate behind her and proceeded along the path to the kitchen, where she put the kettle on for tea and set out on a plate the pastries she had bought at the bake-shop.

Fifteen minutes later she brought a tray to the garden and set it on a small, once-white wooden table that Brennig had cleaned and moved closer to the bench under the willow branches.

"I've brought tea."

"I thank you, milady." Brennig set down his shears, wiped his hands on the seat of his jeans, joined her on the bench and allowed her to pour the tea for him.

She studied him as he added two spoonsful of sugar and a good portion of milk. There was dirt on his clothes; she was amazed that not a bead of perspiration stained his face or his shirt on this sunny summer afternoon.

She said, "Either you're awfully neat in the kitchen, or you haven't eaten all day."

He stirred the tea slowly. "I tend to forget about food when I'm working. This is very nice. I appreciate your thoughtfulness." He was looking at the pastries with interest, trying to decide which he wanted first, and finally chose a jam tart, saying, "I haven't had one of these for a long time."

Ellen was watching him closely. "Why do you say that with such sadness, Brennig? Do they remind you of your childhood?"

"My childhood, aye," he replied, so distracted she wondered if he had really heard her question.

"Does it taste the same?"

"I don't know." He looked up. "I mean, I can't remember."

Most people remember tastes and smells better than anything else, she wanted to say to him. How odd you seem to recall neither. But it seemed inappropriate to say it, too impolite, and the setting created its own misty mood.

At length, Brennig asked, "Why do you keep looking around so curiously, Ellen?"

"I'm wondering where in this garden Brennig Cole died."

"Over there." He pointed to a grassy patch near the stone path that led to the house.

Startled, she turned to stare at the grass, picturing the scene in her mind while trying not to. "How could you possibly know that?"

"Because the wild raspberries grow adjacent to the path. It's . . . an educated guess."

Her gaze moved back to him. "I think you have a vivid mind picture of the murder—his death."

"Each time I tell the story, or walk out here in this garden."

"It's awful to think about it, here where everything is so peaceful with the flowers blooming and the birds singing."

"Time changes everything and nothing," Brennig said softly.

The tree branches above them danced in sparkles of sun. When the sun hit his face through a bright slant of light, the pupils of his eyes seemed to disappear. Like yesterday, when the same thing had happened, Ellen was frightened because his eyes seemed to have no depth to them. For a second or two, she sat, too stunned to move. The teacup trembled slightly in her hand.

He said, "Is something wrong? Are you remembering something?"

Ellen gasped and didn't answer until the color had come back into his eyes with the shifting of the light. "Remembering? What do you mean, remembering?"

He regarded her with an unnatural interest and seemed to be waiting for her to answer her own question. But she couldn't.

Having made no attempt to reply, he picked up another pastry and licked at the confectioner's sugar. In the afternoon hush, grasshoppers and bush crickets sang in raspy bursts. A snipe fly darted by, landed on Ellen's arm and flew away, buzzing its wings when she moved. A thrush gave a concert in the high trees. In the silence that was not silence, Ellen watched his eyes. They appeared normal again, if one could call the extremely pale blue normal. Under the blue sky they had more color than inside, or at night. His eyes reflected the sky.

There were so many things about this man that made Ellen uncomfortable, and yet she liked him. Genuinely. In fact, too much. All during the morning and early afternoon, touring around, she had been thinking about him and wishing he had offered to go with her and act as a guide to places here in his homeland that she had never seen. He had not offered. Maybe she should have asked.

Well, he did have an obligation to do the garden work and it seemed important to him to get to work. He was earning his keep, after all. The guy seemed to have no permanent job and little money.

When he'd asked her if she remembered what she could not possibly remember, had he for a moment thought she was someone else? The injury he wouldn't talk about might have affected his own memory. *Something* was certainly baffling about him. That sullen sadness. The brooding mischief in his smile. She couldn't deny her niggling fear of him.

"You are staring at the spot," Brennig said while he swallowed his tea.

"What?"

"The spot where he died. Try not to think about his death, Ellen. You know there is no such thing as death."

She looked up from the green grass. "The man was murdered, Brennig. He's been lying under the ground for over three hundred and sixty years. It might have happened a long time ago, but he would have had the passion for living that we have now, and the same fears of dying we have now. What do you mean, there's no such thing as death?"

"I mean only that. Death is an illusion."

"You think we keep on living, then, and come back later on in some other life? I don't think I believe that."

He smiled at her, a wise, frustrating smile.

She brushed irritatingly at a gnat. "You're thinking of Nesta, aren't you? You think Nesta is still here."

"I know it, and so do you."

Ellen swallowed. He was right; she did believe it. "And what about the other thing? Reincarnation?"

"It makes sense to me," he said.

"It does? Do you think Brennig Cole could come back as someone else?"

Brennig laughed. "I suppose he would have that choice."

"Choice? It's a matter of choice?"

"Aye. Many people believe so."

Ellen frowned. "Oh. And would the person who was him in a later life know that...? Would the person remember?"

"No. Obviously not."

"Then what's the point?"

"The soul knows," he said, and the laughter in his pale blue eyes was gone.

She leaned closer. "Do you think the spirit of Nesta hangs around because the spirit of Brennig is still here?"

He pursed his lips. "No one has ever thought so."

"You don't think the house and garden are haunted, then?"

"By his spirit? Perhaps."

"By Eira's?"

"No," Brennig said with conviction. "Remember, Eira crossed over the bridge. She couldn't come back in death, because of Nesta's curse."

Ellen watched the light play on his handsome face as sun danced through the willow branches over them. "I don't see how you could know all that, Brennig."

He smiled thinly. "The legend."

So much information in a legend? Maybe so, or at least implied. Yet something was nagging at her. Intuitively she believed he was lying—not about what he was saying but about how he knew.

CHAPTER NINE

The following morning, when Ellen opened her bedroom shutters and looked down through the tree branches, she saw Brennig already in the garden kneeling on one knee trimming back dogwood vines. The sun was high and burning through flimsy, floating clouds.

It wasn't like her to oversleep, but it had been another sleepless night of hearing Brennig moving about the house in the dark and wondering if he had the eyes of a cat. It seemed he didn't get tired, didn't get hungry. Well, there had been some trauma in his life recently; he'd said as much. Probably he still hadn't recovered from whatever awful accident had befallen him.

She showered, dressed in her jeans and made tea in the kitchen. The sound of Brennig's voice singing came through the open window, a voice so beautiful that she closed her eyes and sat listening, lost in a sound that brought pictures to her mind of people of medieval times dancing on the heather-draped hillsides. Where the picture came from she couldn't imagine, except the Gaelic sounds must have conjured up imaginings of history.

The singing grew louder, until it abruptly stopped. When she opened her eyes, Brennig was standing in the doorway holding a large bunch of freshly cut flowers.

He smiled. "For you, milady."

Her heart fluttered. "Oh, Brennig! How nice!"

"Beautiful flowers for a beautiful lady."

Suddenly her blue jeans felt out of place. She should walk toward him with petticoats rustling and reach out with a lace-trimmed sleeve. But since Brennig, too, was wearing jeans, it was quite impossible to hold on to the make-believe fancy. The flowers, though, were from an ancient garden. Had the blacksmith ever brought in a wild bouquet like this one for his wife? Chances were, he had. And she had looked at him with love.

She gathered the flowers into her hands, smiling radiantly, filled with excitement because this gift was his way of telling her he desired more than merely a casual friendship. This was the gesture—combined with the apprehensive expression in his eyes—of a man intrigued by a woman.

"Thank you, Brennig! I must find a vase for these." Self-consciously, she began opening cupboard doors until she found a large jar. Her hands were not as steady as they should have been when she filled it with water. This man...this incredible mystery of a man... found her attractive! He was sincere, even a little shy about conveying it. The gift of flowers spoke for him.

Or, she thought, maybe he was just being polite the way she had been yesterday when she brought tea out to the garden. Who was she kidding? She'd brought tea because she was so drawn to *him*. And he had known it.

She said softly from behind the flowers, "I heard you singing in the garden."

"I like to sing."

"Your voice is lovely. It was hard for me to tell exactly where you were, because it's like an echo from the nearby hills. From a distance, your voice takes on such an echo, Brennig. Have other people told you so?"

"No."

"It's quite fascinating, really. Sometimes even your speaking voice takes on that echo. And sometimes your voice kind of fades away, and then it comes back."

"When I'm not concentrating, I suppose," he answered vaguely.

"It's...very unusual, though." She grinned. "It's very sweet of you to bring me the flowers. I was about to come out and ask if you wanted any help in the garden."

This seemed to please him. He took the vase from her and set it in the center of the table. "I wouldn't want those lovely hands soiled with dirt or scratched by twigs. But I would like the companionship."

The pleasure showed in her face. "I'm not any good at watching other people work. What shall I do out there if you won't give me a pair of shears?"

He held out his hand. "Come. I'll show you how to make a bracelet of vines. A wee craft I learned in my youth."

Brennig was feeling downright playful this morning. And why not? It was a beautiful day. Ellen took his hand, luxuriating in the cool sensations of it and allowed him to lead the way.

In the midst of a concert of bird song, Brennig gathered vines, cut them in equal lengths and piled them neatly on the lawn. They sat on the grass while he twisted the vines in a kind of braiding she had never seen done, and made a bracelet. He slid it gently onto her wrist. The stems felt cool, like his hands, and as soon as the bracelet was on, Ellen experienced a hint of vertigo, which she blamed on the sun, knowing it was not the sun.

"Do you want to try to make one?" he asked, fitting more vine stems together.

"It looks too complicated. I'd rather watch you."

"Ach, it's not so complicated," he replied good-naturedly while he proceeded to weave the vines into a second bracelet and slipped it over her other hand.

The vertigo came again, strangely, and then disappeared, and she was left with a feeling of euphoria that had to do with Brennig. She gazed down at the pretty bracelets wound around her wrists like handcuffs and wanted to say, it looks like I'm your captive. But she didn't say it because he might not understand what she meant. She herself wasn't sure why she would react to the vine bracelets that way—she almost *felt* as though they were handcuffs.

Handcuffs or not, she couldn't resist the charm of a man who was so gentle, even though something about him hinted he might not always be gentle. Those eyes would captivate any woman, and he probably knew it.

Brennig suddenly got to his feet and reached down to help her up. Standing, looking at the bracelets, Ellen thought that this bracelet weaving must be a very old tradition and probably had meanings he wasn't sharing with her. She looked up quizzically to see if she could determine what he was thinking, but all she could see in his eyes was the usual mischief mixed with sadness.

"What other games did you play in your youth?" she asked.

He shrugged. "Hide-and-seek."

"A garden like this would be the perfect place for hide-and-seek."

"It would," he agreed. "Very well. I'll be a gentleman and allow you to be the first to hide."

She laughed. "Now? You want to play?"

"Why not? Do we have something better to do on this sunny morning?"

There was quite a change in him, she noted, and wondered if it had anything to do with her. Certainly he seemed more at ease with her than he had at first. Maybe it was just the adjustment getting easier, for both of them—this odd business of her renting a house with him in it—this guy who said he believed there was no such thing as chance.

The sun warmed her shoulders. She took a deep breath and allowed the fragrant, fresh air to fill her lungs. "All right." She grinned. "You're it, then. Stand by the tree and cover your eyes."

From the tree, he called, "I'm going to count to one hundred. Then I'm coming."

"No peeking!" she called back, darting to the opposite side of the garden. She crouched behind some rocks where a fat, wild clump of bilberry was growing, laden with its purple berries.

"Time is up!" Brennig yelled.

She waited, barely breathing, until she heard him say "Aha!" He was standing over her.

"How did you manage to find me so fast?"

He shrugged innocently. "I know the garden better than you do. I know all the good places."

"Maybe, but you're bigger, too. I don't think you can hide from me."

"We will see," he challenged. "Cover your eyes."

Her heart pounded, not from the excitement of the game itself but because of how it felt to be running around in this ancient garden as carefree as a child.

"I've counted to a hundred and I'm coming!" she called to the empty garden. No sound. She checked all the obvious corners and hedges and thick trees. He seemed to be nowhere. The garden wasn't that big. How could he hide so well?

Two or three minutes passed, and Ellen was certain he had sneaked out either the side gate or the back gate, yet she hadn't heard any hinges squeak.

"Brennig! I give up! I can't find you!"

From a hedge immediately behind her came his voice. "I'm right here."

A chill shot through her. Her heart thundered. "Omigod! You scared me half to death! Where were you? I looked behind there!"

"You just didn't see me."

Hand on her pounding heart, she was gasping. "I looked everywhere and not a sight of you, not a sound! And then you pop up like a ghost! How could you—"

"I'm sorry, Ellen. I swear I didn't mean to frighten you." He reached out with one hand, then with both and pulled her toward him.

In the next second she found herself wrapped in his arms, her head against his chest, and he was holding her tightly, comfortingly.

"I didn't mean to," he repeated. "I don't want to do anything to frighten you."

Instant calm dropped over her as if someone had slipped a warm cloak over her shoulders.

"I'm not afraid," she mumbled into his chest. "I just was startled for a second."

"Let's forget about the game," Brennig said gently into her ear, and then he muttered, "the sun in your hair is so warm against my face...so soft... I had forgotten how soft a woman's touch can be...."

Something was happening to cause her body to go weak. Her legs trembled. Her heart began to race as much as before but in a different way. A frightening and familiar way...that of her body's response to wanting a man.

Then his lips brushed her forehead, her cheek and her mouth. The kiss was gentle at first and became more firm with each passing second. Ellen leaned into him, allowing his weight to support her body as the kiss lengthened. For some uncountable seconds, her mind went completely blank and black, as if she had stepped off the earth into a floating nothingness.

When she finally was able to open her eyes, his eyes were closed. She drew away; he released her only reluctantly.

"Brennig..." It was only a whisper.

"My sweet lady, don't draw away from me." His voice was a whisper, too, barely audible above the warbling of a songbird perched in the highest branches and the chorus of grasshoppers in a nearby patch of parsley ferns.

"But I..."

For a moment, Ellen couldn't remember what it was that felt so wrong. Some dark shadow was brooding near her heart, and, so stunned was she by the power of Brennig's kiss, that it seemed a long time before she identified the shadow as her memory of Brent.

Brent. The guy who loved her. Trusted her. Waited to come to her. The sweet, handsome, desirable guy she loved—only a shadow behind the blinding radiance of the Welshman's kiss.

An awful ache started in her heart. When Brennig cupped her face in his large hands and looked down into her eyes, the ache began to lift magically—so magically that she became confused as to just what it was that had caused the pain in the first place.

His lips pressed against hers once more, and the shadow moved away, and she was lost.

And found. He whispered, "How beautiful you are. How soft and warm your lips are. How I've longed—"

"Brennig! What's happening? This is wrong...."

"Wrong? Why?"

She fumbled and tripped over her own words. "Because...we don't even know each other... it's so soon...."

"We do know each other, Ellen. And it isn't soon to me."

"Two days..."

"Aye, two days of thinking of you each moment adds up to a great many moments." He pushed her hair back from her face gently with two fingers, and his deep voice melted into her consciousness. "There isn't much time," he said. "That's why I didn't wait a more proper lapse before I kissed you. There just isn't much time."

She nodded. "I know. My month here is going to fly."

"And we must make the most of it."

"What about you, Brennig? How long are you going to stay?"

"Another three weeks or so."

"Three weeks..." she repeated thoughtfully, sadly. Just about until the time Brent came. Her heart constricted, and her thoughts reached out in a strange desperation. Brent...where are you?

His eyes closed as he moved his fingers gently through her hair. "Like silk..." he muttered. "Ah...it's been so long...."

She blinked. "So long?"

His breathing changed slightly. His eyes opened. "So long since I've touched... silk."

She thought he might be thinking about his wife. He must be missing her. And yet Ellen had also been aware of his curiosity about her before this, of his studying her face when he'd thought she wasn't looking, of his unexpected questions about what her favorite color was or what month she was born or what her house in America was like. Little things most strangers would not ask.

Brennig Cole was no longer a stranger, though, not now. That same curiosity was not in his kiss; rather, he came to her like someone who had kissed her many times before, and already knew her responses and the taste of her lips. Why? Was he wishing she were someone else? His wife?

When he looked into her eyes, though, she felt he knew her. They were eyes trying to see into her heart.

He looked at her with love.

Something in Brennig's pale eyes made her forget she knew another life before him and would go back to another life after. His eyes made her forget everything but him. Those beautiful, mysterious eyes ...

In the garden where long ago a young blacksmith had died a painful death, Brennig held her. Ellen felt herself sliding out of her own world and into his, and it was all right. The nagging fears, the guilt, seemed to have evaporated like dew in sunlight, and it was all right.

She welcomed Brennig's lips.

His kiss tasted like the wild wind, wrapping untamed energy around her, energy too strong to resist, for her memories had become caged by the force of Brennig's will.

Trembling, Ellen clung to him as if from a fear of falling. In his arms she heard music where none had been before; the birdsongs blended magically into a symphony.

"I hear the music, too," Brennig whispered, reading her mind, moving his fingers through her hair as though he couldn't get enough of touching her.

How could he know? Did Brennig feel the magic, or was he creating it himself?

Ellen closed her eyes and let herself drift deep into the magic. With him, she became so keenly aware of being alive, all other days, all other sights, faded away in a haze of uncertainty.

She shouldn't be here. With him. But she forgot there was anywhere else.

They were standing near the gate that opened to the side yard after following the fickle flight of a butterfly over a spangle of lavender flowers. Brennig said in his thick Welsh accent. "I can't believe how deeply I feel. I didn't know the emotions would be so strong. Have I forgotten and it is you reminding me?"

"You say the darnedest things," Ellen replied. "And you ask questions that have no answers."

"All questions have answers somewhere, my sweet lady. They are just not within grasp right now. Someday there will be no questions left."

"There, you see. These are remarks I barely understand. How can there be no questions left, unless we knew every answer to everything?"

He smiled and took her hand. "Not answers to everything, Ellen. Only the answers about us."

This startled her. "Brennig? How can there be an us?"

His laughter was as gentle as the mysterious music. "My dear, there will always be an us. Memories are never forgotten, those we have and those yet to come. The memory of our kiss, just now, will be with me forever."

"For me, too," Ellen said honestly. And she thought, *our first kiss.* Already she was longing to feel again the touch of his lips on hers. Her heart had still not stopped fluttering. Something seemed very wrong with this aching for Brennig's touch, but just now the dark shadow was out of reach; she could barely remember what it was.

On the street a woman was walking a small dog on a leash. As she passed and saw the man and woman standing inside the garden gate at the back wall, the dog halted, whimpered and began to bark.

His mistress, embarrassed, called the dog's name and then apologized over the sound of the shrill yipping.

"I don't know what's got into him! He never barks like this."

"It's all right," Brennig said. "Dogs don't like me."

Ellen's head turned swiftly. "Dogs don't like you? Why? It isn't mutual, is it?"

"Ah, a dog enthusiast, are you?" he replied. "Of course it's not mutual. It just seems to be a fact, as you can see."

The woman on the street was pulling on the dog, urging it away from the cottage with some difficulty. "I do apologize for the bad manners of my dog...I just really do not understand why he would do this...."

Brennig rested a hand on Ellen's shoulder. "You seem upset. Don't let such a small thing upset you."

She gazed up at him. "Is there an answer to this, too? Why dogs bark at you?"

He nodded slowly. "Aye, sure. At the moment it is not a concern, though. I can think only about you and how good it feels to be near you. All the feelings are here, Ellen." He paused, as if he had just said something he hadn't meant to, and then added, making a loose fist over his chest, "Here ... in my heart."

For a long time she didn't speak. The garden that once had known death now symbolized love for her. If the ghost of the blacksmith was still here, it was all right. He, too, had been in love. He, too, would know.

"I'm afraid of my feelings," Ellen said after a long, contemplative silence.

His arm tightened around her shoulder. "Don't be afraid. It's all right."

"But you don't know my feelings."

He smiled softly. "I know your kiss. You told me with your kiss and the way your arms embraced me. Those parts of us which respond to each other also communicate with each other, whether we are consciously aware of it or not."

"I'm afraid," she repeated. "Saying I shouldn't be doesn't change it. I feel like something is very wrong."

They began walking the stone path that led to the kitchen door. He said, "You have someone at home, in America."

"Yes."

"What is he like?"

Ellen found herself straining to remember. Trying to shake off the powerful spell of Brennig so she could think about Brent was not an easy thing to do at this moment, with Brennig's shoulder touching hers and his hand wrapped over her own.

"He's a very good man. Intelligent, kind, honorable."

"You would not choose less."

She lowered her head, while a shard of that terrible sense of loss shot through her like an arrow. It didn't linger as it had on the bridge; it struck with searing pain and then gradually began to lift.

"He loves me," she continued, her voice weak.

"I'm sorry," Brennig said.

She looked up at him. "What do you mean?"

He opened the kitchen door for her and motioned her inside. "The curse of Nesta."

She stared. This was something she had tried very hard not to think about. "The curse...Brennig, is that why I find it difficult to think about him, to remember...?"

"Aye."

"But how could you know that?"

His voice became almost a whisper. "I know, that's all. I just know."

Tears welled up in Ellen's eyes. "I believe you. I don't want to, but I believe you...."

He took her in his arms again. "Try not to cry, my sweet. Remember, there is a reason for everything in this life. It is as if it were meant to be, because now I am here, and I want your thoughts to be of me."

Ellen tensed. It didn't take much intuition to realize that this man was as possessive as he was desirable. It was flattering, exciting, but also disquieting, and, above all, puzzling. She looked down at the braided bracelets on her wrists. Brennig's gifts to her. The bracelets gave her joy and trepidation at the same time. It was silly; they were made of vines, not iron. Not gold.

In the kitchen, washing his hands at the tap, Brennig looked out at the sky. "The high clouds have blown off. There will be no rain. Do you have plans in mind for the day?"

"I want to drive around the countryside and take some photos of the scenery."

His face brightened. "Ah! You mean in the automobile!"

She nodded. "Would you like to come along?"

"I most surely would." He dried his hands on a kitchen towel. "I'll be your guide, insofar as things are as I remember them. Are you ready?"

"Sure. I'll just get my purse and camera and meet you out by the car."

He was there before she was trying to open the door of the small white sedan.

"It's locked," Ellen said, fumbling in her shoulder bag for the key.

She unlocked both doors, started to get into the driver's side, and stopped. "Do you want to drive, Brennig? I'm not used to driving in Britain—on this side of the car or this side of the road. I have to concentrate every minute to keep myself from pulling into head-on traffic."

"I was hoping you would invite me to...uh...drive."
He grinned. "Where did you get the automobile, then?
Surely you didn't buy it for just three weeks."

She cocked her head. He must be kidding; he'd have to
assume she rented it. "It belongs to a friend who lives in
London. She was kind enough to loan it to me while she's
spending the summer in Italy. I was really lucky there, because car rentals are more expensive than I could have
managed."

He nodded thoughtfully and slid into the driver's seat,
waiting for her to go around and get in. His manners were
normally so perfect that this breach of etiquette startled
her.

He was studying the dash, just sitting and staring at it
with a frown on his face.

"Is something wrong?" she asked, clicking her seat belt
closed.

"This is new," he muttered, not looking at her.

"Fairly new, yes, but it's an easy car to drive."

"What do I do?"

Ellen hardly knew how to answer. "It's automatic, of
course. Just switch on the ignition and move from neutral
to reverse."

He was looking at the dials in front of him in silence.
Finally he said, "I've never had a car."

"Really? You can't mean you've never driven...?" She
caught herself before her surprise became too obvious.
After all, she knew nothing about the Welsh community
in which he lived. People probably didn't have cars galore
like they did in America, and yet there were plenty of au-
tomobiles around Wrenn's Oak. It had evidently been
presumptuous, though, to presume everybody in this
country owned a car and knew how to drive. Brennig

would have driven up from the town he lived in if he'd had a car. Still, how could he not have driven?

"Well, not a car like this," he was mumbling, fiddling with the knobs and dials. "If you'll drive a short distance and let me observe, then I'll take over from there. I learn fast."

"Okay, sure," Ellen said doubtfully, opening her door.

When he got into the passenger seat, Brennig said, "I should have thought of it."

"What do you mean?"

"Cars," he replied, already using her name for them instead of his. "I mean I ought to have..." He stopped, intent on watching what Ellen was doing as she turned the key in the ignition.

Taking care that she stayed to the left, she pulled out onto the narrow street. There was no other traffic. She drove the short distance to the edge of town and down a country lane through lovely bucolic scenery. Sheep with bushy black tails grazed peacefully on the green hillsides. Scattered farm buildings and small houses nestled on the valley floor.

Brennig was silent, enjoying the breeze through the open window while he watched Ellen drive. After a short time, he said, "I'll have a go at this machine now."

"I'm looking for a place to pull off."

Brennig's impatience was obvious. He acted as if he expected her to just stop in the middle of the road. This was not the first example of his impatience; he seemed to be impatient about everything. Like kissing her, not waiting what she considered a more reasonable amount of time considering the fact that they were thrown together by circumstance, not by their own doing.

Where a shoulder widened, she pulled over and stopped. Brennig was as impatient as a boy to get behind the wheel.

He put it in drive and pressed the gas pedal so heavily the car lurched forward like a pouncing cat. Ellen gritted her teeth and called on all the forces of her willpower to keep silent. What kind of cars had he been driving, anyhow? Well, he said he could do this. So let him.

Luckily there was almost no traffic. Brennig was taking his half of the road out of the middle.

When it was impossible to keep it inside any longer, she howled, "You're going awfully fast!"

"This is good," he answered. "This is fine. I like this, Ellen."

"It's dangerous on this road. Watch out, a car is coming toward us!"

"Have faith, fair lady."

Brennig swerved the car over but just in time and barely slowed down doing it.

Ellen's heart was pounding in her throat. "Have you no fear of death?"

He looked over at her. "Have you?"

"Of course! I don't want to end up a crash statistic, and we're going to if you keep driving like this. Damn it, slow down for this curve! You're scaring me, Brennig!"

His foot lifted from the gas pedal. "I didn't realize you would be frightened."

"Who wouldn't be?" She started to complain that he drove like someone who had never been in a car in his life, but it might be cruel to keep pounding home the fact because he might be so poor he hadn't even ridden in many cars. But still, there were such things as common sense and respect for the safety of another person.

"Very well," he conceded. "I will stop being the child and drive sensibly. For you."

After that it was better, but he still did irresponsible things like running a stop sign, and he liked to speed up and slow down for no good reason, and he always hit the brake too hard. The more used to the car he became, though, the better it was. No question, he was having great fun.

"Where would you like to go?" he asked after a time.

"To the castle on the hill."

This brought a smile. "Aye, I should have guessed you would want to see the castle."

"Doesn't everyone?"

"It is not such an ominous one anymore," Brennig answered. "It is merely a ruin, but from its hill is a fine view of the valley and the river."

The towers formed a dark silhouette against the sky. Two rose tall, two more had crumbled away. Brennig told her of ancient battles fought here, of enemies storming the fortress walls.

The road ended halfway up the hill. They parked and walked the rest of the way, hand in hand. Ellen was aware that she was enjoying herself more than she had in a long time. It was the newness of Brennig, the ancient beauty of his country, the country of her ancestors—and his—and the adventure of seeing it with him.

He read her mood. "You seem happy."

"Happy to be out of that car with you driving," she teased, and then, seriously, "Yes, I am happy. I'm having fun. Aren't you?"

"I don't remember having more fun."

She squeezed his hand. "I get the feeling it has been a long time since you really had some pleasure in your life. Am I right?"

"It has been longer than you think."

"You were hurt, you said."

"Aye. I was."

"Do you want to talk about it?"

"No, my sweet lady, I do not. These hours are so pleasant with you. We won't speak of unpleasant things. There is no need to."

"You're right. We shouldn't. We're both here for a holiday. We'll just enjoy ourselves."

Up close, the castle was scarcely more than a shell. The roof was missing and many of the stairs were damaged. They wandered through weathered stone chambers and up a dark, winding tower stairs to reach the ramparts, which looked out over the countryside. Here they paused, Brennig's arm about her waist. A gentle wind blew against their faces and the soft warmth of the sun fell on their shoulders. Except for the distant cry of a bird, there was only silence where once fierce battles had taken place. Even the memories seemed mute.

"It's beautiful," she said. "The colors of green in the fields and the sheep. And the dark green stripe of river winding clear to the horizon."

"Destiny, too, is beautiful," he said as he leaned down slowly to kiss her. "Your destiny and mine...as intertwined as the vines that grace your lovely wrists."

Accepting his kiss, Ellen allowed his love to flow into her. She felt it enter her body through her beating heart and flow through her bloodstream.

Love was in Brennig's kiss.

"Your destiny and mine..." he repeated in a raspy whisper.

In the fragrant, fresh breeze of the Welsh countryside, on the ramparts of a medieval castle, Ellen held her body close to his, feeling now, since his kiss, that she had known him forever. She had no idea what he meant when he spoke so mysteriously of their destiny, but Brennig knew, she was sure.

He knew she was falling in love with him.

CHAPTER TEN

Love had caught them in its talons as if it were a giant soaring bird, seizing them, carrying them high and higher into sunlight and weightlessness. When they walked, he held her hand and the very touch of him would unbalance her heartbeats with a seizure of need. When they ate by candlelight, Brennig would reach across the table to close his fingers over hers. They would smile at each other spontaneously. And in quiet moments, he would take her into his arms and kiss her in a way she had never known before, and they would hear the music.

Feeling his male body hard against hers, Ellen's own run-away emotions would rush up like flames to her eyes. Through the flames, she could see his handsome face as if in a dream. He would reach out through the heat tremors, luring her into the dazzling heart-core of his love.

The music turned into colors, and pieces of rainbows fell over them when Brennig whispered his love for her. In the rainbows and the sunlight and the flames, they had become lovers without the final surrender of their bodies to each other. To her surprise, Brennig didn't even try—didn't touch her, except to caress her face or hand or shoulder lovingly. These sweet caresses and his kisses expressed his love and his need for her. Nothing more.

It was incredibly refreshing. The man had a different code of ethics; his was simultaneously a gentle and possessive love. Although he made it clear he would not take advantage of their unique living situation, he wanted to be with her every waking moment. Ellen wanted it, too. Wanted his time. Wanted him. His kisses brought visions to her mind of soft days and peaceful nights, always with him.

Yet she knew so little about him. And when she asked, he hedged saying the past was not important in these new days, only the future mattered.

A future with Brennig? That hardly seemed possible, especially since he never talked about himself—not his home nor his work nor his life plans. After all, she had another life with someone else, somewhere else ... it was just hard to recall the details of home....

For two days they toured the environs of Wrenn's Oak. Brennig knew his way around very well, but some things, he said, had changed since he was here when he was young. That second evening, when they got back to Afan House after a late dinner in the pub, a letter was waiting for Ellen on the doorstep. Mrs. Jenkins had brought it over because the cottage had no mailbox and it had been delivered across the street.

Ellen experienced a sinking loneliness when she picked up the envelope. In the gloaming the writing was not clear, but it was easy enough to recognize that the handwriting was the unassuming, familiar scrawl of Brent.

Brent. Oh, God.

"Is something wrong?" Brennig asked, opening the door for her.

She slid the envelope into her handbag. "No. It's a letter from home."

"From him."

She nodded. "Oh, Brennig, I feel guilty."

His eyes were sad. "It's not something within your control, my sweet."

"*I* control my actions."

"But not your feelings, and not fate. And not the hooks of Nesta's curse."

She looked at him doubtfully. "The curse will affect us, too, won't it?"

"Perhaps not." He was evasive, hesitant.

"*Why* not?"

He became deliberately distracted with switching on the lights in the lower hall.

"Brennig, why aren't you answering me?"

He sighed. "It can be different for us, Ellen."

"I thought you were so convinced the curse is real!"

"There are some mysteries about it," he replied evasively. "You and I had both crossed the bridge before we met, not after."

"And that matters?"

"I think so."

Ellen felt like crying. "Oh, but, Brennig, it's all so unreal. I don't have much time left here. I don't know what to do with your feelings for me or mine for you. I think we shouldn't have allowed ourselves to..." She started to say "become lovers" and then stopped herself, because actually—technically—they weren't lovers. So why did she feel as if they were?

He held her close. "It's all right. Please trust me when I say that. It will be all right, in time. Why don't we have a little wine together in the parlor?"

"No, I don't think I should. It's been a long day and I'm tired. I think I'll go upstairs and wash my hair and have an early night. These last days have been so overwhelming, I've hardly slept. I just want to wind down and have a little time to think."

"And to read the letter."

She nodded. "Yes. That, too."

It was obvious Brennig didn't like this at all. He wanted to be with her, and she was telling him she would rather be alone—and with the letter from a man who loved her. She saw a flash of anger in his eyes, and his jaw stiffened, but he chose—wisely—not to say anything more. Instead he leaned forward and kissed her.

"Good night then, my sweet. I hope you sleep better tonight."

"I hope you do, too, Brennig," she answered gently. "I hear you walking around in the night all the time. Don't you ever sleep?"

"Not much."

"But what do you do at night?"

"I suppose I pace a lot, out of restlessness. I didn't know I was disturbing you."

"You're not, really. I just...wonder why you walk around so much and never bother with the lights."

He smiled. "I can see in the dark very well. Anytime you feel like pacing with me, let me know."

What did he mean by that? Was it only a joke or was it an invitation to spend the night with him? It was so hard to read him. It was so hard to *think* with Brennig so near. When she pulled away from his embrace, Brennig released her easily and remained standing in the foyer while she climbed the stairs.

"Good night," she called back. "Sweet dreams."

Alone in her room, Ellen pulled the shutters, closing out the night, the electricity of Brennig's last kiss still tingling on her lips, the touch of his hands still throbbing on her shoulders. She sat on the bed and stared at the floor, trying to calm herself after the effects of his nearness.

Her eyes came to rest on the bracelets he had made and placed on her wrists. The green vines were changing color from green to iron brown, and as the strands dried, they tended to shrink. Each day it was a little harder to get them off. Rolling them over each hand, Ellen wondered still again what it was about those bracelets that bothered her and made her think of handcuffs. There was no logical reason for her paranoia about them; Brennig had woven them of his love, and it pleased him that she had worn them each day since. He had mentioned it a time or two.

Who the hell was Brennig, anyway? Why did he love her? Why did she love him? It was a blinding, bewildering kind of love that had come fast and dazzling and, Ellen thought, ill reasoned. It perplexed her that the longer she knew him, the more he seemed a stranger—and yet the longer she knew him the more she loved him. It made no sense. That he should be more mysterious to her now than he had been the day they met was just plain eerie.

And even though he had been nothing but kind to her, his possessiveness was something of a worry. She couldn't figure out what Brennig wanted from her.

He wanted something, though. At the very least, he wanted her love. And Ellen? What did *she* want?

At this point, she didn't know. How could she love a man like Brennig? How could she *not* love him?

She set the woven bracelets on the table beside the bed with a slight, unexplainable sense of relief that they were off, even though they weighed almost nothing and, when Brennig was with her, she was mostly unaware of them. Turning on the lamp with a trembling hand, she lifted Brent's letter from her handbag.

He must have written immediately after she'd phoned him from the hotel when she'd checked out that first afternoon. It had been important to let him know she was staying at a charming cottage on Pembroke Lane that unfortunately had no phone. She had given him Mrs. Jenkins's name and address. He must have sent this letter by express mail that same night.

Tears filled Ellen's eyes as she looked at his familiar handwriting on the envelope. The guilt seemed to paralyze her fingers; she thought she couldn't bear reading the letter Brent had written to a woman he believed was in love with him. Damn. She *was* in love with him.

And now with Brennig, too? A hard lump formed in her throat.

Brent did not normally write letters at all; he'd often mentioned that. This one was not thick. She unfolded the paper slowly.

My dearest Ellen,

I was glad to hear you found your way safely from London. I worried about you on those British roads. Not that I don't have all the world's confidence in you, honey; it's just that I have tackled those crazy roads myself and I know it's not easy. But never mind, you made it. By the time you receive this you will be settled into your little old house, and hopefully thinking of me and wishing I were with you.

I wish I were, too. I miss you more than I thought I could ever miss anyone, and I'm sorry I didn't come with you like you wanted. The place is lonely and empty without you. My whole life is empty without you. You are so much a part of me.

If I could, I'd change the plans and hightail it over there to share your cottage. I've got some tough business commitments now, though, and the ticket, which can't be changed, and I know you want some time to be alone and rest and do your research, so I'm forced to wait another three weeks. Watch out when I get there. I'm going to grab you up in my arms, and I just

might never let you go. Then the world will feel right
again. I love you, darling. More than you know. I
think even more than I know. I want to feel your love.
I count the days till we're together again.

All my love, Brent.

The words on the page were so blurred with her tears,
Ellen had to keep blinking in order to read his letter. The
pain in her heart was almost more than she could bear.
Guilt. Sadness. Overwhelming love for Brent. What was
the matter with her? What was happening? Was that curse
really in effect, or was Brennig manipulating her to believe so?

Brennig was the sort of man, she had figured out, who
would stop at almost nothing to get what he wanted, and
he wanted her . . . at least he wanted her while he was here
in Wrenn's Oak. Would he lie about the curse?

He hadn't lied about the curse, she was sure, because she
had felt it take hold of her on the bridge. There was no
question about that. The awful sensations of having lost
everything, of being alone...no, Brennig hadn't lied about
the curse. The hate for Nesta that showed in his eyes was
frightening. No doubt he blamed the ghost in the river for
the loss of his own love. And he took for granted that Ellen, too, had now lost Brent. Maybe that was why he didn't
hesitate to declare his own love for her. He believed she was
destined to loneliness.

But *why?* Loneliness? Brent loved her. Oh, no! Did it
mean that something awful would happen to him the way
it had happened to Brennig's wife, unless she left Brent's
life forever?

If something happened to Brent, she couldn't stand it.
What if it did, and it was her fault for not taking the damn
curse seriously? Maybe Brennig was trying to *help* her!

No. Brennig was trying to possess her. Could she allow that to escalate? Could she stay with Brennig to save Brent's life? She loved Brennig, to be sure, but she loved Brent, too. And to hurt Brent, without his ever understanding why—Brent didn't deserve that. He had always been so good to her.

The letter dropped from Ellen's hands. She let it lie on the floor at her feet and curled onto the bed, sobbing into her hands, wishing she had never met Brennig. Wishing she had never crossed the cursed bridge. Part of her longed for home and normalcy—for the first time. The familiar part of her embraced the adventure of an enchanted Welsh village and the love of a mysterious Welshman. But in moments like this, without Brent, the adventure seemed hollow.

How long she lay on her bed crying, Ellen wasn't sure. But after a time, she heard Brennig's footsteps on the stairs. The house otherwise was as still as death and her room was chilled. The bed pillow was wet from her tears, and the one small lamp cast cold light across the floor. Dark shadows filled every corner.

She sat up. *This place is haunted!* a voice within her screamed. There was a strong presence here, she could feel it, and the presence was not human. The strange footsteps— Maybe they *weren't* Brennig's—at least not all of them. A ghost was in this house. Brennig had tried to talk her out of the notion each time she'd mentioned it, but tonight, here alone, the feeling was too strong to deny. Surely he felt it, too, and just didn't want to scare her.

She shivered and pulled the quilt around her. "Who are you?" she whispered into the dimly lighted recesses of her room. "You're here, I know you are!"

There was movement in the shadows and a slight rustle of the curtains, as if the ghost were answering her quivering plea to acknowledge its presence.

Ellen knew her voice was shaking, even in a whisper. "Who are you?" she repeated. "Are you someone who died here? Are you him?"

Nothing more. The room quieted. Perhaps he had not liked the question and had drawn away through the darkness.

She woke to piercing arrows of light shooting from the window. The shutters hadn't been tightly closed, and the strong east sun pushed through. It had been a restless night with the sounds of Brennig moving about and the end of her recent denials that the house was haunted. She knew now for sure that it was.

In the light of morning, she felt no unwelcome presence. Why was it spirits chose to stalk the darkness and rarely, if ever, the light?

A debilitating heaviness gripped her body this morning, and her eyes were swollen from crying, but it had nothing to do with the ghost. Brent's letter still lay on the floor where it had fallen from her hands last night.

Brent's letter...

It had to be answered and at once, she had decided this in the sleepless hours of tossing. Brent had to know what was going on here, at least he had to be told about Brennig and her own confused feelings. Ellen believed in honesty, and Brent certainly deserved honesty.

With effort, she sat up and opened the drawer of the bed table where she had put her journal and a writing pad. The journal had been neglected since Brennig. Her thoughts were so jumbled and confused, her whole life seemed to be upside down and wrong side out.

Do it now, before you get up and find some excuse to put it off, she told herself with fierce determination. And, propped up against pillows with the quilt over her chest, Ellen began to write.

Dear Brent,
There is something you have to know. A man is here in this house who is named for one of my ancestors, which makes him a cousin of some sort, and this cousin and I have been ...

Ellen read over what she had scrawled, let out an involuntary groan and ripped the page from her writing pad, crumpling it with vengeance. The truth was terrible! Too terrible to write. She couldn't do it.

After all, she reasoned, there was no future with Brennig. She would leave here and all this would be over. Forever. Except for memories that would slowly fade as time went by. What was to be gained by hurting Brent?

How different everything looked in the cool light of morning. Okay, so she had been aware of a ghost here last night. The thing couldn't hurt her. Okay, so there was supposedly a curse. It was three-and-a-half centuries old, for Lord's sake, how could it hurt her now?

And what, really, was there to say to Brent? She and Brennig weren't lovers. It was true she felt guilty as hell for leading him on, for returning his dazzling kisses, for getting caught up in the fantasy of an ancient story. But hurting Brent over it all would only make Brent suffer and make her feel worse. The only one to gain anything by it would be Brennig, who made it pretty clear he didn't think she should be involved with anyone but him, even though he had to know she couldn't stay in Wales. He hadn't even *asked* her about the possibility of her staying, so how damn serious could he be?

It was just an adventure, this fascination with Brennig Cole, because he was foreign and mysterious, with a voice and an accent too much like Richard Burton's to be fair, and eyes that could haunt because they were too pale to sparkle and a body a model would envy. What woman wouldn't be smitten with a man like this? And Brennig would know that, he would have to know.

He had a way of drawing her to him that was too mysterious to define.

Ellen threw back the bed quilt, welcoming the cool. She picked up Brent's letter from the floor, muttering, "It will be all right.... *What* will be all right? I don't even know what I'm talking about! I don't even know what's happening!"

Carefully she folded the letter, slipped it back into its envelope and set it in the desk drawer with the blank pad of paper, thinking of Brent's infectious smile and the prints of his bare feet on the wet pool deck and the black onyx ring he wore on his right hand...parts of him that were a part of her world. No, she wouldn't hurt him, wouldn't tell him.

Maybe the curse wasn't real. Maybe Brennig was wrong, or lying.

The woven bracelets sat on the bed table. Ellen gazed at them for a moment before she slipped on her robe and went to shower, still telling herself that this exciting love she felt for Brennig was a fantasy, and like all fantasies, it couldn't last. She was practical, if nothing else. And it was easier to reason in the light of day.

Dressed, ready to go downstairs, she remembered the bracelets. She pulled them on, noting how much tighter they were than before because the vines were still shrinking. The blur of vertigo she had felt when Brennig's hand slipped the bracelets over hers returned. Odd. Was it something in the vines, affecting her?

Holding out her arms in front of her, gazing at the beautiful works of Brennig's hands, Ellen smiled. How caring and gentle he was, and how romantic, to make these bracelets for her, and to give her flowers from the garden. How loving was his kiss, how sensuous his hands when they touched her arms or her shoulders or her face...

There was no question that she loved him.

Where would he be this morning, anyhow? In the garden, probably, trimming weeds and waiting for her to come down and play. Suddenly Ellen ached to see him, ached to run into his welcoming arms.

Wearing Brennig's bracelets, she rushed downstairs, never looking back at the closed drawer of the bed stand where Brent's heartfelt letter lay shut away.

CHAPTER ELEVEN

The kitchen was in chaos. Brennig, with blood on his chin where he had cut himself shaving as he did every day, stood stirring the contents of a deep pan on the stove. The room smelled of something burning, a charred dish was in the sink, along with a pile of bowls, and the refrigerator door was standing open again.

Ellen closed the refrigerator. "What's going on down here?"

"I'm cooking porridge."

Noting a box of oatmeal was open and partly spilled on the countertop, she answered, "It looks like you're making a real ordeal of it."

"I know. I burned it on the first try, but this looks better now. I finally figured out how this gas stove works."

How could a person burn oatmeal? The guy was completely helpless in a kitchen, which confirmed her suspicions that it hadn't been very long since his wife died. He must have led a very sheltered life in a remote place.

"Do you want some help?"

"No, I've got it now," he said.

"Brennig, you really should be more careful about closing the refrigerator door. It will run up Mrs. Jenkins's electric bill and maybe even ruin the fridge."

He looked at her as if he were trying to figure out what she was talking about, then nodded in agreement. "Do you want some porridge? I made it for you."

"You're having some, I hope." She took two bowls from the shelf and set them on the counter by the stove.

"Aye, I'll have some, too." He proceeded to serve oatmeal that was so thick it stuck to the wooden spoon.

He had already set out milk, butter, honey and spoons on the table.

Sitting down, Ellen said, "This was very sweet of you, Brennig."

"I want to do things for you." He smiled. "Things that will please you. Here. The tea is all made." He lifted the polka-dot tea cozy and poured.

The oatmeal was surprisingly good, and she told him so, and the compliment made him laugh with pleasure.

He asked, "What would you like to do this fine, sunny day, milady?"

She sipped the tea, which tasted better than it did when she made it. "I'd like to have a picnic."

"A picnic? Aye, a fine idea! We shall buy some fresh bread and some cheese, some wee cakes . . ."

"Yesterday I noticed the picnic basket on the high shelf in the pantry. I couldn't reach it, but you could get it down. We could get some cooked chicken to go with the bread, couldn't we? And maybe some apples or pears."

He nodded, eating the porridge he had labored over. Ellen noted he never ate very enthusiastically, the way most men did, and he rarely finished his meals. Food didn't interest him much. Perhaps it was because he had been ill and his appetite hadn't returned.

Brennig said, "The castle on the hill is a good spot for a picnic, with the view of the countryside. There isn't any wind this morning. . . ."

"I want to picnic on the riverbank," Ellen replied.

This brought a frown to Brennig's handsome face. "A few miles downstream from the bridge are some wide ar-

eas on the riverbank. I can't think of any spot specifi-
cally, but I'm sure we can find a good place for a picnic
under the trees.''

"Not downstream," Ellen said. "I want to go to the
spot opposite the church, where the blacksmith and Nesta
had their picnic.''

A shadow crossed his eyes. "Why?"

"Why not? The legend fascinates me. What I remember best of the stories my grandfather told was of the
blacksmith's grave and the mystery surrounding his death
at the hands of his wife. Now I learn from you that it
wasn't his wife that killed him and the ghost of the witch
who did resides in the river. And what's more, I was
somehow led to the house where it happened, and to you,
a descendant of his. It's a great story, Brennig, and I'm
going to write it down for my children and grandchildren.
So I want to experience all I can of it. I want to sit on the
riverbank where they were and imagine Brennig and Nesta
picnicking there and his discovering she was a witch.''

The look on his face told her he didn't like this idea.

"Oh, I know the legend can't be totally accurate," she
admitted, assuming he was having a problem with her
taking the story too literally. "But those two young lovers
probably really were there, and I want to be there, too.''

"If you want," he conceded. "I, personally, don't like
to get that close to the spirit of the witch, but, very well, if
it's important to you, I'll show you the place.''

Ellen set down her spoon. "What do you mean, you
don't like to get that close to the spirit of the witch? You're
not scared of a ghost in the water, are you?''

"No, not scared. She can't leave the water...and
couldn't hurt me even if she did. But she might try to hurt
you. Her presence brings up rage in me, and rage is not

good for the soul. I want desperately to destroy her, and I can't."

Ellen drew back fearfully. "You talk like the witch is real!"

"She is real," he answered. "How can you doubt it when you saw her yourself?"

"I don't know what I saw," she said weakly.

"Sure you do, Ellen. Not wanting to acknowledge her won't make what you saw go away."

She tried to shrug off the memory; it was too horrible to think about. "Well, she presents no danger to picnickers, so shall we get the basket down and get organized?"

Brennig shrugged, giving in, but he seemed to do so with trepidation.

Around Wrenn's Oak Bridge, three swans swam in the calms, as always, gliding peacefully and giving no attention to the two people who sat on the grassy strand behind the veil of reeds. Dipping willow branches provided dappled shade from the noonday sun. The warming sky was blue and clear, except for some white fluffy clouds over the far hills. A hawk soared in the sky. Songbirds chirped and warbled in the high branches. And the river sang its slow, musical path southward, giving no hint of any evil dwelling in its depths.

It was very easy to forget that evil was there, with Brennig beside her and the fragrance of grass and flowers on this summer day. He lay propped on one elbow, humming.

"I've heard that melody," Ellen said. "You sing it in the shower. What is it?"

"You hear me sing in the shower?"

She laughed. "How could I not? You sing loudly. Oh, no, don't frown. I like to hear you. Your voice is so..." She wanted to say "deep and sensual," because it was, but stopped short of that. "Nice," she finished, self-consciously. "Your voice is very nice to wake to in the mornings."

He grinned. "It's an old Welsh folk song. My mother used to sing it when I was young. I've been trying to recall the words, and gradually they're coming back."

"Would you sing it to me?"

He did, in low, melodic tones, and it sounded more beautiful than the birds and the river combined, but she couldn't understand a single word of the Welsh language he sang in.

"What is it about?" she asked when the song was finished.

"About love. About two people who meet and fall in love and then are separated by war, and finally find each other again."

"There has always been love," Ellen mused, watching the movement of white swans through the reeds that filled the shoals.

"And there always will be," he said.

Brennig refilled their wine goblets and handed her a slice of cheese and bread. They sat in silence for a time.

He ate a small cinnamon cake, and, brushing confectioner's sugar from his hands, gazed at her with a faraway sort of look in his eyes. "Tell me more about you, Ellen. Your past. Tell me what made you decide to come to Wales ... to Wrenn's Oak. I don't mean just your grandfather's stories. A lot of people grow up with stories. I mean, at this point in time, why did you leave your life in America and decide to come?"

Ellen sipped her wine thoughtfully. "It's hard to explain, actually. I had always wanted to, as I said, because of my grandfather. And I've always had the urge to travel and seek out adventures as opposed to leading a so-called sensible, mundane life. And I have traveled some, but I've also been sort of strapped to Tucson because I have a business there. A friend and I run a garden furniture shop. I do all the designing and she takes care of the retail part of the business. I'm not as confined as my partner is, but it is a tie, nonetheless. It's been okay, this business, but lately I've been feeling a need to pursue the dream my grandfather had of visiting Wrenn's Oak. Maybe it's because I've been faced with some thoughts about settling down and putting aside my search for ancestors and the adventure of walking where they walked. I wanted some time to think about that, and what better place than here?''

"You were drawn here," he said. It was a statement, not a question.

She remained thoughtful. "I seem to have been."

"You were led here by forces from the past."

His words frightened her, without her knowing why. "What does that mean? What forces?"

Brennig shifted on his elbow. "The past is never dead, Ellen. Its forces have energy, and energy cannot be destroyed. You carry the blood of the Coles who lived here centuries ago, and the blood is strong. I ought to know. I have it, too."

"You believe that a longing for this homeland is in my blood?"

"Aye, that's so, and in ways that would be difficult to understand. There are forces from the past and they are not bad forces, dear lady, they are good."

"You're speaking in riddles again, Brennig. I don't understand."

He smiled and reached over to touch her cheek gently. "But you will. Sometime soon, you will."

"Oh? *When?*" Her voice sounded more sarcastic than she intended, Ellen knew, but she was getting a tad fed up with these sudden comments that made little sense.

"I can tell you only that it has to do with love," he said. "You and I and all of us are powered by the force of love. It is strong enough to transcend oceans and even centuries. There is no stronger force."

Cocking her head, she straightened and looked down at him as he lay stretched out on the grass. He had closed his eyes to sun dapples coming through low branches; his breathing was soft and light, as if he were falling asleep.

"How could I have been drawn here by the force of love when my family has been away for generations?"

"I'm here," he said without opening his eyes.

"But I didn't know you."

"I wasn't aware of you, either—an ocean away. But I believe we remember love from another lifetime."

The remark should have surprised her, Ellen thought, but somehow it didn't. Nothing seemed surprising in this enchanted place. She smiled. "Does that mean you think we've known each other before, in another lifetime? Here?"

"It's a possibility."

"But do *you* believe it?"

"Aye," he said from behind his closed eyes. "Because of the coincidences that can't be coincidences . . . a butterfly leading you to Afan House . . . that sort of thing . . ."

The afternoon sun was lulling her into calm, as it was lulling him. "You're sleepy," she said, and smiled.

"I am. And it feels rather good."

"It should, because you are up so much at night."

"I don't mean to disturb you. I have trouble sleeping."

She ran a finger along his bare arm. "Could that be because there is a ghost in the house?"

He opened one eye, halfway. "What?"

"There is a ghost in that house. I feel its presence and I know it's there. Surely you must feel it, too. Surely you must hear echoes and feel warm and cold brushes sometimes. It's a very haunted house, but the ghost doesn't feel unfriendly, well, not really. You just won't admit it because you don't want to scare me."

The eye closed again, sleepily. "I don't want to scare you."

"That's what I just said."

"Mmm..." he muttered, moving closer to settle his head onto her lap.

Ellen sat quietly, gazing down at his face, at the shadows of his eyelashes on his cheek, at the pattern of sun speckles moving gently over his skin. Brennig was beautiful, almost too perfectly beautiful in this light. Any woman would fall for him, helplessly, as she had done... as she continued to do, losing herself deeper and deeper to that love. Knowing virtually nothing about him but wanting him anyway.

He knew that, of course. He acted as though he bloody expected it. But then, he had told her he didn't believe in chance.... Love. And guilt, because there was another man at home who loved her. When she thought of Brent, he was somehow behind a veil of mist. Brent... Brennig... their names were so much the same, one of those coincidences Brennig said he didn't believe in.

Suddenly terribly restless and uncomfortable, realizing she couldn't sit this way for long with his head on her lap, Ellen touched Brennig's dark hair. "Go ahead and sleep," she told him softly. "I'm just going to take a little walk along the shore."

He stirred but didn't open his eyes. "Don't go near the water... the river is dangerous...."

"I'll be fine. Don't worry."

"The river is dangerous...." he repeated.

"I know. I know." Ellen lifted his head from her lap as gently as she could, pulled her full skirt from under his shoulder and stood up stretching, because she had been sitting so long on the grass.

She took off her shoes to feel the moist grass between her toes. The day was becoming warmer; the afternoon sun this far north was so directly above her she had almost no shadow at all. A deep sigh pulled in all the peace and beauty around her, and the freshness of the air and the smell of fresh grass and the damp air of the river.

Three glasses of wine were in her bloodstream, relaxing her, causing some of the dreamy feeling that put her in awe of the beauty of this place and of the man sleeping so near. This was enchantment if there ever was such a thing in the world.

Enchantment...

Insects buzzed in the grass. The sun felt warm on her shoulders. A stone's throw away was the ancient blue-green river, ever flowing, ever whispering, shadow-bruised from sunlight tangling in water, cold with memories.

The river is dangerous, Brennig had warned.

On such a lovely day, how could it be? What could a river do to someone only passing by, or wading in its glassy shallows? The water would feel refreshing on her feet.

Ellen found herself moving closer and closer to the water's edge. The grass was wet, the soil warm and spongy. Dragonflies and water flies darted over the reeds. She waded in to her ankles, remembering wading in a canyon river of her childhood on long summer afternoons. The clear water was deeper than it appeared; before long she was in all the way to her knees.

For a second the image of the witch's face came to mind . . . the haunting shadow-eyes. It was directly under the bridge, though, and she was several meters downstream from there. She had wanted to come down to the place where Brennig had rejected Nesta's love when he'd learned that she was a witch. She had imagined that long-ago day and had tried to get Brennig to talk about it during the picnic, but he wasn't in the mood. He didn't enjoy talking about Nesta.

Now Ellen didn't want to think about Nesta, either. The day was too beautiful. Forcing the image from her mind, she did her best to reject the notion of a curse. Superstition, nothing more. Had to be. Curses weren't real.

All at once the river darkened to a brooding, cruel gray. Standing in sparse reeds, Ellen watched vibrations of feeble shivers on the surface churn stronger until the water seemed to be shaking.

An arrow of fear struck her heart. Ellen turned and tried to push her way back to shore, but she could move only slowly in the spongy mud. Some force in the river reached out, snaring her, and pulled her in.

With a shriek, Ellen fell backward into the water. It was deeper than she had imagined. A strong current spun up and caught her, pulling, pulling, away from the safety of the shore. She began to struggle, but it was no use. The tide that pulled and held her was stronger than she was. Horror numbed her for several seconds before she began to struggle wildly. Her scream was drowned by the churning water as she yelled Brennig's name.

Her cry to Brennig brought a stronger, harder pull. It felt like waterlogged claws holding her under the surface. Panicking because she couldn't breathe, Ellen opened her eyes and saw the face of Nesta writhing just in front of her—moving in the depths of the river, her hair rippling as it floated, her shadow-mouth grinning with evil. And anger.

Anger that rode on the weight of centuries. Anger that never forgot.

With terror gripping her heart, Ellen felt herself sinking into the black depths of the river.

CHAPTER TWELVE

There was no doubt in Ellen's mind that the force pulling her, drowning her, was the spirit of the witch who had just shown her face in the roiling water for the second time.

In her panic, kicking, she felt a strong tug unlike the water's claws. For a second she wrenched away from the force in desperation, before she realized Brennig was in the water with her trying to get in close enough to grab her around the chest with both arms. He was kicking hard, struggling with the raging currents and trying to push Ellen toward the surface.

For some crazed moments she couldn't tell which tugs on her were which—the water claws or Brennig's desperate pulls. It was a hideous kind of battle. Kicking and flailing, she fought to be free, fought for air, and thought she was going to pass out. Everything around her turned to echoes and gurgling green.

Then suddenly air. She felt a cold shock of air on her face and took a great gulp. In the struggle, she sank again, but this time managed to stay close enough to the surface to come up for another breath. The water was gasping and shaking in a dance of evil, determined, it seemed, to kill.

And Brennig was still under.

Almost too exhausted to help herself, much less Brennig, Ellen tried to swim to the safety of shore. In moments, gasping, she felt the soft river bottom under her feet. Brennig was nowhere in sight. The water in the middle of the river was still shuddering. Desperately she wanted to go back and try to help him, but her body wouldn't move. The fear and the fight for her life had left her with barely enough strength to breathe.

Had he drowned? *Had her disregard for his warnings cost Brennig his life?*

Hysterics kicked in. As little breath as she had left, Ellen began to sob helplessly, desperately, calling his name, falling to her knees in the shallows, watching the surface for any sign of him while endless seconds dropped into a pool of time....

Fear that Brennig had drowned drained the last bit of strength from her. Her body went limp. In such a weakened state, the spirit was too strong. Water tentacles grabbed her again and pulled hard. She slipped back into the trembling darkness.

I can't get out! she thought desperately. *With the river pulling me, I haven't the strength to get out....*

Strong arms came up beneath her, then around her—Brennig's arms—lifting her. Ellen went limp and heard the splashing of his steps and felt the bending reeds scratch her legs as he carried her through the shallows. It was more dream than real being lifted out of the darkness and into the light to safety.

Gently he lowered her onto the grass and knelt beside her, touching her fearfully. "Ellen?"

"I'm all right," she panted. And she was, and apparently so was he, but something was very, very wrong. They were both saved, and yet something was not as it should be...something, but she couldn't think what it was.

Nesta. Brennig had been struggling with the spirit of the witch, and Nesta had shown her incredible strength. He had had trouble getting out of her evil clutches, and Brennig was a very strong man. Did the witch want him more than she wanted Ellen? Whether she did or not, Brennig had taken the spirit's wrath from Ellen in order to save her life. He *had* saved her life!

She lay back onto the soft blanket of grass, breathing hard, unable to hear Brennig or the river or anything else over the sound of her own gasps. The warmth of the sun took away the chill, even through their wet clothes. He sat beside her, leaning on his knees, and stared out at the river. The fury in his eyes at that moment actually became sparks of red. Ellen shuddered at the sight of his eyes and looked away.

Was he mad at her for getting into the water when he had warned her two or three times not to? Certainly he had reason to be angry, but how could she have been expected to believe the river would actually try to kill her? To kill them both? No one could have anticipated such a thing!

No one, perhaps, except Brennig.

"I'm sorry," Ellen whispered on an exhaling breath.

He looked away from the river and down at her, and said softly, "She tried to kill you."

Ellen swallowed. "She tried to kill you, too."

"No," he corrected. "It's you she wants. I tried to tell you."

Ellen gazed up at him, the sun in her eyes. "How could you possibly know that?"

"I know her," he replied, and his jaw muscles went tight and the angry sparks returned to his eyes.

Unsuccessfully trying to calm her pounding heart, she propped herself up on her elbow. "You've had encounters with Nesta before!"

"Aye," he said in a faraway voice.

"A ghost tried to kill you?"

"She can't kill me."

Her curiosity growing wildly, Ellen waited through a silence for him to continue, and when he didn't, she said, "It looked to me as if she were trying hard enough. Why can't she kill you?"

"Because she killed Brennig Cole." He paused, looking at the river, still grinding his jaw and finally added, "She is not strong enough to harm me, too—not the way she is now. But it's different with you, Ellen. She could kill you and she will if she gets a chance."

"Why will she kill me? She doesn't even know me."

"You are descended from Eira Cole."

She sat up. "What? I don't know that."

"It has to be, though. There is no other explanation. I was sure of it when you first told me you had seen the face in the water." He took a long breath, trying to calm himself. "Remember, Brennig was the man Nesta loved. Even when he betrayed her, she kept on loving him and vowed to find him again, which is one reason she died so young. But Eira. Eira *married* him. Nesta was insanely jealous of Eira. It was Eira, not Brennig, she meant to kill."

Ellen shook her head. "Nesta sure is a stupid ghost if she can't tell the difference between Eira Cole and me. Does she think Eira could be alive after three and a half centuries?"

He gazed at her for several seconds with her questions hanging in the air. "Who knows what the witch thinks, except that she needs someone to vent her rage upon, and you carry the blood of the woman who, in her eyes, destroyed her life and took from her everything she ever wanted."

"But Eira didn't do anything to her. Brennig did."

"Brennig married Eira. Worse, he loved Eira...far more than he ever loved Nesta. He loved Eira with a soul-deep love and Nesta knew it. Everyone knew it, I think, even though Nesta tried to start a lot of rumors that their marriage was unhappy in order to take some of the sting out of the entire village witnessing his rejection of her. Some people saw through her, and it enraged her even more, and it was Eira she wanted to get even with.''

"It happened so long ago, Brennig. How can all these details have survived?''

He smiled. "In a village like this there is no such thing as time. The stories are as alive today as they ever were."

She returned the smile, grateful that he didn't appear to be angry about her wading in the river. Her wet clothes felt heavy, but, oddly not cold. Nothing seemed to matter except being here... right here on the riverbank with Brennig. "I think I understand why you're so intrigued with the legend of the blacksmith, since you carry his name, as well as his blood. It's your heritage."

"And you, sweet lady, are involved because you carry Eira's blood."

"And his..."

As Brennig nodded, Ellen recalled the fire sparks in his eyes when he was kneeling on the banks, looking at the river. She felt the something-wrong feeling again. For one thing, his connection with Nesta seemed wrong. Ellen could explain it away by his name and his blood, and it made sense. But that terrifying fire of anger in his eyes when he spoke of Nesta or looked out at the river after their struggle with her was spooky. That spirit was so *real* to him.

Damn, it *was* real to her, too! She had seen it, felt its power, almost been drowned by it. Still, Ellen couldn't connect with it personally the way Brennig did. Maybe she just hadn't been here long enough.

Or maybe he knew something about Nesta that he wouldn't reveal.

"I am sorry," Brennig whispered gently, leaning over her. "Sorry you were so frightened." He smoothed her damp hair away from her forehead.

"It wasn't your fault. You tried to warn me about the river."

"But I should not expect you to understand things that are unexplainable." He reached out to stroke her face lightly, lovingly. A dreamy smile formed on his lips. "You are so beautiful... touching you is an incredible sensation... the feel of your skin... your warmth..."

Ellen's heart began to pound again, not from fear this time but from sensations even stronger, as this stranger who was not a stranger... this man who had just saved her life... began to make love to her with his fingertips, softly and so sensually she could find no voice to speak.

"I can feel your laughter in your throat," Brennig continued, holding his fingers lightly on her neck. "I can feel your laughter and your tears. I can feel you fearing me and wanting me at the same time." He stroked her throat. "There is no need to fear me. I have only love in my mind when I think of you."

Leaning closer, he brushed his lips against hers. She felt his lips press harder as he wrapped his arms around her and pulled her to him, cradling her against his chest. The kiss became so passionate, Ellen lost hold of reality. Her head began to spin, and it felt as though not just her head but her whole body were being lifted and floating weightlessly on the summer air. Imaginary clouds seemed to be moving around them and over them, touching them— spell-like—with silver mist.

Ellen heard the word *love* ring in his voice like music echoing as if from the hills at first, then coming closer until it touched her heart and formed a song there, and the

NO RISK, NO OBLIGATION TO BUY...NOW OR EVER!

GUARANTEED

PLAY "ROLL A DOUBLE" AND GET AS MANY AS FIVE FREE GIFTS!

HERE'S HOW TO PLAY:

1. Peel off label from front cover. Place it in space provided at right. With a coin, carefully scratch off the silver dice. This makes you eligible to receive two or more free books, and possibly another gift, depending on what is revealed beneath the scratch-off area.

2. Send back this card and you'll receive brand-new Silhouette Shadows™ novels. These books have a cover price of $3.50 each, but they are yours to keep absolutely free.

3. There's no catch. You're under no obligation to buy anything. We charge nothing – ZERO – for your first shipment. And you don't have to make any minimum number of purchases – not even one!

4. The fact is thousands of readers enjoy receiving books by mail from the Silhouette Reader Service™ months before they're available in stores. They like the convenience of home delivery and they love our discount prices!

5. We hope that after receiving your free books you'll want to remain a subscriber. But the choice is yours – to continue or cancel, anytime at all! So why not take us up on our invitation, with no risk of any kind. You'll be glad you did!

NOT ACTUAL SIZE

You'll look like a million dollars when you wear this lovely necklace! Its cobra-link chain is a generous 18" long, and the multi-faceted Austrian crystal sparkles like a diamond!

DETACH AND MAIL CARD TODAY!

"ROLL A DOUBLE!"

PLACE LABEL HERE

SCRATCH HERE

SEE CLAIM CHART BELOW

200 CIS ALAZ
(U-SIL-SH-12/93)

YES! I have placed my label from the front cover into the space provided above and scratched off the silver dice. Please rush me the free books and gift that I am entitled to. I understand that I am under no obligation to purchase any books, as explained on the back and on the opposite page.

NAME _____

ADDRESS _____ APT. _____

CITY _____ STATE _____ ZIP CODE _____

CLAIM CHART

 4 FREE BOOKS PLUS FREE CRYSTAL PENDANT NECKLACE

 3 FREE BOOKS

 2 FREE BOOKS

CLAIM NO. 37-829

THE SILHOUETTE READER SERVICE™: HERE'S HOW IT WORKS

Accepting free books puts you under no obligation to buy anything. You may keep the books and gift and return the shipping statement marked "cancel." If you do not cancel, about a month later we will send you 4 additional novels, and bill you just $2.96 each plus applicable sales tax, if any.* That's the complete price, and – compared to cover prices of $3.50 each – quite a bargain! You may cancel at any time, but if you choose to continue, every other month we'll send you 4 more books, which you may either purchase at the discount price...or return at our expense and cancel your subscription.

*Terms and prices subject to change without notice. Sales tax applicable in N.Y.

song grew more melodious with each passing second. And she felt the pieces of rainbows falling.

Then, from the bright yellow air, a rumble like thunder. A chill shot through Ellen. The rumbling sounded like a deep-throated threat. She tensed in Brennig's arms and suddenly her wet body turned cold. "What is it?"

His voice came as if from far away. "The river. The ghost of Nesta is furious."

"What?" She tried to pull herself back from the cloud-soft euphoria of his sensual kiss. "Why is she . . . ?"

The expression on Brennig's face gave her the answer. Nesta was furious because he was kissing her...because he had saved her life and he was holding her lovingly... kissing her.

In blatant defiance of Nesta! He was doing this here by the river to defy her!

Why? Ellen wondered, shivering in his arms. Why would he do that? And why would the spirit hate her so? The anger of the river was so terrible, her shivering became uncontrollable.

Although she couldn't feel it now, the sun was bright overhead. Still in Brennig's arms, Ellen opened her eyes and looked up at him, but for several seconds she couldn't see him. *An illusion because of the sun's rays,* her protective inner voice exclaimed. *The sun's rays blinding me!* Yet she could see clouds above them and she could clearly see a blackbird flying low in the sky. Only Brennig—for those seconds—was gone. She was resting in his arms, yet he was gone!

No, only an illusion, she told herself fiercely. The fright in the water, a close brush with death by drowning, had left her a little crazy, and why wouldn't it?

Brennig was back in her vision now, still holding her protectively, trying to give her warmth, but his body felt as cold as hers.

He might have read her thoughts, for he said, "We need to get home and into some dry clothes. Are you all right, my love?"

"The river...it's scaring me. The waves are moving and that...that hideous sound..."

His arms tightened around her. "The river can't hurt you as long as I'm here. I won't let it." He got to his feet, helping her up with him. "Here, love, let's get away from here."

They followed the shore to the place of their picnic and quickly gathered up everything, taking no care to pack the basket neatly. Then, Brennig carrying the basket with one hand and holding Ellen's shoulder against him with the other, they left the rumbling river. The blue-green water had turned almost black. Even the sky seemed darker than before.

Ellen said, "You knew what would make her angry, Brennig. You kissed me in her presence on purpose, didn't you? Knowing she would be furious. How did you know? Why would your kissing me cause all that?"

"Nesta is as jealous in death as she was in life," he answered.

"But you and I have nothing to do with her."

"Apparently she feels otherwise. She is confusing us with them."

"Them? Brennig and Eira?"

"Aye."

"But..." She brushed her hair from her eyes. "Hey, it's been a few years since they were here. Can't she figure that out?"

"Time is different to a spirit, Ellen. I think she believes you are Eira...the woman who took everything she ever wanted. I sensed this. That was why I didn't like the idea of you being too close to the water." He gazed at her thoughtfully. "Even your names are similar."

"And your name..." Ellen mused. "The same as his." She thought with a shudder, and Brent's name, so like yours, too. This is all too strange....

She said, after a silence, "You didn't really answer me, Brennig. Why did you kiss me here by the river, knowing...knowing what you know about her jealousy?"

"She has no right to interfere in our lives. She may as well know I'm going to fight her."

Ellen picked up her pace, longing for the warmth of the cottage. She was getting colder by the second, and his words were more chilling than the cool breeze against her wet clothes. "*Fight* her? What are you talking about?"

"Now that I've found you," he answered.

He walked in silence for a time, as if he expected her to understand what he meant. She didn't. Not exactly. "What are you trying to say, Brennig?"

"Now that I've found you," he repeated, and then, reluctantly conceding that this wasn't explanation enough, he continued. "Nesta has taken love away from me before...with her bloody curse. She won't get away with doing it again. I'll fight her with every bit of strength I have."

The anger almost shook in his voice. Ellen didn't look at him because she didn't want to face again that same horrible anger in his eyes. She asked with trepidation, "How can you fight a...a ghost? Especially a ghost as powerful and mean as this one?"

"I'm trying to figure it out," he answered. "There has to be a way."

As they crossed near the business street, Ellen noticed people were staring. Why wouldn't they, when their clothes were wet? But when she thought more carefully about it, their clothes weren't *that* noticeably wet. Something felt extremely odd, as if strange forces were vibrating all over the town.

From the moment she'd stepped foot in the village of Wrenn's Oak, Ellen had noted the town had strange vibrations. Sometimes, it simply didn't *feel* like other places, which gave her the impression the whole town was haunted. Now—walking home from the riverbank—the atmosphere fairly crackled with unwelcome energies. A cat ran out from under a bush, took one look at the humans there and turned back into the shadows, hiding. A small brown-and-white dog—a friendly dog Ellen had seen before—who had been sniffing along the curbside raised his head, ears back and skittered away. They couldn't hear the songs of birds that should be chirping everywhere on such a fine summer day.

Something was wrong. As they walked, Ellen heard a baby crying in a cottage behind shutters closed in midday. Why were the shutters on most of the houses closed? "What is it?" she asked. "What's going on?"

"It is the wrath of Nesta," he replied. "The moods of the river affect the people deeply, they are greatly bothered by its emotions. When the river is filled with vengeance and fury, everybody feels it." He squeezed her hand protectively. "A river has tremendous energy. Nesta uses that energy for her power, and it is strong."

She swallowed. "Then they all are aware of Nesta?"

Brennig frowned. "Not by name, necessarily. To my knowledge, no one here has actually seen her face in the water. The appearance of the face is only legend to them. But they feel her, just the same, even when they aren't aware of what is causing such a black mood...in the river and in them."

Ellen wouldn't have believed this if she weren't seeing it with her own eyes. The ghost's shadow covered the town! And the chill from the shadow was terrifying. The whole day seemed dark, even though the sun was shining as brightly as before.

"I just want to get home," she said, mostly to herself, while he heard the discomfort in her voice.

"Don't be afraid of anything, Ellen. Not this town and not the power of Nesta. I'll protect you. When we get back, I'll light a fire for you so you can get warm and dry."

They were on Pembroke Lane, nearing Afan House. "Don't you feel cold, too?" she asked him.

"The cold doesn't bother me."

"Even when you're wet?"

"Even then. Don't worry about me. If you don't understand me, don't let it worry you. You will understand me better one day."

A sudden sadness washed over her. "You speak as if my time here weren't limited, Brennig. But it is."

"What is time? One day time will have no more meaning to us."

She looked at him as she so often did when his remarks made no sense to her, and replied, "Time to me is the number of days I have left to spend in Wrenn's Oak. That has quite a definite meaning, because I can count them."

"I can count them, too," he said with a kind of omen in his voice that she sensed more than heard.

Thinking of the limited time made her sad because she didn't want to leave Brennig. Every moment by his side was more magical than the one before. Everything about him was so beautiful...his body, his voice, his face, his strange eyes when they looked at her in the shadows. No doubt existed in her mind that she had fallen in love with him, and he with her. As impossible as that was, it was true. He had known it even before she had and he had been denying it less. He had known it long before he risked his own life to save hers.

Brennig waited for her to unlock the door of the cottage.

"You don't have a key?" she asked.

"Not any longer."

"Oh, damn. It must be at the bottom of the river."

She set her key on a hall table inside. Brennig followed her back to the kitchen and to the back porch where he brought in two large cut logs to build a fire, as he had promised. He didn't light the kitchen fireplace, but instead proceeded through to the cozy parlor and made the fire there. In a few minutes, by the time Ellen had returned downstairs in dry clothes, the fire was burning high. Brennig, too, had changed into dry jeans and a sweater and was standing warming his hands by the flames, waiting for her.

"How did you get the fire roaring so quickly?" she asked.

"I've built many fires in my life." He stepped to a sideboard, where he had set out a bottle of claret and two goblets, and poured.

She accepted the goblet he handed her, feeling as though this house, this room, were suspended in time. So old-fashioned, so full of memories of other days, other centuries, being here with this Welshman felt almost like going back in time. Ellen was giddy before the wine ever touched her lips.

The room was gray and shadowy, for the single window did not let in much light, and the heavy curtains were mostly closed. The fire sent out a bright, soft orange-pink glow, and when Brennig turned toward her, his face in the fire glow was the most handsome face she had ever seen. His eyes reflected the flames in such a mysterious way, almost like mirrors. Her heart fluttered wildly. There could be no other man in the world like this man. No man as exciting, no man as inviting, no man as persuasive...

He wanted her and she knew it. Standing next to him in the warm, pink, flickering light, she wanted him, too.

Brennig took a slow drink and set down his glass. He waited in silence while she drank a sip or two, then reached for her goblet and set it on the table beside his.

He held out his arms, and in a silence filled only by the popping of the logs in the fire, Ellen came to him.

For a long time, he merely held her, as if the woman in his arms were the most precious thing in the world to him. The building of love in his embrace caused the fluttering in her heart to change to fast, hard beats. The sound of the fire grew louder in the silent house, a reminder that they were alone here... alone in space, alone in time... alone in the secret of their love.

Something wrong, a voice inside Ellen's head echoed weakly, the same echo she had heard on the riverbank. *Something wrong...* But in Brennig's arms, the echo grew weaker and weaker until it was too dull to be heard any longer over the sound of Brennig's sighs of contentment and yearning. His every word, every action, every soft guttural sigh conveyed to her the attitude that their being together was neither new nor forbidden. It *was* new, and it was forbidden, but Brennig didn't think so, and under the persuasion of his eyes and his touch and his deep, magical voice, Ellen couldn't deny the newness, but she soon forgot that this was forbidden love...soon no longer could hear the warning deep inside her head... *Something wrong...*

He drew away and looked down at her, stroking her hair lovingly. His lips moved over hers, unhurried, somehow so familiar now in a kiss that caused her head to spin far out of her control.

"My love..." Brennig whispered into her ear. "My sweet love... I've waited so long for you...."

His hands moved slowly and possessively down the length of her body.

"Brennig... when you're so near, I can't... can't even think..."

"Don't think, just allow yourself to feel. Feel my love for you. Feel my body next to yours. Feel my breath. Feel my need. Feel me, my sweet. Feel us... *together.*"

He kissed her again, holding her head, his fingers in her hair, his body hard against her.

"Surrender to me, Ellen. Surrender to me...."

CHAPTER THIRTEEN

"How softly you come to me," Brennig said. "How tender is your touch. You must trust me. Do you trust me?"

"I trust that you love me," she answered, moving her hands along his chest, feeling the hardness of his muscles under the thick wool sweater he wore.

This brought a gentle smile to his lips. "If you trust that I love you, that is all I ask. Your trust is what I want most."

She laughed. "Is this primarily about trust, then? I thought it had more to do with passion."

"Passion without trust is not worthy of us. I have lusted after women in my lifetime, but I have loved only once." He paused and qualified, "Only once before."

While she guided her hands over his chest, Brennig slipped the sweater over his head. He was wearing nothing underneath the sweater.

"I want to feel the fire's warmth on my skin," he said, closing his eyes and kneeling in front of the hearth. "Ahh, how good that feels! Sensations of earth and of life."

"One forgets the more simple sensations of earth and of life," Ellen mused, kneeling beside him, holding out her arms to the warmth. Behind them, the room felt cold.

"You must feel it, too." Brennig touched her sweater. With gentle, deliberate movements, he pulled it over her head and tossed it aside with his. Ellen felt the heat of the fire intensify on her skin. He touched her breasts over the lace of her bra and finally tugged at the bra hooks unsuccessfully. For a second or two this surprised her. Didn't all men practice unhooking bras with one hand in the dark as part of the ritual into manhood? Obviously not this guy. She reached back and undid the hook herself.

The heat of his hands and of the fire seemed one and the same; she could scarcely tell them apart. All Ellen knew was that she was inundated with sensations unlike any she had ever known. Brennig's touch... like a fire's warmth... filling her body and her soul.

He was cradling her breasts in his hands. Then he wasn't. He was unfastening the buttons of his jeans, and saying, "I'll have all of it, all of the sensation, all over my body."

He stripped off the jeans. To Ellen's surprise, he wore nothing underneath. The orange glow of the fire reflected on his skin, the flames flickering against the shadows. She experienced a sensation that none of this was real, couldn't be. No man really looked this beautiful, no fire really burned this bright, sending up blue and green colors from its coals. No moments could ever be this exciting or filled with so much wonder—not in the real world.

"It feels fantastic," Brennig was saying. "The warmth. I had forgotten."

"You don't wear underwear?" she asked with a mischievous smile, touching his bare buttocks.

"Too confining," he answered, returning her smile. "I don't like to feel confined. Clothes are confining enough, as they are. I prefer being naked. It feels... free." He reached under her skirt and caressed her thigh. "Don't you agree?"

"I haven't thought that, no. But I must admit the heat of the fire feels marvelous."

"Ellen," he whispered sensuously, leaning over to kiss her while he continued to stroke her leg. "My sweet . . . let yourself be. Just let yourself be with me. Just let me love you. . . ."

The tingling and twitching deep in her stomach and her loins responded to the stimulus of his touch and his voice and bid her surrender to every impulse he drew on. The slow, circular strokes of his hand moving higher along her inner thigh. The caress of his other hand over her breasts. Exploring fingertips, acquainting him with her body, urging the responses that were welling up in her, aching to be expressed. Aching to be fulfilled.

He knew. Oh, yes, he knew.

A small, quick chill the moment she was free of her clothes, and then the warmth filled in. Warmth of the fire and of him. His hands. His lips. His body pressed against hers, so heated from the fire, she was surprised by the heat of him. So hard from desire, Ellen knew there could be no turning back, no turning away. His body wanted hers more than he could probably control any longer. Her desire soared and burned, left her weak and strong at the same time. Afraid and unafraid.

One thing was sure: they were here alone in a time and space they had somehow created together, and there was no going back from here. Not today. Not ever.

His kisses, his touches, were as hot as the fire. The firelight glazed his skin and hers, and in the orange glow, their bodies melded like heat and color, forming a tapestry of sight and sound and emotion beyond anything familiar in the physical world.

"What sorcery have you used on me?" Ellen whispered, closing her eyes while his kisses moved along her neck. "I am spellbound . . . unable to think of anything but you . . . and only us. . . ."

"Love is sorcery in its own right," he whispered back. "Because love tangles all that exists outside it...memories, wisdom, doubts, fears...all tangled up in an illusion of runaway time. Everything else but love is illusion, my darling. With love there is no such thing as time."

"You speak like a poet sometimes."

He smiled. "Perhaps because you are a beautiful poem that I want to express. You are a song, Ellen. You are a dream returned to life...my dream. You are everything to me."

How could I be? the small, naggy voice inside her cautioned. If the question had an answer, she didn't want to know what it was—not this moment, wrapped in Brennig's strong, bare arms. Not in this cone of happiness. If the happiness she felt was misaimed...*no.* This love she felt could live and thrive in the real world outside this haunted cottage. It *could.* It would.

"My love is forever," Brennig said, as if reading her thoughts.

"Forever," she repeated, but the word frightened her when it came from her own lips.

His arms cradled her again. She felt oddly weightless, scarcely aware of the wool against her back as he slid her down onto the soft hearth rug, kissing her, caressing her, exploring her.

He lay beside her and guided her hand. "Touch me, Ellen. I want to know your touch again."

"Again?"

"I have known you in my dreams...and now you are here."

His eyes closed. He moaned softly in response to her caresses. "It feels so good...."

"And you, my love..." he whispered, reaching out to her. "You feel so good...so..." His voice trailed away into the silence of the room, and he was lost in the luxury of her and the sensations of her.

Ellen's breath caught and heaved—a reflex to his intimate touch that stirred her overheated blood. She lay back, eyes closed, floating in the rapture of his touch.

Then, with a whisper of words she could not quite understand, his body moved over her...into her...and a gasp like a spasm came from her throat.

"Brennig..."

His response came as a fevered breath. "You belong to me...I love you."

Ellen lost herself in the rhythm of his love; reality melted in a blur of pleasure.

Beneath him, she opened her eyes. And she could not see him! For a second, he was gone, just like on the riverbank, when she'd opened her eyes and Brennig was not there. On the riverbank, though, the sun had been in her eyes. Here there was no sun to blind her, yet still, for an instant, she couldn't see him.

But she felt him there, making fiery love to her, filling her with the wildest sensations she had ever felt...and in a second, he was in focus again—so flushed and so handsome in the fire glow, she reached up to touch his face.

"Brennig...who are you...?"

"The man who loves you...never anyone but you," he whispered in jerky breaths.

Her passion caught fire from his as he thrust faster, harder, until his body tensed and a loud moan shuddered from the depth of his throat. His pleasure, in its intensity, sounded like pain.

The intensity overwhelmed her senses; Ellen too began to shudder, and she cried out deliriously.

Brennig gazed down at her. "The sound of your pleasure is like music to my ears."

Moments later, he lay beside her, holding her.

He said, "I still can hear the music. Don't you hear it? The music falls like silver dust around us, covering us."

"Yes, I do hear the music. I thought it was coming from my heart."

"It is. From your heart, and mine."

"You have made me believe in magic, Brennig."

He smiled. "I have always believed in magic, but even more so now. Now that you are here. Now that you love me. Magic is very real."

His total commitment still worried Ellen. "Brennig, you scarcely know me."

"I know you very well."

"No, you don't. You can't. And I don't know you, either."

He shifted. "Do you love me?"

"Yes. I love you, but I don't know you."

"You will. For now, it is the love that matters."

They lay for a time, listening to the sounds of the fire. Little light was coming from the curtained window across the room, a sign that the sky must have clouded over. Clouds formed, she thought, from the river mist.

"You saved my life today, Brennig."

He caressed her arm slowly. "Were you afraid?"

"I was terrified. I nearly drowned."

"Does death frighten you?"

She stared at him. "Of course. I sure don't welcome it. I have a lot of living to do. It's a funny question. Doesn't death frighten you?"

"There is no such thing as death," he answered.

"Oh, I don't know. Corpses are pretty real, if you ask me."

"Corpses are merely shells after the spirits—the souls—have left."

Ellen didn't like this morbid subject. "I believe that, too, of course. I know there are ghosts about. Like the ghost in this house. I can feel a ghost here."

Brennig looked thoughtful. "Can you feel it now? Here?"

"Not in this room, no. But in the night. Especially in the small hours of the morning. Do ghosts not sleep?"

Brennig laughed and squeezed her hand. "You don't seem like someone who is frightened of ghosts."

"No. But I don't like the idea of him spying on us."

"Him?"

She nodded. "I think the ghost must be your ancestor, the blacksmith. After all, he was murdered here."

"Aye. Perhaps you're right." He stirred. "The fire is burning lower. Are you getting cold?"

"I'm beginning to feel a little cold, now that you mention it." She wriggled up into a sitting position.

Brennig threw another log on the fire and handed Ellen her wine goblet. He raised his own. "A toast to our love," he said. "Forever love."

Forever love. The words echoed in Ellen's ears. Forever Brennig Cole in her life? It made no sense at all, and yet it was just as impossible to imagine leaving him and going away, back to her other life—that other life that was becoming fuzzier in her mind each day...and that other man whom she had lost through a witch's curse.

"Forever love," Ellen repeated, with a sinking feeling that she had no idea what she was saying or what it meant. But if the curse had taken Brent from her, wouldn't it take Brennig, too?

Gazing into the firelight, watching the new log begin to spark and flame, and sipping slowly at the wine, Ellen asked, "Brennig, what does Nesta have to do with us?"

He stretched out beside her. "What do you mean? We talked about all that."

"Can she keep us apart?"

His jaw went tight. "No. She can't. I'll make sure of it."

"How?"

"I don't know how. But I give you my word."

Ellen rested her hands on her knees. "I don't see how you can meet a spirit on her level . . . or on any level."

He stroked her hair. "Try not to worry about Nesta, my love. Think only good thoughts. Think of us."

That night in her bed he came to her again, savoring the sweetness of their love. And afterward he snuggled in beside her with an arm around her. I am deliriously in love, she told herself giddily, with her body fitting so perfectly into the curves of his.

Delirious, excited, too excited to fall asleep, while Brennig lay so still she knew he must be sleeping. *Think of us,* he had said. Not Nesta, not the curse.

Not the man she had lost, whom she also loved. But deep in the night, when the shadows were still, Ellen lay awake, her eyes staring out at the darkness, and thought about Brent with an aching heart and terrible guilt. It was perplexing and bewildering how blurred her images of Brent were; she had to concentrate to bring the memories forward, and, lying in the dark, she worked hard at it, until the mind and heart pictures wrapped themselves around her, in almost-forgotten warmth. The two of them standing at the rim of the Grand Canyon . . . hiking into old Fort Bowie . . . lazing in a paddleboat in the sunshine at Pena Blanca Lake . . . Brent's Jacuzzi on a cold winter night . . . margaritas at poolside with the laughter of their friends . . .

Brent could not know he had lost her, could not know she was lying beside another man, spent from lovemaking. He wouldn't understand any of this. Confusion mingled with the agony of guilt. Brennig had such a hold on her, like a spell. Could he be some kind of sorcerer? Could it be that Brennig had lied about the effect of the curse on her relationship with the man back home? Lied for his own purposes because he wanted her?

No. She had seen and felt Nesta's awesome power in the river today. She had seen the witch's fury when Brennig kissed her there. The curse was real, all right. Even those villagers who had never seen the face in the water feared her power, shuddered under her rage. Just what Brennig could do about this, she couldn't fathom, but there was no doubt he was forming some kind of wild plan in his mind. Ellen didn't want to be around to find out what it was. Nesta had nearly killed Brennig today, whether he was willing to admit it or not. Next time the loathsome witch might be more successful.

At some time in the night, Ellen became aware that Brennig was not beside her, although she hadn't heard him leave. She must have dozed longer than she'd thought. Lying there, still feeling his touch all over her body, she listened for the sounds of the house and of Brennig prowling around as he always did, so restlessly, in the night. But this time, to her surprise, she could hear nothing. A strange kind of peace had settled over the cottage.

The peace somehow settled over her, too, and she was able to drift back to sleep. At one point, she woke and Brennig was beside her again in the bed, holding her as if she were a prized possession.

CHAPTER FOURTEEN

In the morning when she woke, Brennig was gone again. Because she was such a light sleeper, Ellen was amazed she hadn't heard his restless movements in the small bed, but then she must have been exhausted after the physical strain and the emotional overload of yesterday.

Her first thoughts of him came with a surge of warmth and love that filled her heart and made it sing along with a warbling bird outside her window. She threw off the quilt, slipped into a robe and opened the shutters to welcome the morning.

The clouds of last evening had not blown off. The smell of rain was in the air. It was a fresh summer scent blending with the singing of birds and the fragrance of flowers. The grisly gloom of yesterday afternoon had lifted from the village, the effect of the river's rage no longer felt. Everything was normal again.

Everything and nothing.

She had given herself, heart and body, to a man she scarcely knew, and now, in the morning, she loved him even more, longed for him more than ever. Lovingly she touched the bracelets on her wrists. Brennig's sweet gifts...

Ellen was not surprised to see him down there in the garden, working diligently. The garden seemed more important to him than it did to Mrs. Jenkins.

From her upstairs window she watched him work. She watched children playing down the street. Two women out walking their dogs stopped along the sidewalk to chat. Both were carrying folded umbrellas. The postman, with a leather bag flung over his shoulder, stopped at the house next door, and then, proceeding on his route, paused in front of Afan House, opened the gate and started up the path to the front door.

Startled out of her reverie, Ellen tightened the belt of her robe, slid into her slippers, and ran down the steps, combing her fingers through her tangled hair and wondering if last night's lovemaking still showed on her face.

Maybe not; the postman had no reaction to her appearance. He merely smiled, asked if her name was Ellen Cole, and handed her a letter. As soon as the envelope touched her hand, an outflow of sadness spiraled around her.

Brent.

Trembling, she thanked the postman with a false smile and closed the door, and then stood in the dim entry alone with a letter Brent had sent her, surely written in faith and love. Her heartbeat quickened. She hurried back to the privacy of her bedroom and sat down on the side of the bed, closing her eyes.

It was hard to bring a clear picture of Brent into her mind when Brennig's image was now so much a part of her. In fact, it was difficult to think of Brent at all when she was in this enchanted house. Hard to remember... It had to be the curse at work; there was no other explanation.

Trying to force thoughts of Brent into her mind, she thought of an Arizona sunset and Brent sitting on the cool deck of his pool with a drink beside him, writing a letter to the woman he loved... the woman he believed loved him. The woman who *did* love him! Sharp stabs of pain shot through her.

What was happening? What was happening to her?

Shaking with guilt and the awful undertow of sadness that made the gray skies loom even darker, she opened the letter. Brent was the same, always the same. His letter was chatty and somewhat hurried, but not as hurried as the last one had been, and filled with missing her and with loving her. He hadn't heard from her, he wrote, and was certain it was only because the overseas mail could often get delayed, and her letters would probably all arrive in Tucson at once.

"I think of Wales and the things you told me about Wrenn's Oak, the way you described it on the phone, and I find myself really longing to see it, in a way I never thought I would. Maybe it's because of my ever-increasing desire to share what's important to you. I wish I'd been more supportive of your interest in history all along. Now, thinking of you there, I want to be with you, walking those ancient hills with you, crossing that old stone bridge from England. I look forward to our meeting there more than you can know. I miss you and I love you...."

A chill rustled through her, turning sadness into something like fear. Brent had mentioned the bridge! Well, why wouldn't he? It was on many photos of Wrenn's Oak, a significant historical structure, and it was beautiful, one of the most beautiful stone bridges she had ever seen. Brent imagined walking over that bridge.

Brent was coming here. Expecting to stay at Afan House with her! A wave of nausea went through Ellen, horror built of guilt and confusion. Could she tell Brent not to come because the bridge was cursed and therefore she couldn't see him anymore, and anyway she was all involved with this Welshman living in her attic...

Could she tell Brent she didn't love him anymore? She could not, because it wasn't true. She *did* love him. She knew him well and loved him, trusted him. Yet she knew Brennig not at all, and loved him, too, and had no idea whether she could trust him or not, or even if she should try. In the next couple of weeks she would have to get some perspective on her confusion and find a way to figure it all out. Had a witch who lived nearly four hundred years ago really ruined her life?

Was anything in Wrenn's Oak real? Was Brennig? Was the river spirit? Maybe it was truly enchanted, like Brigadoon, and she would leave here and it would all have been a dream.

Last evening was no dream. The electric magic of Brennig was still with her, all over her, and wouldn't go away by trying to think of another man. Ellen began to wonder if the touch of him would ever go away... or if she even wanted it to. No, she never wanted it to.

Numbly she showered and dressed, drank a glass of cranberry juice in the kitchen, and went out to the garden. When Brennig saw her, he set his shears on the ground and came to greet her with a hug. His shirt felt cool and damp, like the air.

"Good morning, milady."

"Good morning," she replied, her heartbeat quickening at the nearness of him, a reminder of how much her heart had come to love him.

The mysterious magic of the garden surrounded them, even in the grayness of the morning. She said, "Brennig, the garden looks so different from the way it did when I first saw it. You've really done wonders here."

"There's more to be done. Beds to be thinned and some to be replanted. More vines to trim. And the little fountain won't hold water any longer, it needs to be mended."

She began to stroll along the stone path. "This spot where you said the blacksmith died. It was grass before, and you've planted flowers here. For any particular reason?"

He shrugged. "It seemed like a good spot for blue tortoiseshell. Butterflies are particularly fond of tortoiseshell blooms."

Interesting that Brennig would associate butterflies with the blacksmith, Ellen thought, since she had seen the butterfly flitting around his tombstone . . . that special brimstone butterfly who had led her to this house. As if it knew . . .

"You know a great deal about plants," she said.

"I've told you, I enjoy gardening. It feels good to get my hands in the soil."

"Can I help?"

"Ach, no. It's not a lady's work. Besides, I think it's going to rain."

He looked up at the sky. Ellen did, too, but not before she noticed that as he raised his head toward the light, the pupils of his eyes faded to the color of ice-blue water, the way they had the first time she saw him. It was easy to blame the sun that first day, but there was no sun now, only the light gray sky turning his eyes to the same pale color. When he lowered his gaze and met hers, the pupils were very slow to return. She felt that without them, he could look down into the deepest part of her and see her soul. With a shudder, she imagined that those eyes could see the feelings in her heart, the deep feelings for him, and if he could see the love, he could also see the fear. This moment, his eyes frightened her.

His velvet voice with the Welsh burr had the opposite effect.

"Is anything wrong?" he asked.

"I was just looking at your eyes," she answered. "You have such unusual eyes. Sometimes I can't see the pupils."

He looked concerned for a moment before he said, "Reflection of the light, I suppose. Come, love, I felt a raindrop and it's getting cooler. Let's go into the kitchen and I'll build a fire and you can make some tea while I go down to the bakery for fresh bread and some scones. I think it's a good morning to stay inside. What do you think?"

She smiled. "Inside with you sounds dangerous and exiting."

"Good. And so it is." He wiped his hands on the seat of his jeans, and circled an arm around her.

The morning ahead was heart-throbbing anticipation. Giddily Ellen thought, he's leading me down the garden path...literally! No one had ever explained exactly what was at the end of that proverbial garden path. But she knew this morning where it led...and it was all right. It was so good with Brennig.

By the time they reached the kitchen door, Ellen realized that although his arm was around her, just like yesterday walking home from the riverbank, it felt different now. Yesterday his touch had sent her senses flying in anticipation of their closeness. This morning's anticipation was wilder still, for now she knew the magic of his love. And yet, oddly, his arm circled her so lightly she could scarcely feel it. His skin was exuding no warmth that she could feel, either. Out here working in the damp cold, his body felt cool, even though he claimed he never felt the cold.

In the kitchen, he had the fire glowing hot in minutes. Drops of rain coming down through the chimney spit and

hissed in the flames. Rain hitting the window glass re
fracted like tiny prisms in the firelight.

As it began to come down harder, Ellen said, "It's s
cozy in here."

"I won't be gone long," Brennig answered. "I want t
get something good for you—for us—to eat. All celebra
tions must have food."

"Is this a celebration?"

He smiled. "We are celebrating our love, are we not
The communion of our bodies, each to the other. Th
blending of our hearts together. Our love, Ellen. Afte
waiting so long, so very long, to find each other."

"You make us sound old." She laughed.

He laughed, also, and his laughter faded into the shad
ows of the room like a disappearing echo.

"Stay right here, my love. Let the firelight warm you
beautiful body until I return." He hurried down the hall
way toward the front door.

When he opened it, she felt the cold breeze mov
through the hall. "Brennig, it's raining hard," she calle
after him. "Aren't you going to take an umbrella?"

"Ach, sure," he muttered, as if he should have though
of it, and helped himself to one of the two in the umbrell
stand in the foyer.

Ellen put on water for tea and sat down, and stared int
the fire flames. Was he so in love he could dash out into th
rain without thinking about how wet he was going to get
Brennig puzzled her with so many things he did...lik
cutting himself shaving every day, as if he'd never learne
not to. Like knowing nothing about cars. Like not wear
ing underwear. Like not wanting to talk about his life, a
if there were something he didn't want her to know.

Brennig's mysteriousness was uncomfortable. Ironic
because Ellen had often thought of Brent as being to

predictable. She longed for some of that predictability now. But when Brennig was near, his presence blinded her; her love blinded her. When he was away, like now, Ellen had to admit to herself that in some way—some unidentifiable way—she was afraid of him. The fear did not feel good. She was unable to put a name to it.

Fear? While she sat here counting anxious minutes until he returned?

They stayed inside the rest of that day, and Brennig made love to her again, with the rain singing against the windowpanes.

"You are mine," he said in the heat of passion. "I won't ever let you go."

Snuggled in his arms, she asked dazedly, "If you won't ever let me go, where do you plan to take me, Brennig? You don't live here, after all. We couldn't stay here in Mrs. Jenkins's cottage, could we? Would you take me home with you?"

He hesitated before he answered, "Aye, my love. I will take you home."

"What is your home like?"

"It's a place where people live in peace with each other and where love is the most important thing that exists."

"How could there be a place like that?"

Brennig smiled and held her closer. "There is such a place, I promise you. You'll see when I take you home."

Ellen sighed. "But, Brennig, I can't just go home with you. I have a business in America. Obligations. I can't just pretend I don't have any other life."

"Sure you can. If you want to."

"Well, I don't actually want to. I have no idea what I'd be getting into. Maybe you could come to the States for a visit. Would you consider that?"

"I don't think I could do it," he answered with that strange echo in his voice that tended to fade his sentences before he was quite finished.

She touched his skin, which felt quite cool, even though she herself was still hot from passion. "Loving you is going to get complicated."

He stroked her hair while he looked deeply into her eyes. "I love you, Ellen. That is what you must remember above all else. I love you."

He said the words as though they had never been said before, by any man, anywhere. He said the words with such sincerity, Ellen felt she had never been loved like this, hadn't known it was possible to be loved like this.

Two days later, the village was busily preparing for a celebration. Preparations were in progress for a community picnic on the riverbank, complete with fireworks. Stirred by the excitement, Ellen returned to the cottage from a walk to the village all aflutter, anxious to learn what was going on.

"It's a celebration for Glyn something," she said, as always confused by the local language.

"Glyndwr, who led the Welsh against the English a very long time ago." Brennig scratched his head. "I can't believe this holiday is still celebrated here."

"How long ago was this altercation between Glyndwr and the English?"

"Fourteenth century, I think."

She was slicing fresh vegetables for a salad. "I love these old, old traditions, Brennig! Don't you? The picnic begins in midafternoon. It sounds like great fun. There are going to be games and music and some dancing."

Brennig had joined her at the kitchen sink to help wash the lettuce and tomatoes. "You want to go to this affair?"

"Of course I want to go. Surely you want to, too. Don't you?"

"It's on the riverbank, Ellen. People will be swimming in the river. I don't think you ought to get near the bank again."

Slicing cucumbers, she didn't look up. "If I don't go into the water, why wouldn't I be as safe as anyone else?"

Brennig turned off the water and dried his hands. "Tonight the moon is full. The spirit of Nesta is especially powerful during a full moon."

She stared at him. "How could you possibly know that?"

He hesitated before he said, "The family legend. You've experienced for yourself the power of the witch Nesta."

"You actually believe she's singled me out because I'm related to Eira, don't you? But it's so *distant*, Brennig. It was so long ago. When you kissed me on the bank and such hell broke loose in the river, do you honestly believe it was her jealousy?"

"You saw it for yourself, my dear. Our earth concept of time is not a spirit's concept. For Nesta maybe it has not been so long."

She set down the knife. "I did see her jealousy, but I just don't understand! There is something so weird going on around here, Brennig. Totally weird, and you're so matter-of-fact about it all, like none of the strange happenings throw you at all!"

He smiled. "You must remember I grew up with the legend. I have known Nesta for a very long time. Nothing she does surprises me. It's a fact about the danger of the full moon, Ellen. The witch can take power from the moon. The villagers know this. In fact, they have their party on the riverbank more or less in honor of her. They fear her more by tradition than actual experience, because they haven't seen her face. When they feel her rage, as yesterday, they acknowledge Nesta's presence. They call their fear 'the witch's gloom'."

Ellen knew he was speaking the truth; she had seen too much not to believe him. "What do you mean, they go to the riverbank to honor her? Why *honor* her?"

"Honor is perhaps the wrong word. Defy might be more accurate. You know how people are about fearful traditions, they welcome the intrigue and the danger. It's always been so."

She nodded. "Yes. And I can defy her, too, Brennig. She's not going to keep me away from the fun of the celebration. After all, this damn witch has been dead for over three and a half centuries, and I am alive...."

"Thanks to me."

She blinked. "Yes, thanks to you. But the point is that I am alive and she is dead, and she can't hurt me at the picnic if I stay out of the river. I don't care *how* bright the moon is."

Brennig smiled and shrugged. "Very well, my love, we'll join in the celebration by the river, in honor of brave old Glyndwr. We'll drink and dance with the others. But promise you'll stay with me. Don't wander off. Whether you want to believe me or not, you are in danger anywhere near the river. Nesta will see us there and be as jealous as before. So stay close beside me, my love. Stay beside me where you will be safe."

CHAPTER FIFTEEN

There was dancing on the river shore, and laughter. Tables were spread with sandwiches and cheese and cakes and biscuits of all flavors. Children darted about playing tag among the trees, and many of them were swimming along the shallows, splashing and shouting.

Wine and ale flowed freely; Brennig, like most other men of the village, did not stop at a few. He allowed himself to be caught up in the spirit of the festival as though he had celebrated it many times before.

When she asked, he told her, "When I was a lad, I celebrated the festival of Glyndwr."

"You didn't tell me that," Ellen said, helping herself to a chocolate biscuit.

"You didn't ask."

"Well, I hope you didn't drink so much ale when you were a lad."

"Aye, of course I did. Why not?"

They were standing on the shore with the other villagers, watching the children frolic in the river. Ellen wondered how the kids could tolerate the cold of the river, but these summer days were as warm as it would get in this northern country—swimming days for hearty youths. Fireworks burst softly overhead as twilight shadows began to fall in the valleys of the nearby hills.

She asked, "Aren't there laws?"

"What do you mean?"

"About kids drinking. You said you drank a lot when you were a boy."

From the look on his face, she knew he had no idea what she was talking about. Brennig was very distracted, with eyes fixed on the water.

"Nesta is angry," he said.

A qualm of fear grabbed at her. "How can you know that?"

"Take my word for it, she is angry. It is because you and I are here. It is because you and I are in love. It is because we have found each other. I'm not sure we should be here, Ellen. I'm not so sure we should stay."

As crazy as this kind of talk sounded, Ellen no longer doubted Brennig's intuition. He couldn't know these things about Nesta's feelings, and yet he did know, somehow. Still, she really wanted to stay. "We're safe enough on shore," she said.

"We are, perhaps. But all those children in the water— I'm afraid for them." He shook his head, muttering, "The moon is full and the children playing in the river were born of love. Each one represents a love child she wanted and never had. I'm worried that the children aren't safe."

She looked at him, concerned. "Should you warn them?"

"Warn them how? Tell them the witch in the river might harm them because she is jealous of two strangers in their midst?"

"Should we leave?"

"Perhaps it's too late for that, Nesta knows we're bonded together now. The best thing, I think, is for me to keep an eye on the swimmers. You stay on the shore, Ellen, promise me you won't get even one foot in the water."

The illogical fear hit again. "You're going in? You can't!"

"Promise me you'll stay well on the bank!" he demanded.

"All right. But don't go in, Brennig, please!"

"Nesta can't harm me," he said, removing his shoes and socks.

"Damn it! How do you *know* she can't?"

"She can't, Ellen. You'll just have to believe it." He removed his shirt and tested the water. "I have a strong feeling there is danger here. I have to watch. I have to try to put a stop to the danger. This village has taken just about enough from Nesta."

He waded into the water at the same spot Ellen had gone in the other day. The moon had risen early in the eastern sky, sliding up bright yellow over the crests of the distant hills. The castle was sinister in silhouette as the color of the sky changed and the moon became strong and bold. Its beams penetrated the water, slashing a gold stripe across the river.

How can he know there's danger? the voice inside her kept asking as Ellen watched him move out further until he was in to his waist. And how could he presume to have influence over the evil water spirit? How could he influence a dead witch who took her power from the river and from the rising moon? Maybe all the ale he'd taken in had stirred his blood too much, and he was drunk. Maybe he was wrong about being in no danger himself. If jealousy was the reason for the rage, why wouldn't Nesta go after *him* as she had gone after Ellen? Of course she would!

"I've had enough of her evil doings," he growled as he waded in among a group of swimming children and dived under. Ellen held her breath, waiting for him to surface. Seconds went by and then more seconds, and Brennig didn't come up. He'd gone under to try to confront the spirit! Panic began to rise like fever tremors. *Come up!* she screamed in silence. *Brennig, come up!*

More seconds passed. A full minute, then another. The children in the water were acting as if nothing had happened, as if they hadn't seen him at all. But they'd seen him dive in, they must have! Desperately Ellen began to run from one man to another on the shore, pleading for help. "The man I'm with is drowning! He dived into the water and hasn't come up!"

People looked at her as if she were insane. "You saw him go in," she said to a farmer who had been standing next to them.

"Saw who go in?" he asked, drawing back.

"The man I was standing here with."

"I saw no one," he said, scowling.

This was madness! The people had been standing right there. How could they *not* have seen Brennig? Ellen rushed to the edge of the bank and scanned the water. Not a sign of him. He had been under now for several minutes. *Nesta had drowned him.* He had underestimated her power and she had drowned him!

Heart thundering, pulse pounding in her temples, Ellen was so desperate it was all she could do to keep from diving in. And she very well might have, had she known where to look. The children were playing in the spot where he had dived—shouting and splashing with no awareness whatsoever that anything was wrong. What had happened?

She had to find out.

Just as she was kicking her shoes off, Brennig surfaced. He came up very near to where she was standing, brushing the hair from his eyes, acting perfectly normal. No gasping for air. He wasn't even breathing heavily.

"How is the water?" a man with an ale asked him. It was one of the same men who, only moments before, had denied seeing Brennig at all.

What was going on here? How could Brennig possibly be alive after staying under water so long? And he wasn't even winded?

"The water is warm after a bit," he answered the man.

Gooseflesh formed on her arms. This place was crazy! Nothing was real. Now, watching Brennig in the beam of the full moon that reflected in his eyes, Ellen suddenly knew what had bothered her that other day, when he'd come into the river to rescue her—*he'd stayed under too long then, too!* Minutes without breathing...

No *mortal* could do that. With a moan, Ellen grasped at a barrage of hideous truths assailing her. No mortal man could go so long without breathing. No man could have disappeared when she blinked those times or lost the pupils of his eyes in the light.

Brennig was not alive.

Shivering uncontrollably, she remembered his strange eyes...his touch, always cold. His arms hugging her in the night so lightly she could scarcely feel them. His voice fading to an echo sometimes. His inability to smell or taste. The reaction of the dog to him. The wild ride in the car with him behind the wheel. His odd relationship with the ghost of Nesta...

The truth washed over her like a great, drowning wave— Brennig was spirit, not man.

She had been living with—*sleeping* with—a ghost. With her heart sinking and tears streaming down her cheeks, Ellen watched him move, dripping wet, out of the dark river, as if nothing unusual had happened. When he approached, she involuntarily shrank away.

He saw her tear-streaked face. "What's the matter?"

She fought down hysteria. "What's the matter? You stay under the water for three or four minutes and you ask what's the matter?"

She could hear her own voice, but it didn't sound like her voice. Nothing seemed right. Brennig didn't answer at once, merely looked at her, obviously upset because she appeared on the verge of collapse. He blinked a time or two, took another step toward her, and Ellen moved back again, in fear.

At last, weak and shivering, tears streaming down her cheeks, she found her voice. In a series of squeaks, she cried, "You're him, aren't you? You're *him*...still here!"

Brennig merely looked at her. His eyes were soft. In the deep Welsh brogue, he said, "Let's go home, my love."

Her heart pounded. "No!"

"Please, Eira..."

She started to feel faint. "I'm not Eira!"

"Ellen," he corrected gently. "I will explain. But not here. Please."

"You're not denying it."

"No," he whispered. "How can I deny what you already know? But I must explain. I must explain many things."

She shook her head. "I can't take this. It's a nightmare and if I just wait, I'll wake up. I can't take this, Brennig!"

"My dear," he said quietly. "I think you have known all along who I am. Part of you has always known. That's why you came to Afan House."

Her head throbbed with confusion. "I came because a stupid yellow butterfly was..." She stopped when he smiled. "The butterfly?"

He nodded. "I led you to our house, aye. But you came to Wrenn's Oak by yourself because you knew I was here."

Numbly she shook her head in torturous denial. "No..." But even as she said it, Ellen recalled how drawn she'd been to the tomb in her grandfather's stories. *No!* the voice in her protested. She couldn't possibly have known the blacksmith was...still here....

"Oh, God..." she mumbled feebly.

Brennig had inched near enough to reach out and touch her shoulders with both hands. The moment she felt his touch, light as it was, strength seemed to surge into her veins. New strength, and a magical kind of calm. She knew he was sending the strength and calm to her somehow, but he couldn't stop her tears.

People were staring at them. Brennig circled his arm around her and whispered again. "It's all right, I promise. Let's go home."

"And talk?"

"Aye. And talk."

She found the courage to look at him. The flowing river reflected eerily on his face. The moon overhead had turned to white, and cast a white glow over his skin and over all the world. Fireworks popped not far away, lighting up the dark water, and the music of fiddles and an accordion had begun just behind them, in the clearing.

Ellen felt suddenly so alone. She loved Brennig, but who was he? *What* was he?

"Are you afraid to go home with me now?" he asked.

She swallowed and shook her head. "I don't believe you mean any harm to me."

"How could I harm you, my dearest? I love you."

"You'll explain...?"

"Of course. I have wanted to explain from the start. I just haven't known how. Now I'll have to...find the way. It's all right, my sweet. Believe me, it's all right."

This Ellen did believe. Brennig meant no harm to her. He had loved her as no man ever had; there was no denying this. She didn't talk as they walked the short distance from the river to the cottage, and neither did he. His arm around her felt light and heavy at the same time.

Earlier, Brennig had set up a fire, ready to light in the kitchen fireplace. He lit it quickly, and then put a kettle on for tea while Ellen sat on a chair staring at him.

"How can you walk around here acting so...so normal?"

"How else should I act?"

"Like..." Her voice trembled. "Like a ghost?"

Brennig knelt beside her chair and took her hands in his. "You mustn't be afraid of me."

She kept staring at him as the fire warmed the room. "Are you a ghost?"

"I am Brennig Cole's spirit, yes."

She shook all over. "You're not alive?"

"Of course I'm alive, dearest. But not by your definition."

"Not by...I can't stand this, Brennig. I really can't. I've felt this house was haunted by him...the blacksmith. I've felt the presence of a ghost. But...but *you*?"

"I came back here to Wrenn's Oak and to this cottage a very long time ago," Brennig said. "I came to wait for you, in hopes you'd come. I had faith you would someday return, just as you have."

"Me? Why me?"

He rose, pulled up a chair and sat beside her, speaking softly. "Because of Nesta's curse, I have been unable to find my wife. She escaped over the bridge, and I desperately wanted to reach her, but I couldn't get across. I can't cross, even in death. I've waited here, hoping Eira would find a way to come to me...to find me so we could be together forever. I have waited over three and a half centuries.''

Tears filled her eyes. ''How awful!''

''A long time, even for me.''

She whispered, ''And have you given up?''

Brennig's smile came suddenly. ''One day,'' he said softly, ''I saw her again. She was a little changed, of course, but only a little, and she was as sweet and as beautiful as before....''

Her breath caught. ''You saw her? Where?''

''Beside my tombstone. Her eyes were glistening like blue gems, the way I remember. Her fingers were trembling when she touched the old stone. I knew she had come at last, to find me.''

Ellen stared at him, speechless. ''She...she found you...? Then why...?''

He looked directly into her eyes. ''My wife is in mortal form, reincarnated once again. I knew she would not remember me. But she would remember love.''

''You knew she would remember love...'' she repeated, staring at him.

Brennig took her hand. ''Please listen to me. When I realized Eira was here, I was given one chance to come back in my mortal body. I was given four weeks—only one weak moon cycle of grace in the density you call Earth. Within this time of grace in human form, I must bring her home.''

She stared, openmouthed. ''I'm completely baffled, Brennig. Eira isn't here!''

''Aye,'' he whispered. ''She is. *You* are Eira.''

A wave of pure horror moved from her head all the way down to her toes. ''No,'' she protested. ''I'm not.''

"Ahh, my sweet. You think you can't remember, but you remember many things on a deep level of your mind, or you would not be here."

She shook her head in protest, becoming afraid of him, yet almost afraid to argue. He was mistaken! Could a ghost be mistaken?

He caressed her arm soothingly. "When you first crossed the bridge and saw Nesta's face, and then when you went looking for my tombstone, I knew you were Eira, reincarnated to another mortal life in order to find me. You have returned to me as a living woman because neither of us could get across the bridge...you could not reach me any other way but this way."

With her thoughts spinning, Ellen tried to comprehend what he was telling her. It was true that she felt a familiarity with the village of Wrenn's Oak and with the cottage, and she *had* felt a fascination with Brennig—what woman wouldn't be fascinated by a man like him? But she couldn't be Eira and not know it. She had never felt a connection with Eira, and didn't now.

"Brennig, you are wrong. I am not Eira. I'm sure I would know if I were."

He said, "I want to gently remind you that you crossed an ocean to a small Welsh village, a dot on the map. And you saw Nesta's face in the water, something other mortals normally cannot do. And you knew the butterfly was guiding you, and you followed it."

"You were guiding the butterfly?"

He nodded. "Aye. I guided you to Afan House, and you loved it at once and wanted to be here because deep in your mind you remembered that it was our house, yours and mine." He leaned forward and kissed her forehead. "And need I remind you of how easily you loved me?"

"It can't..." Her voice faded away. "Be true..."

"It is true, my love."

Her gaze moved from him to the fire, which was blazing. Staring into the flames, she tried her best to suppress the fear that was building in her. What if Brennig was right? What if she were his wife, Eira, returned all these centuries later to reunite with him? Even if that were true, she was alive and he...wasn't. How could a mortal reunite with a ghost?

Brennig had said he had only one moon-cycle—four weeks—in human form. But then what?

Supposing she *were* Eira...even if she were, which Ellen didn't believe...but even if she *were* Eira, what good had it done for her to find him, or for him to find her? They could only be together these short weeks. Maybe those weeks were enough, all he wanted....

What did it all mean? Shaking, Ellen struggled to find courage enough to ask Brennig the dreaded questions. She began haltingly, "You said you had only four weeks. Over half that time has already passed. What happens after? I mean, if I were her—Eira—which I'm not—"

"You are Eira," he interjected firmly.

She swallowed nervously. "Even if I were, we're still separated by death...and life. In that sense, we're very far apart. So just what are we supposed to do?"

The awful truth lay in his ghostlike eyes. Ellen trembled with unease, deeply and instinctively afraid to hear an answer to her question.

The fire crackled in the silence, before he finally answered gently, "We have found each other again, my sweet love. You are my one true love and we are destined to be together forever. That's why you came here . . . to find me, and that's why I didn't leave Wrenn's Oak but waited for you to come back. I had faith that even with the curse, you would find a way to get back to me."

"Destined to be together forever..." she repeated numbly.

"Aye, sweet lady. Forever."

"How? You already told me you can't remain a mortal much longer."

"I can't live as a mortal, no. But you can live forever as a spirit."

She stared in alarm. "You want me to die?"

"I want you to join me."

"I would have to die to be with you!"

"Aye. To stay with me. Now that you have come, it is to stay."

"Brennig, I thought you loved me! How can you ask me to die?"

"I want to take you home."

"Home?"

"Where we belong. Where we can be together forever. I have said that death is not death, but merely a journey to another plane of life. I have been there, but I wouldn't stay, without you. This is all I am at liberty to say... only that it is good and there is love there. And I have been given only this one short chance to come for you."

Was all this a nightmare she couldn't wake from? It had to be! Ellen looked into his eyes, realizing what she should have recognized all along—they weren't human eyes; they were the eyes of a ghost. And the ghost—who had made passionate love to her—wanted her dead.

"I don't understand," she said weakly. "I would have drowned in the river. Why didn't you let me drown? If you wanted me to die, why did you save me?"

Brennig's voice echoed sadness. "You were fighting for your life in the river. We could have no chance that way, Eira. You must come with me because you want to. You must love me enough to want to go with me... willingly."

"Please don't call me Eira," she said, her head down, looking at the reflection of the fire flames dancing on the floor.

His eyes closed, and he sighed. "Do you love me?"

"Yes, you know I do. I don't know how it happened. I loved you almost from the moment I met you."

"Because you already knew me and you had loved me for a very long time." He squeezed her hand. "Like I told you, you don't consciously remember me, but you remember our love. This I know."

Tears sprang to her eyes as the magnitude and gravity of what Brennig was telling her began to seep in. She was in love with a ghost! A man who had died hundreds of years ago, whose name was fading on a weathered gravestone. *She was in love with a ghost who wanted her to die to be with him.*

"I can't absorb this!" she cried. "I can't make any of this ... real ... it just can't be."

Abruptly she rose from the chair and tore out of the warm kitchen into the garden, which was darkening with shadows. A chill was out here, a chill that would not go away, not ever. Her eyes went to the tortoiseshells Brennig had planted on the spot where he himself had died so long ago. This garden—he must have been trying to make it look as it had then.

Away from him, the hoary truth began to penetrate her consciousness—a truth she had noticed but never been able to understand—Brennig's touch was now lighter than it had been when she'd first met him. His eyes were more pale, and his footsteps were becoming so soft she often didn't hear him approach. His heartbeat was becoming weaker and his skin colder, his voice sounding more like an echo.

Brennig was changing. He was less alive now than he'd been when she'd met him two and a half weeks ago. He was fading—slowly changing from human to ghost right before her eyes.

His time was running out.

CHAPTER SIXTEEN

Night sounds descended with the darkness. From somewhere in the high tree branches came a terrible noise that caused Ellen to jump with fright until she decided it must be the screech of an owl. The garden was as cold as a tomb. What she was doing out here, Ellen didn't know, except that she'd had to run from the ghost who haunted not only the house, but her heart, as well.

It was impossible to think of Brennig as a ghost. Yet it was equally impossible, now, to think of him as anything else; she had seen for herself that he couldn't be a living man. Confused, she felt the tears on her cheeks turn cold. She shivered with misery, pacing restlessly along the flagstone path to try to keep warm, to try to hold on to her sanity. He led me down the garden path, all right, she thought in desperation. Masquerading as a human being when all the time he was... *Oh, God...*

Brennig said he loved her. He had demonstrated that love in the most sensuous and beautiful ways, and had convinced her it was true. Now to learn he actually wanted her to die—and in the name of love? What kind of love was that? He had cast such a spell on her. What bizarre plans did he have for her? What the hell did he expect her to *do? Kill herself?*

She thought, this just isn't happening. People don't fall in love with ghosts!

But she had. Her love for him was too powerful to deny. She loved him not for what, but for who he was.

Through the large paned window, she could see the reflections of the fire burning in the kitchen fireplace, casting an orange glow onto the walls. Warmth was there, and yet Ellen remained in the garden, pacing and shivering, unable to face the house or the man.

"Ellen . . ."

His voice startled her. He was standing beside her, but she hadn't heard him approach. When she turned, she saw his face in the shadows and the blue of his eyes catching light from somewhere even though there was almost no light at all.

"Ellen. Dearest, it's cold out here. If I frightened you, I'm sorry. The last thing I wanted to do was frighten you."

"Why the devil didn't you tell me the truth about who you are?"

"I was going to tell you. I was waiting for the right time. Perhaps a time when you would believe in me so much, you wouldn't be frightened. Foolish of me, I suppose. I've been taking my mind back to the time when I was on earth before, and trying to remember how most mortals feel about encounters with spirits. The skepticism and fear form barriers. I do remember that now, and I understand this is a shock to you."

"To put it mildly."

He nodded. "The thing most people don't realize is how thin the line is between the planes of the living and the spirits. That other side is closer than mortals imagine. And not frightening. There is nothing to fear."

"Nevertheless," she said, "I am afraid . . . of you."

"Why?"

"I'm afraid of your love."

"No, don't be." He reached out his hand to her.

Ellen hesitated, but then took his hand as she had done so many times before. His voice was so soft and so caring, it served to assuage some of her fear.

"I can feel how cold you are," he said. "Let's go back inside where it's warm. We'll sit beside the fire and talk."

"I have a lot of questions to ask you, Brennig." Her voice trembled. She thought the fire would feel good; the cold penetrated all through her, although the night wasn't very chilly.

"I thought you might have questions. I'll answer them all, my sweet. I just want you to trust that I love you and therefore you must not fear me. We'll talk. All right?"

She nodded and allowed him to lead her back inside the house she had always known was haunted. The touch of his hand was not warm, as it should have been, nor as strong as it once had been . . . nineteen days and a lifetime ago.

In front of the stone hearth in the kitchen, Brennig sat on the floor at her feet.

"I see you changing," Ellen began weakly. "Your hands aren't as warm, nor your touch as strong.... I noticed both just now, walking in from the garden. Almost from the first day I met you, I've turned around sometimes and couldn't see you. That's happening more than it did. And your eyes . . . Sometimes they're so silver I can't see the pupils. That's more often, too, than at first." She waited for a response from him, and when there was none, she continued, "It's frightening, Brennig."

His voice, which also tended to fade at times, was soft. "I am having difficulty hanging on to my human form."

Ellen closed her eyes, not wanting to face the gravity of this.

He sat for a long time in a silence filled only by the popping and hissing of the fire, before he added, "I have no control over these things. Coming back hasn't been easy. So much has changed since I've lived on the earth plane, so much to try to adjust to, and I wasn't given a lot of time. I have realized for a few days now that I am—" he cleared his throat "—that my body is fading."

Her heart was scarcely beating, even though she was afraid. It was a different kind of fear—a quiet horror comprised of woven emotions of confusion and grief.

"Fading . . ." she repeated in a monotone of disbelief. "You are slowly changing from human to ghost right before my eyes. . . ."

"Aye," he admitted softly. "I am. I realize it, but I can't stop it. My time here is running out, Eira."

She looked up at him, wanting to scream, *Don't call me that!* but what use was it to ask? Nothing she could say was going to change his mind about who she was . . . or wasn't.

She sat wringing her hands on her lap. "Brennig, when you were in the river at the picnic, underwater so long, I told several people, and no one would help. They acted like they hadn't even seen you—people we had just been talking with a few minutes before. It was macabre! Then when you came up, they were talking to you as though nothing had happened. I don't understand their strange behavior."

"People can see me when I'm around, and I look human to them, as I do to you. But when they can't see me, they don't remember having seen me at all. No one can, except you. Not even Mrs. Jenkins, who has no memory that I am living in her house when I am not actually in her presence."

She stared, incredulous. "But how? Why?"

"It can't be any other way. I am not allowed to leave any marks on the village by my presence, or by my actions, or even by any gossip that might start because of my name or my staying in the legendary blacksmith's house. I was allowed to come back for the woman I have always loved, but nothing more. Just as ghosts have no reflection in mirrors, our image will not stay in mortal's minds unless we wish it so."

"But you said you were worried about the children swimming in the river. If what you just said is true, you couldn't have saved one of them, could you?"

"Only by encountering Nesta and making her back off from taking out her anger on innocents." These last words brought back the hideous image of the face in the water. She forced herself to look directly at him. "Why—truly—did you stay under so long?"

"To confront Nesta. My returning—disguised as a mortal to get you back—has her in murderous fits. I was so angry when she nearly drowned you, I wanted to have it out with her then, but I was too concerned with getting you to safety at the time. Today in her lair I warned her not to cause any more trouble in the village and no more trouble with us."

"You warned her? Did she answer you?"

"Aye, with a voice as wicked as it ever was. She said it didn't matter that you'd found your way back to me through the world of the living, that her curse will hold no matter what, and she will see that it does."

Ellen swallowed. "So it did no good to warn her."

"No good at all. She takes her power from the river, the power of centuries. Has always done. I can't match it."

Ellen's shivers replayed his words: *It didn't matter that you'd found your way back to me through the world of the living—her curse will hold...* These words meant only one thing: Nesta, too, believed she was Eira. When Ellen first crossed the bridge, Nesta had shown her face.

She shuddered and insisted weakly, "I'm not Eira."

Brennig took both her hands in his. "You *are* Eira. You are my wife, the mother of my children, the woman who cared for me when I was hurt, who gave me love unselfishly and completely. Who never wanted another man but me."

Tears sprang to her eyes. "How can you *know* that?"

"Spirits have different eyes. I recognized you standing by my grave."

Ellen sighed a protest, her heart beginning to pound again.

"You force me to repeat myself," he said. "Very well, I shall. I stayed in Wrenn's Oak because I knew someday you would come back to me. And you did. You came right to my grave ... and then to our house."

"You *led* me to our ... to this house. You admitted it."

"You followed a butterfly. Would anyone else have?"

Her head bowed. "I don't know. It's all so incredulous, Brennig, why haven't you looked for another love? Why does it have to be me—her?"

"I will have no other. I can love no other but you." His pale eyes looked into hers, mesmerizing her as they had done so many times before. "Don't you see, my dearest, that it was the power of our love that brought us back together again?"

She frowned. "If I were Eira, reincarnated, wouldn't I have chosen a place closer to Wrenn's Oak to live this lifetime?"

"What difference does it make? You got here. You always wanted to come to Wrenn's Oak, and you did come, that's all that matters."

She studied his face, so handsome she had been drawn to it from the first moment she saw him standing in the weed-grown garden. His smile had charmed her, and the way he moved, and the way he laughed...everything about him had captured her imagination and her fascination from the start. There had been no resisting him, as if she were caught in a magical spell whenever Brennig looked at her. Had he been doing that to her because he had the power to do it, or was it something else?

Was it memory, as Brennig said?

Was it possible that everything he had been telling her was true? Could she really be Eira?

If she were, it would explain Nesta's rage, the vibrations of which the whole village had felt. Could spirits be mistaken? Could Nesta?

Could Brennig? Was it possible Brennig was so desperate to find his wife that he had made himself believe what wasn't true at all?

If she were Eira, could she love Brent?

The thought of Brent caused the life to go out of Ellen; the little energy she had left drained away. Her shoulders sagged, and suddenly it was impossible for her to sit here by the hearth any longer, or look at Brennig any longer wondering, if she were to close her eyes and open them a bare second later, whether he would be gone . . . or half of him would be gone . . . or his eyes would be staring through to her soul.

"What's the matter?" he asked, rising quickly to his feet.

"It's . . . all this is too much for me," she mumbled. "My head is spinning and I feel faint. I have to rest, Brennig. I have to try to think."

"Why don't you lie down in the parlor, and I'll make a fire there for you?"

She thought, I want to be alone, and then realized there was probably no way for her to be alone in this haunted house. Brennig moved all around in the night without being seen. Could he stand beside her and not be seen? Too exhausted to ask, she merely nodded. "A fire in the parlor would be nice."

He circled an arm around her as though she were unable to walk without his support, saying, "It will be all right, I promise you. Try not to be so upset. You're not afraid now, are you?"

"I don't know, Brennig."

"Rest, my sweet. Just rest. I won't bother you, but I'll be nearby if you need me."

She lay down on the love seat in the parlor and curled up, pulling a cushion under her head. The cushions were soft. With eyes closed, she heard Brennig building the fire in the brick fireplace, and soon came the sound of burning logs. How nice it would be to stay here, she thought, and not have to search for answers to the awful questions looming just on time's horizon.

Was she Eira?

All the evidence seemed to point that way, if she looked at it logically. But the idea had really shaken her: could Eira love Brent? What strange forces were at work here, anyway, that Brent's name would be so like Brennig's? Had she sought him out for that reason? Brent's last name was Cole, after all, and so was hers.

Okay, so Brennig might be telling the truth. Damn. Even when she'd believed Brennig was a human being, she'd been puzzled by him and hadn't thoroughly trusted him. How could she completely trust him now that she knew he had actually died centuries ago? How could she live with him...no, that wasn't right; he didn't want her to *live* with him, he wanted her to *die* with him.

Lying with one arm over her eyes to shut out the light of the old-fashioned parlor, Ellen struggled to pull in thoughts of Brent. Brent . . . who was so normal, so kind. Maybe he didn't offer the adventure a ghost could, but he offered all his human dreams to her, his life and his love, and asked nothing in return except that she love him. Brent, though, was lost to her, because of Nesta's curse.

Ellen sat up with a start, gasping. *Brent lost?*

From across the room, Brennig asked with concern, "What is it?" He was sitting on a rocking chair near the brick hearth.

She turned to look at him. In the firelight, his face was so beautiful, his strange eyes so full of love for her. "Oh, Brennig! This is really difficult for me. You say everything will be all right. I don't have any idea how to take that."

He answered carefully, "We love each other. We'll be together."

She swallowed. "Well, that might sound simple enough to you, but it spells major trouble for me. You have no intention of going back to death without me, have you?"

The shifting expression in his eyes confirmed the truth of what she had just said. He had no intention of going back without her.

He replied after a long pause, "I said you must come willingly, Eira. I would not in any way force you. The choice must be yours."

She gazed at him for a long time, the fear forming again in her chest. Finally she asked softly, "And if I should decide to stay here? What then?"

His eyes closed and he looked away. "Then I shall have to return alone."

Alone, she thought. When he said it, the word echoed hollow like a deep voice in a black cave, falling into nothingness. *For eternity?*

Would she be able to send him away—into eternity—alone?

CHAPTER SEVENTEEN

It was the loneliest evening of her life. While Brennig was beside her, attentive and kind and taking care not to mention any more about the reasons they had met, there was a gap between them that had not been there before. A space between the planes of the living and the dead. It might not seem such a far distance for Brennig, who had experienced both, but for Ellen the expanse was immeasurable.

She was less interested in conversation than with studying every detail of him. He had admitted he was fading. His whole image, from across the room, was less clear than it had been. Only love had been powerful enough to bring him back. Ellen's heart went out to him. Ached for him.

Miserable, she finally excused herself from the warm parlor, and went upstairs to her bedroom. Away from the fire, the house was cold and eerie—haunted by the ghost who had entered her heart, and her bed.

Her flannel nightgown was thrown across a chair, along with her robe. Ellen closed the shutters at the window as she always did, undressed and put on the nightgown, sliding under the blankets. In the glow of the lamp on the bed table, she sat staring at the far wall, imagining that the shadows were moving, imagining she heard the familiar footsteps on the stairs. Loneliness closed in around her, nearly strangling her.

Poor Brennig! If she was feeling this lonely tonight, what must he be feeling? Was he afraid she wouldn't go with him? She certainly had given every indication that she wouldn't. Yet he was determined to convince her for the sake of their love.

Ellen forced herself to face what she'd been trying to avoid thinking about—she was slowly losing him. As Brennig gradually faded back into his spirit form, she was losing him!

This brought tears to her eyes. She didn't want to lose Brennig. She loved him! He was still Brennig, after all. Still the same Brennig she had come to love so deeply in the magical time they had shared together. Whoever he was, *whatever* he was, he was a man she had wanted. And wanted still. Lovingly she caressed the vine-woven bracelets on her wrists, gifts given in love. They were quite tight by now and wouldn't slide off.

Was this terrible loneliness fear of losing Brennig? Ellen didn't want him to be alone tonight, didn't want to be away from him, after all. She looked about, wondering if he might be in her room, even now, invisible. Would he do that? Had he done it before when he'd slipped so quietly in and out of bed without her hearing or feeling a thing? The room felt horribly empty.

She pulled back the covers and got out of bed, padding in her bare feet across the worn rug. From the top of the stairs she called down to him, assuming he was still in the parlor, or else in the kitchen.

"Brennig! Are you there?"

His voice came back like an echo from somewhere in the house; she couldn't tell from where. "Aye, I'm here."

"Where? Where are you?"

In a moment a figure appeared in the middle of the stairway. Just a gray shape at first, then, as it ascended the steps, the color came, and the features, and then Brennig was before her.

He said, "You look frightened. What's wrong?"

Didn't he know that he had just appeared the way ghosts do—out of the nothingness?

"Ellen? Are you all right?"

"No. I'm not all right. I'm confused and sad, and very lonely."

"Lonely, with me right here?"

Tears formed in her eyes. "Are you right here, Brennig? Are you really here?"

"I won't leave you, ever. You know that."

"Are you going to sleep beside me again tonight?"

His voice lowered to a whisper. "You told me downstairs you wanted to be alone."

"I know I said that, but I've changed my mind. I can't bear to be alone in my room."

"My poor darling, you must never be alone, nor ever lonely. There is no need to be. I'm here and I'll always be with you."

She tried to smile. "Your voice is gentle, Brennig. It can be so calming."

He took her hand and walked with her into the bedroom where he stripped off his clothes and slid into the small bed beside her.

His body didn't feel as warm as she wanted it to. Maybe it would never feel warm again; maybe it was already too late. When he began to caress her shoulder and her breasts, Ellen savored his touch because it was a touch so filled with love. No man had ever touched her with such magic fingers that could send sensations through her bloodstream to every part of her body.

She ran her hands over his back and chest, exploring, and when she did, his skin seemed to become warmer. He felt more solid, still her mysterious lover.

Gently he guided her hand down over his body. "You see, I am still very much a man." He smiled. "And filled with desire, wanting you."

When she touched him, he moaned with pleasure.

After a time, she whispered, "Brennig, what is it like where you come from? Do none of these earthly sensations exist on the plane where you live?"

"Love exists there," he answered huskily. "It isn't the same. For us—for you and me—it will be even better."

"It couldn't be better than this."

He hugged her to him lovingly. "Ah, but it can be. You'll have to take my word for it until you can see for yourself."

Sighing shakily, she begged, "Hold me. Hold me close to you. Stay with me tonight, like before. Make love to me . . . like before. . . ."

His groan of pleasure filled the silence of the dark room. "I want to make love to you forever. Our lovemaking is even better now, in the twentieth century, than it was before, in ours. I wish you could remember, but I can tell you that it *is* better now. I savor these days and nights with you on the earth plane, in honor of all the old memories. Once we are on the other side, your memory will return and you will be able to tell me what happened to our sons after you fled from Wrenn's Oak, and if they became strong men like their father. And if our third child was another son or a daughter. I know our children grew up and married, because we have descendants from the union of our blood."

Her pleasure threatened to fall into fear again. "Could we please not talk about that anymore tonight? You said we wouldn't. I don't want to talk about dying."

"I'm sorry. It's easy to forget that it's such a difficult subject for you. Very well then, we'll embrace only the night." He began to caress her gently again. "I want to

take away your loneliness, milady. As I have done before.''

When he touched her, the rest of the world seemed to
disappear. There were only the two of them and their love.
Brennig moved over her and began to cover her body with
feather kisses that caused her to shiver with passion.

In the height of their lovemaking, while she grasped his
shoulders tightly, and hung on with all her strength, a
strong voice inside her began to mutter and moan. *Never
let Brennig go,* the voice commanded. *Never leave him.
Never let him go away.*

And from his own throat came words that sounded like
an echo, ''I love you. My dearest, I love you.''

The morning dawn was disguised as an ordinary day.
Sunlight slanted in like bright dust stripes through the
shutters of the east window. Brennig wasn't in the bed; he
had risen early. With a start, Ellen remembered why it was
that he could come and go so silently and never be heard
unless he wanted to be. The weight of yesterday's shock
felt so heavy, she didn't want to move from the warm
comfort of the bed where he had made love to her so tenderly.

Her love for Brennig was strong and the time with him
so precious. Had she only dreamed that crazy business of
his being a ghost? In the cold light of morning, it was too
absurd to be true.

But the deep self could not be manipulated by a sun-
rise. The deep self knew Brennig was a spirit, not a man.

Yet she loved the feeling in her heart when she watched
him work, the feeling in her stomach when he touched her
a certain way. Pain rushed into her heart and shocked her
body when she thought of losing him. There was so little

time left before he had to leave...and she had to return to America....

Unless they left together, as Brennig wanted. A thought too frightening to comprehend and too tempting to toss away. If she were to go with him, they would have each other forever, have their love forever. What more could anyone want?

Ellen went to the window and threw open the shutters as she had done every morning since she came. And, as every morning, Brennig was down in the garden, working. She watched him from the window, wishing yesterday had never happened, wishing nothing had changed, aware of how precious were these memories from her window, greeting the morning with Brennig in it. If only this could go on and on....

If only she wasn't slowly losing him. This thought—and her choices—were so painful that Ellen couldn't think about them, not now in the fresh sunlight of a Welsh morning when the world looked so beautiful and so normal.

The world *was* beautiful; she certainly didn't want to leave it. But if she stayed, would it remain beautiful with Brennig gone?

Forcing herself not to cry—time for tears would come later—Ellen showered, dressed and went down to join him. None of this routine was new; what was new this morning was the fear of tomorrow.

It was the warmest morning yet. Propping open the heavy kitchen door, she felt the sun and smelled the flowers. Looking around, unable to see him for nearly a minute, Ellen watched Brennig's husky form appear in a far corner of the garden. With a hammer and nails, he was guiding ivy vines onto a trellised wall. His fading and suddenly appearing were happening more often. One day would he just not . . . come back?

"Brennig?"

He turned at the sound of his name, and smiled. "Good morning, milady."

"Good morning." She attempted a smile. "I've just come down, lazy me. Do you want tea?"

"Of course I'll have tea with you. Is it ready?"

"Not yet. But I'll make it in just a bit." Ellen didn't move, though. She stood on the flagstone with the sun in her eyes, watching him. For an instant she thought she saw his body shimmer in the light, but talked herself out of it. Damn, she thought. All she was doing now was looking for signs of something going wrong. Where before she had ignored the signs, now she was trying too hard to find them.

She walked toward him. "Every day the garden looks more beautiful."

He smiled and nodded, straightening the trellis.

She bent to smell some lilac-colored blooms, and asked thoughtfully, "Tell me, though, how can you do it? I mean, you told me you weren't allowed to leave a mark or change anything. Yet you're changing this garden from an overgrown, neglected patch to something truly beautiful."

He lay the hammer down on the stones. "It's my garden. I planted it with many varieties of flowers and bushes that are still here. I built it and cultivated it, and I died in it. So it belongs to me. I wanted to see it beautiful once again, the way it was when I was here before, the way I planned for it to be." He looked about at the trees and flowers with a smile of pleasure. "When I leave, I suppose it will eventually go back to neglect, but it won't matter to me, then. Working here with the soil has put me in communion with earth again. I used to love earth, Ellen."

She gazed into his eyes. "Only used to?"

"Well, I love it now, being here, because one can't help but admire the beauty that's here. But there are better places. Kinder places. You'll see."

She swallowed, wishing he would stop talking about that faraway, mysterious place he now called home, which she called death.

"I'll . . . I'll go make the tea," she said.

"I'll go in with you. I like to watch you moving about the kitchen, like in the old days. You were the one who designed the kitchen and I built it to your specifications. The oak table is the original one that was here, that's why it fits so well. A friend of ours, a skilled carpenter, built it. I'm pleased the later owners have left the house so much as it was. Luckily people appreciate old houses as part of their heritage."

Inside, Ellen ran water into the teakettle. "Brennig, I get a very odd feeling when you talk like that. I don't remember anything. Not anything."

"I know you don't remember. I don't expect you to. It's very rare for mortals to remember their past lives, even though the past lives are connected to the present ones. But the memories are there, nevertheless, deep in your subconscious. We know that because you came here and we know that when you saw me, you remembered me."

"No, I didn't."

"Ah, my love, you did. I saw it in your eyes."

Ellen felt like arguing her side of this. "I was looking at *your* eyes, Brennig, and thinking they looked strange the way they caught the sunlight. It was positively ghostlike, and now I know why."

He cocked his head and studied her. "But you weren't afraid of me."

"I was, though. I always have been a little afraid of you. Instinctively, I guess I knew something wasn't quite right.

But it wasn't because I remembered you from long ago, it was because you were just...sort of mysterious, and you said odd things. I've always thought it was strange how important Nesta and the legend were to you. My lord, I had no idea why you knew so much about it. It's still hard to comprehend that you're actually...who you are.''

"And you are who you are," he said stubbornly. Picking up a knife from a drawer and an orange from a bowl on the counter, he began to peel it.

She scowled. "I'm not convinced."

"Then you'll just have to take my word for it and hope that somehow you will begin to remember. You must trust me as you did then."

Ellen pushed her hand through her hair and frowned at him. "That's asking rather a lot, Brennig."

"Not if you love me."

"When I fell in love with you, I assumed you were a man."

His lips formed what was almost, but not quite, a smile. "My personality is the same as when I was a man. You're making a very great thing out of this temporary transformation of mine."

"Oh, well, sorry, it's only death we're talking about here. No big deal." Her sarcasm came with a sigh. "I can't think about this like you do, because my perspective is so different." She looked over at him and gave a start. "Brennig! You've cut yourself!"

"Have I?" Letting go of the half-peeled orange, he looked curiously at the knife and then at his hand. The flesh was deeply cut but there was little blood.

She winced. "Don't you feel it?"

He glanced at her in a way that told her clearly he couldn't feel anything.

"I wasn't paying attention to what I was doing. It's nothing."

"It looks like a very deep cut to me."

"A cut isn't going to hurt me," he said evenly.

She blanched. "Oh. Oh, great. The nick on your chin bled, but this hardly does. Is that because...?"

"Aye, because I'm losing my human body."

Calculating how short a few days would be—only eight more days—Ellen felt pulled into her own dread of what was coming. *"And then what? I won't be able to see you at all?"*

"I hope it won't come to that. I'll keep my body as long as I can, until your time here is up."

"I have only ten days left before my return flight to Arizona."

He looked at her steadily. "You won't be on that flight. You'll be leaving with me."

"I haven't said so!"

He smiled calmly. "It's what you want. Everyone wants a forever love. We are luckier than you know. And incredibly lucky to have found each other again, especially with Nesta's curse in place."

She'd placed a paper towel over the cut on his hand, to blot the blood, but it bled only a little. Gazing at the wound, Ellen said, "Speaking of Nesta's curse—why won't it go on keeping us apart? If you...if...we...couldn't get together in death before because of that curse, why do you think we could conquer it now?"

"I can't be absolutely sure, but I have studied and tested Nesta's strength. It is built on hate energy. I think our love coming together, on both planes—the mortal plane and the spirit plane—will be too much for her. It is jealousy that energizes her, and jealousy is a shallow emotion compared to love."

"I don't know about that, Brennig. Jealousy can be a powerfully destructive force. The curse is proof enough of that." She'd begun wrapping his hand in one of Mrs. Jenkins's linen napkins because the cut gaped open and she didn't like to look at it.

"Nesta may not have the power she once did. The centuries have corroded and rusted her memories along with everything else. I believe if you love me enough to come with me, she won't be able to stop us."

A chill ran through her. "Yeah? And suppose she *is* able to stop us?"

"I'm determined she won't."

"But she'll try, damn it. The curse might hold! And then...oh, my God..."

He took her arm. "Eira, please. You have to have faith. Our faith and our love will win this time. I've been planning this for a very long time, knowing, through my faith, that you and I would find each other somehow. And after all the waiting, you are with me at last. No witch, no power, will ever take you from me again, I swear it."

At this moment, his eyes were vacant of all emotion save that of determination. In that determination was power strong enough to frighten her. *Was he giving her a choice?* Even though he had said he would? Or would he overpower her as he was doing now?

Helplessness coiled through her like a choking serpent as she stared at Brennig's strange, commanding eyes. Ghost's eyes. Her heart, constricted, seemed suddenly bent on claiming her for itself. From somewhere down deep in her, Ellen was aware of the silent tremor of her own voice calling out. Calling reality.

"Brent..." the small voice called, and then again, louder. "Brent...help me...."

CHAPTER EIGHTEEN

With a gasp, she turned and ran from the kitchen to get away from the ghostly eyes that wanted her. Feeling trapped, she needed to think, *had* to think.

"Eira?"

"Give me some space, Brennig."

"Where are you going?"

"To the bathroom, do you mind?"

"It's an odd time to take a bath."

Ellen rolled her eyes. She was halfway up the stairs. "The WC, if that's all right with you. We humans have body functions to worry about in case you've forgotten."

"I don't know what you're acting so upset about..." His voice faded as she reached the top of the stairs.

"Right, Sir Ghost," she muttered to herself. "Why would anybody be upset?" Get real, she thought, and then, closing the door, burst into hysterical giggles at the unintended joke. *Real?* He couldn't get real.

She had gone into the bathroom to be alone. Surely Brennig would have enough respect not to walk through these walls. Sitting on the edge of the tub, Ellen closed her eyes and made herself think of Brent—something that was extremely hard to do when Brennig was present. Even now, it took conscious will. The flickering thought of Brent, still vibrating from a few minutes before, threw her into a deep blue funk.

"Brent. Brent, I need you," she mumbled to the white tile floor. He'd stopped writing, as if he sensed she was involved with another man. Sensed? These past weeks, under the spell of Brennig Cole, she had written only one quickly scrawled note, in which she'd been unthinking enough to mention that she and a Welsh gardener were sharing the charming Afan cottage. If Brent was disgusted with her, it was her own doing. Originally he'd planned to join her in Wrenn's Oak for a few days, and she hadn't mentioned it since she first came, much less encouraged it. Brent wasn't stupid; he would have read those signs easily.

Brent must have changed his mind altogether about coming and figured if she was too involved to write to him, he wasn't going to write, either. Perhaps it was just as well, because if he did come to Wrenn's Oak, he would pass over the bridge from England and the curse would fall upon him, as well as on her, and they would have no chance to be together anyhow, even if they wanted to be. The curse was already in place. They surely had no chance.

And yet thoughts of Brent banged at her conscious mind harder and harder as the reality of her dilemma sank in. As her fear of Brennig grew.

By mid morning five days later, welcome memories of Brent were moving in and out of every hour of her life. He seemed so far away, further than the mere ocean between them. Yet special moments they had shared kept surfacing. His smile was there before her, his eyes—real, deep, caring...squinting in the desert sun, soft in candlelight, dreamy in the orange glow of twilight.

Why was this happening? Some deep part of her heart was desperately trying to communicate with her head. Growing fear of Brennig—entwined with her love for him—was only part of it. Something else was pushing through from somewhere.

Ellen sat on the shaded bench in the back garden of Afan House calculating that it would be about seven in the morning in Tucson; Brent would not yet have left for work.

"I'm going to walk down to Main Street to do a little shopping," she told Brennig.

He was clipping plants in a corner of the garden where a small stone fountain had once stood. "I'll go with you."

Brennig had been moody for more than a day now, doubtlessly because things were not going as he had planned, and, according to her calculations, he had only two or three days left of his "moon-cycle." Ellen was not accepting the fact that she was his wife, and she was not leaping at the chance to go with him when he left, which had to be very soon. Was he planning something she didn't know about to lure her to his world? He had been spending a great deal of time at the window, looking out at the Welsh landscape and the castle on the hill, and the sky. He might be remembering the past, she thought, or maybe thinking about that mysterious place where his spirit lived now. Or maybe planning her death ...

Even through some moments of fear, her heart went out to him. It was impossible for her, Ellen knew, to have any concept of the loneliness he had experienced ... of the loneliness he faced without her ... without his wife. She couldn't let that happen. Nor could she leave without ... without Brent knowing, without talking to him again ...

"There's no need for you to go with me to town," she responded, as casually as possible. "I just want a bit of exercise and to pick up a few things from the greengrocer. I won't be gone long. No need for you to interrupt your work." She almost added, *I know you want to finish your work before you run out of time,* but thought better of reminding him, especially when his mood had been so foul of late.

When he responded, his voice caught on a small wind that wafted down from the high wall and across the garden.

"Speak louder, Brennig. I can't hear you."

Exasperated because his voice, too, was losing strength, Brennig shrugged heavily. "I'll put my work tools down by the time you return. I'll make you tea."

She nodded sadly. He no longer bothered to pretend he enjoyed the human frivolity of tea. He ate very little anymore and slept not at all . . . if he ever had slept.

Perhaps he had not slept in three and a half centuries.

She hurried toward the kitchen door before he could change his mind about walking into the village with her, and called, "I'll be back soon, I promise."

Normally Ellen would have taken time for a little makeup, but how she looked was the last thing on her mind as she ran upstairs for her handbag, and then ran back down. Closing the front door behind her, she thought, why the hell hadn't she done this days ago? It was frightening that so much of the time when Brennig was around, she was unable to think clearly. What she had attributed at first, and for such a long time, to love, now seemed a kind of remarkable influence he had over her.

So much influence she couldn't effectively fight it, couldn't leave. Couldn't stop loving him. Yet she also couldn't stop loving Brent.

By the time she reached Main Street, Ellen was out of breath. Not just because she'd been walking at a fast pace, but because of the emotion building in her as she drew nearer to town. Glancing at her watch for the dozenth time, she stepped into a small shop to get a handful of change for the telephone.

Her hands were shaking as she stood at the phone booth on the sidewalk outside the corner pub. "Brent, please be home," she prayed. He should be, this time of morning. What she would say to him, Ellen was still unsure. The walk to town had produced one rehearsal after another, but no words seemed right. The truth would only make him back away, thinking she'd managed to lose her mind in a few short weeks. Brent, a practical left-brained kind of guy, was certainly not ready to hear such a tale. "A ghost that I fell in love with wants to take me with him back to ghost land before his body disappears..." *Right.* Well, she thought, just ask if he's coming. But then, he surely wasn't if he hadn't written to confirm it. Damn.

The longer Ellen stood beside the telephone booth, the more uncertain she was about what she could say, and yet the stronger the desire became to hear Brent's voice.

And if he's coming? she asked herself for the thousandth time, *will Brennig let me stay? Will Brent try to help me? Will he even want to after he learns the mess I'm in?* How do you tell your boyfriend you've been unfaithful with a ghost? What if Brennig was able to prove that she really *was* his wife? If she were Eira, she would have to go with him.

For all that, caught up in her love for Brennig, Ellen knew she wanted desperately to connect again with Brent. Once courage took over, it seemed to take forever to get through. Then the phone was ringing, and she pictured him leaving his morning coffee and walking across the breakfast room to answer. Surely he would be pleased to hear from her.

"Hello?" The connection was surprisingly clear, but it wasn't Brent's voice. It was a woman's.

Ellen went cold with shock. A woman was there at seven in the morning? Oh, God.

"Hello. I'm calling long-distance for Brent Cole."

"Oh? Who is calling?"

"Ellen," she answered, knowing exasperation was rusting her voice. "Ellen Cole. And it's important that I speak with him."

"He isn't here."

This last sounded like a lie. The kind of lie that might come from a jealous woman. He was probably in the shower. *Late shower*. Damn. How could Brent have replaced her so quickly? It wasn't like him…not like him at all. Had she hurt him that severely by not keeping in closer touch? He hadn't kept in touch, either. Which, come to think of it, definitely wasn't his style.

"Where is he?" she asked.

"I'm not at liberty to say."

Ellen felt the heat of fury all the way to the bottom of her feet. "Who am I talking to?" she demanded.

"Laura Davis."

Grinding her teeth in jealousy, Ellen nearly hung up. The name was familiar. Laura Davis was a woman she had either met or heard of somewhere. She said, "Tell him Ellen called, please. From overseas."

"I'll deliver the message when I see him."

"Thanks," was all Ellen could manage to say in the fake calm that remained in her voice.

The anger and disappointment she felt when she left the phone booth were debilitating. Brent wasn't coming. He'd found someone else in less than three weeks. After her affair with Brennig, it might be what she deserved, but it was the last thing she'd expected from Brent. Trustable Brent. Who hadn't even written.

Hell, even if he did come over as planned, what could come of it? There was Brennig, and there was the curse, which was the probable cause of Brent's leaving her in the first place—of Laura what's-her-name lounging at Brent's at seven in the morning.

The damn curse definitely brandished enduring power.

Devastated, Ellen barely remembered to stop at the greengrocer shop to pick up something—she didn't care what—to take back to the cottage with her.

There were some very serious decisions to make.

When she returned, Brennig had tea ready as he'd promised. The pot was hot, and a single cup and saucer were set out on the table along with a plate of bite-sized bread slices, spread with butter and herbs. A fresh bouquet of garden flowers, arranged in a blue china vase, graced the table with color.

Brennig was wearing his first smile of the day. Ellen accepted the smile with relief. His sulking was more than she could take, not just the unpleasantness of it; she was frightened of his disapproval.

"This is sweet of you," she said, sitting down and spreading the cloth napkin over her lap.

"In the old days," Brennig said gently, "you were the one who always prepared tea for me."

Ellen sighed. "The old days...that I'm supposed to remember but don't."

He sat down across from her, watching her pour the tea slowly and add milk and sugar. "It would just...it would make this all so much easier if you remembered."

She gritted her teeth. "You mean, if I remembered the things you say I should, I would be ready and willing to die."

"For our love, yes. To be with me again and for always."

"It's a powerful love you're speaking of, Brennig."

"Aye. More powerful than anything of this earth."

Ellen was so moved by the power of his love, tears came to her eyes. Could a woman give up a love like this? Was Brennig right about her being his one love who came to Wrenn's Oak to find him again? It could be true; she'd certainly sought out his gravestone. If it was true—if he was right—she would be giving up an eternal love for a few short years of living.

Wouldn't she?

Brennig, noting the shine of tears in her eyes, reached across the table and touched her hand. An odd sensation now, his touch. Not a human touch, anymore, it was like a press of velvet—soft, with only an illusion of warmth.

"I do not want you to be sad, my love."

She swallowed. "I don't want you to be sad, either, Brennig. I can't bear for you to be sad." She wasn't thinking only of today, but of forever.

He closed his eyes and opened them again before saying, "I don't want to lose you."

"I know." A new rush of tears filled her eyes. "I don't want to lose you, either."

She sipped her tea, welcoming the distraction, but there was no way to distract her mind. "Brennig, if Nesta had caused me to drown—are you sure you couldn't have reached me then . . . in death? Somehow?"

"No." This was emphatic. "Because you are Eira and therefore separated from me by the curse. Only if you make the decision yourself to come with me do we have a chance to ever be together. Our love must prove to be stronger than Nesta's evil."

Trying to comprehend this, and remembering that he had saved her life and fought Nesta's evil in the river to do it, she asked, "What if I were to *choose* to let Nesta drown me?"

"Don't. Giving Nesta so much power would strengthen the curse against us. She wanted to kill you in the first place, in 1631, instead of me. She mustn't have that victory, not even by your choice. If she does, I'm sure we'll be separated again as we have been all these years... probably forever, because I'm certain this is our only chance. Whatever you do, Eira, stay away from the water and from Nesta."

She gazed at his eyes, which were so pale in the window's light they had no color anymore. Staring at him with her jaw stiff, she challenged, "And just what have you got in mind? Am I supposed to kill myself? Just how the hell do you expect me to do that, Brennig?"

Reacting to the hardness of her voice, he hesitated, then answered softly, "I'll help you, my love. There are poisonous plants in the garden. I will stay with you and hold you. My sweet, it is far easier than you think to cross over. Far easier and far more pleasant than you imagine."

Her shoulders heaved in a great sigh. "I don't know, Brennig. If I were convinced you were right..."

"How can you doubt it?"

"I can doubt it because..." Her eyes lowered and she didn't want to say it, but knew she must. "Because of the love I feel for Brent."

She felt a cold wave cross over her. The ghost's anger was cold, not hot.

"What you feel for him is really your love for me. You just haven't recognized it as such."

"No," she protested weakly. "No. I loved Brent before I met you, and I love him now. Whether he loves me or not. It's a very strong emotion, Brennig, and I can't deny it." She could have added, *I miss him horribly and I want him here more than you could know.* But it would serve no purpose to say it, and very possibly Brennig knew her feelings whether she expressed them aloud or not.

His voice strengthened. "In time those emotions will subside. It is only part of the human experience. Our love goes far beyond that."

With Brennig so near, touching her, it was hard to sort through what was real or unreal, true or untrue, right or wrong. One always assumed spirits had greater knowledge than mortals, therefore it was more likely than not Brennig knew who she was.

If only she could remember . . .

Trying to help her, Brennig reached out to touch her hair, musing, "Your curls used to fall halfway to your waist."

He stood up, and urged her to her feet, too. Ellen felt almost light enough to float. What did he do to her to make her feel this way? How did he wield so much power over her? He had powers she couldn't comprehend. The power to make her love him, the power to spin a web around this house with the two of them in it and cause her to forget her other world existed. Even though Ellen had come to recognize and fear this power, it still pulled her in and held her captive under the charm of his smile and the mystery of his eyes and the gentleness of his voice. Held her captive under the sadness that overtook him from time to time.

Brennig, don't . . . she struggled to say as he bent to kiss her. But the words wouldn't come. He held her close, but there was no warmth in his body anymore, nor in his lips.

"Eira . . . Ellen . . . take my love . . . accept it. Let me love you."

"Brennig, I . . ."

His lips interrupted her. His fingers were in her hair, caressing softly.

"I can still manifest the strength to carry you," he said, lifting her.

She felt herself floating—a sensation of lightness in his arms. "What are you doing, Brennig?"

"We'll get comfortable again, upstairs. Like before. And like in the other days."

"I don't think that's such . . ." she began, and couldn't continue. Something was constricting her throat and blocking her voice.

Floating, she did not—or could not?—protest any further as he carried her up the steps and through the upstairs hallway.

He lay her gently on the soft down quilt of her bed, and fell beside her, kissing her neck. "Don't you know how much I love you, Eira? Don't you know how much I missed you when we were apart?" She shook her head as it spun with confusion.

Brennig was unbuttoning her blouse, moving his hands gently over her breasts. His kiss caused her head to spin faster. Something was dreadfully wrong. Dreadfully. And yet she couldn't think what it was. Couldn't remember. There was only Brennig's handsome face and his soft voice saying he loved her. A voice that tended to fade away sometimes so she could barely hear it.

"Love me . . ." he whispered.

The desire for him was strong, because she loved him. His fingers were like feathers caressing her body. They didn't feel the way they'd felt when she'd first known him, but they felt wildly sensual all the same. His kisses drew her in like a magic spell and took her breath away.

Brennig unbuttoned his shirt and his jeans, and pulled them off. He lay his naked body next to her, but she could no longer feel the hot, impassioned body of a man who loved her. And for a split second, when she looked at him, she could see through him.

A small yelp of horror came from her throat.

"What's the matter?" Brennig asked.

"You're...you're changing so fast. These past few days it's frightened me how fast you're losing your human strength and your human body. You're fading right before my eyes!"

"I told you it would be like that. My time is almost up."

"You didn't tell me what it would be like. For a moment, I could see right through you!"

"Don't be frightened. I am here. I am present as much as ever. You just can't see me as well."

She deflected the caress of his hand on her breast—the caress that had thrilled her such a short time ago. "You ask so much of me, Brennig. You ask me not to be frightened of you. You ask me not to be frightened of death. You seem to forget that I am human."

"No, I cannot forget for a moment that your soul is now trapped in human form. It is the barrier between us."

His voice was gentle, and today even more persuasive than usual. On one level his persuasiveness terrified her, and on another, she responded to it—almost involuntarily, which also scared her. He almost had her convinced...

"Eira..." Brennig whispered. As he said it, the room darkened when a cloud drew across the sun. His soft kisses brushed her forehead and her cheeks and her mouth.

I must be Eira... she thought. *I must be...*

He was hugging her. When Ellen put her arms around him, she could no longer feel a hard, strong body. Only air.

And yet she felt his emotions, his desperation, his need, his love. He drew her into his spell as he had done so often.

Caressing her lightly, he slid off her blouse, whispering, "Our lovemaking is good. We will savor these memories just for the sake of memories."

Removing her jeans, Brennig moved over her, covering her with his body, which had once been so heavy and now was so light. Under his loving persuasion, Ellen wanted to welcome his lovemaking as she had done before, but fear was interfering. Like a dark, familiar cloud moving over her, the horror surfaced once again. This time his declarations of love and his gentle voice could quell it no longer. She knew what he wanted from her—what he was convinced he would get from her, and the fear of him grew loud, and then louder in her ears, loud in her heartbeats. She closed her eyes and tried to think, and couldn't, because he was determined to make love to her...to his wife....

And she? *What did she want?*

"Eira..."

Ellen opened her eyes. It wasn't Brennig's face she saw before her in the darkened room. It was Brent's face, instead!

The illusion lasted only seconds, but it was startlingly vivid. She gave a jump, gasping.

"What is it, my love?"

For a moment—a brief moment—it had sounded like Brent's voice, not Brennig's. Brennig's voice was changing as it weakened, becoming less his own.

Brent! Ellen reached out in desperation, but the illusion had already passed. Brent wasn't here.

Fearfully she slid away from Brennig, out from under him and off the bed, pulling on her jeans.

"What's the matter?" he asked, touching her arm. "You're trembling like a willow leaf, Eira, and acting very strangely. What's wrong? I thought you ached to make love with me, just as I ache for you. . . ."

She didn't look at him. "Stop calling me Eira. My name is Ellen."

She stood up, hurriedly dragging on her shirt, afraid to look at him. Brennig wouldn't like this rejection. She didn't want to make him angry; she feared his anger, but his selfishness was getting overwhelming. He wasn't giving any thought to what she was going through. Panicked that he was running out of time, he was thinking only of himself. Instinctively she knew Brennig could be dangerous, even though she didn't know what exactly the danger was. One moment she was aware of her love for him, the next she knew only the fear. What am I going to do? she asked herself. Brennig's time is almost up. I don't know what to do.

"What are you upset about?" he asked.

"What am I upset about?" Finally she turned to face him. "Why should I be upset, Brennig? Just because you're half-invisible? Just because you're a ghost and not a man and you want me to kill myself so we can be dead together? Why would little things like these upset me?"

He seemed scarcely to have heard her. "Why don't you want to make love to me?"

She looked down at the floor, gathering courage enough for honesty before she looked up. "Because you're more ghost than man now. You fade before my eyes. I can barely feel your touch. Even your face . . . fades and changes. I don't want to make love with a ghost. . . ." A voice inside her was screaming, *I don't want to make love with you. I'm not sure I really love you, Brennig, not in the way I love Brent.* She studied him, wondering if he could hear those unspoken thoughts. He evidently couldn't, because he showed no signs of fury. Only disappointment.

"I am no different than before," he insisted.

"You are and you know it. The physical act of love is very... physical. And you're not. You are spirit. You expect too much of me, Brennig. Far too much."

This time he didn't answer. When she headed out of the bedroom, he followed.

She hurried down the stairs. Without looking back, she said, "I have to be alone... to think. Being around you confuses me so."

"Aye. That is because of the part of you that remembers how it used to be with us."

"Maybe. Or maybe not. Maybe it's you, influencing me."

"How could I do that?"

She grabbed her handbag from the table in the foyer. "How should I know? You're the one who's the ghost."

He stopped her by moving in front of the door. "Where are you going?"

"For a walk. I just have to think. I don't know if you're right or wrong about who I am."

He moved aside reluctantly. "Very well. I'll be here waiting when you return. Please don't take too long. I don't have much time."

She nodded. As she started to leave, the image of him faded again, for several seconds this time. She closed her eyes, hesitating, but then she opened the door and hurried outside.

The cloud that had moved over the sun earlier was gone by now, and the late afternoon sun felt warm, almost balmy. Aimlessly she walked the length of the street, and before long, feeling desperately alone, found herself near the bank of Nesta's river.

CHAPTER NINETEEN

South of the bridge, a wide flat of soft green grass stretched out from the riverbank. A few children with a dog were playing there. Their voices lent gaiety and reality to her dismal mood. She sat on the bank a good safe distance from the water, which was moving calmly, lazily along.

Just a coward afraid to die, she thought. Afraid to die for someone who loved her eternally... endlessly. Was it really fear of death, or was it the uncertainty... ?

"Hello, I know you," a small voice said, approaching. It belonged to a young girl Ellen had met in the village stationer's shop. The girl sat down beside her. "I don't know your name, though."

At first irritated by the distraction from her bleak confusion, Ellen decided the child's voice was, after all, a welcome relief. She had noted often, with pleasure, how friendly all the children were in Wrenn's Oak.

"My name's Ellen. What's yours?"

"Caty. I'm eight. What are you doing? Watching the diamonds?"

Ellen felt a smile form involuntarily. "The sparkles in the water? They do look like diamonds, don't they?"

The child sat down beside the woman, imitating the way she hugged her knees. She touched Ellen's wrist lightly, curiously. "What are your bracelets made of?"

"Vines of some kind. A friend wove them for me."

Fascinated, running her finger over a bracelet, Caty said, "I once tried to braid stems of timothy grass, but it slips. Yours are tight. How'd you get them on?"

Ellen stared at her wrists. She hadn't thought about the bracelets since the last time she'd tried to get them off and found they had shrunk too much. "They were loose when the vines were green. They get tighter as they dry."

Wide blue eyes looked up at her. "But how will you get them off?"

"I don't...know."

"Do they hurt?"

Frowning, Ellen tried uselessly to twist a bracelet. "No, but I don't know why they don't." She tugged, but the woven vines wouldn't move.

Caty's small, gentle hands pulled at the bracelets. She looked up and met Ellen's eyes, staring.

Ellen felt a pang of misgiving. "Why are you looking at me like that, Caty?"

"I don't like them. At first I thought they were pretty, but now I don't like them." The child's concern caused her voice to rise.

Ellen looked at her and then at the bracelets. If they were cutting off her circulation, she couldn't feel it. But if they got any tighter...

"They do seem too tight on me now," she said.

"Not just that." The child drew her hands away, not wanting to touch the vines again. "They don't look pretty anymore."

Ellen wondered how anyone could think Brennig's gifts weren't lovely. She remembered when he'd slipped them on, when, for an instant, she'd compared them to handcuffs. Then she remembered the odd sensations that had slipped on with them, as if what had been woven of his love was magical....

Now, in place of Brennig's hands, a child's hands were touching hers, in place of Brennig's ice-pale eyes, a child's clear blue eyes were touching hers with a warning....

Warning? The word shocked when it bounced from her rational mind. She began to tug frantically at the bracelets.

"Do you want them off?" Caty asked.

"Yes. You yourself said they aren't pretty anymore. I do want them off, but they won't come. I'd have to have a knife."

Caty smiled and reached into her pants pocket. "I have scissors."

A kid who carried scissors? "You have? Why?"

"This morning I was cutting nodding bellflowers. The leaves are like the nettle leaves—oh, I don't mean they sting like the nettles, but they don't feel good to touch, so I cut the stems. I made a nice bouquet for my mum with nodding bellflowers and herb Roberts."

The scissors looked dull—too dull for the vines, but Caty seemed to have faith in them. Ellen held out her wrists. "Do you think you could cut these?"

"It will spoil the bracelets."

"You yourself said you didn't like them, though you didn't say why."

"I don't know why. When I touched the bracelet, I didn't like it anymore. I wanted you to take it off, but you can't."

"Here, try."

To Ellen's surprise, it took only a few clips. Either Caty's scissors were sharper then they looked or the vines were weaker. The left bracelet fell off into the grass, and then the right.

Rubbing her wrists, she gazed down at the broken vines, a spinning in her head. The dizziness soon ceased, and in its place came heaviness, then lightness, and finally a stream of energy that began in her hands and, flowing through her bloodstream, filled her body.

By this time the bracelets were a forgotten episode to the little girl. She returned the small scissors to her pocket and looked out on the river again. "The diamonds in the water are miracles. My mummie told me so."

"I believe in miracles, too," Ellen answered, still rubbing her wrists, wondering if she meant it. Once, it had been true.

"There are miracles everywhere in the world. Earth is a magical ball, my mummie says."

"With miracles like the diamonds made from sunlight?"

A happy laugh. "Oh, yes. And morning glories that open in the morning and close at night. And the northern lights. Did you ever see them? And rainbows. And—" the child began to giggle "—and kitten's whiskers tickling. Mummie and I discovered that one ourselves."

"Your mother must be very wise."

Caty nodded. "Are you a mummie?"

"No. But I would like to be." I had forgotten, she thought. I had forgotten my dreams, and now, suddenly, I remember.

"Then sure you will be. You're pretty."

Ellen smiled. "You're very pretty yourself, Caty."

"I look like my mum. When you have a baby girl she's supposed to look like you."

"Yes," Ellen replied. "I know..." Her eyes were filling with tears.

The child, noticing Ellen's moist eyes as she seemed to notice everything, sucked in her breath. "Are you sad?"

"No. I'm happy. You've helped me find something I had lost."

"Really, what?"

"Some wishes, some hopes."

Caty smiled. "It's because of the water diamonds, I think. When you have a little girl, will you show her diamonds, too?"

"Oh, yes. And morning glories along the path, and the kitten's whiskers." Ellen wiped at her tears and touched the little hand. "You're right, Caty. The earth *is* a magical ball. It's full of pretty things and full of love. It's very nice to be here."

"I think so, too." Caty rose to her feet in response to another child's beckoning call. She smiled at Ellen. "Maybe I'll see you again. I like to hear you talk American."

"Thank you for reminding me of the miracles, Caty. I'll always remember you."

In seconds she was gone, running with the other children, with no idea of the gift she had just bestowed on a stranger. A child couldn't know how she symbolized life and hope. Could she?

The energy Ellen felt without Brennig's bracelets squeezing her wrists was also a surge of freedom. Freedom to think clearly again. Rubbing her forehead, she muttered aloud, "My God, I've been in some kind of mental limbo. Brennig has had so much power over me, I've hardly been rational!"

In that moment, Ellen chose life. In that moment, her heart longed for Brent's love again. Brent...who loved her for herself. Who knew her better than anyone and loved her for the woman he knew. It couldn't be clearer than it was now: if she were Eira, she could not love Brent more than she loved Brennig. And she did love Brent more. Brent was life. He was her dreams, her hopes. Brent's love was one of the miracles she had failed to see.

She saw it now. Saw it clearly, at last. She had probably lost Brent, but she loved him. Aching, she couldn't get the phone call out of her mind. Laura Davis. Who was she?

Ellen got slowly to her feet, leaving the bracelets where they fell. Brennig's gifts, unwanted. Broken. Hardly visible in the grass.

Walking home, head down, Ellen watched the cracks in the sidewalk, trying to figure out how to tell Brennig she had decided not to go with him—a heartbreaking task, because he had said he would face eternity alone, with no one to love. It was horrifying to even try to comprehend the enormity of what she was doing to him by not going with him, and yet she believed he was wrong about her being Eira. If she was really his wife, wouldn't she *want* to go?

Her whole body was stiff with dread. How was he going to take this? Brennig had so much at stake, he wasn't above using ghost powers to influence her, and he certainly wasn't the type to stand for being jilted and left alone forever. What if he decided to get mean about it? To use his powers, whatever they were? He'd been sweet and loving to her because he believed she was his wife, and because he was trying to persuade her to die for him. Once he discovered she wasn't going to do as he wished, he would be angry. What was she facing?

One way or another, she had to try to get away from Brennig. With the clouds cleared from her eyes, she was sure that Brennig could be dangerous.

When Ellen returned, he wasn't in the house. She went upstairs to the bedroom, where she looked down and saw him working in the garden. His obsession with the garden was puzzling, although he had tried to explain it. Maybe he was out there cultivating the poisonous plant he ex-

pected her to make use of. Was it the same poisonous plant
he himself had died from?

Shuddering, Ellen felt the urge to run, but she couldn't
just leave. After all, Brennig loved her. Loved her perhaps even more deeply than she knew. She had returned
that love, and a part of her still loved him and always
would. And she cared what happened to him. The least she
owed him was to talk to him and try to explain why she
couldn't do as he asked.

She couldn't just—just watch him fade forever! Knowing his spirit was leaving for the last time, it would be hard
to say goodbye to him—depart forever from this charming cottage and all the memories. She'd been intending to
take some photos of the house, and now was a good time,
when Brennig was outside and the camera was handy on
the dresser.

She snapped a few shots of the bedroom and the hall
and the other bedrooms, and then paused by the stairs that
led to the third floor, where Brennig's room was. Ellen had
been curious about the dormer floor, but hadn't wanted to
invade his privacy. Now, with camera in hand, she made
her way up the stairway to the small room under the roof.

It was furnished simply, with a narrow bed covered by
a thick maroon quilt, a short oak wardrobe and a squat
dresser with a mirror over it. A patterned wool rug covered a wooden floor that hadn't been polished in many
years. There was a thin layer of dust everywhere. Had she
come here sooner, before she'd known that Brennig wasn't
a human being, she'd have been shocked that the occu-
pant had no possessions except a change or two of clothes.
Nothing else. Absently she opened the top drawer of the
dresser, expecting to find it empty.

Instead, she saw several unopened envelopes. At the
very first glance, she felt a sinking in her stomach. Her eyes

focused on the handwriting. *Brent's.* His printing was distinctive. Her name on the top envelope jumped out at her. Ellen picked up a letter, and then another, and another. There were four in all.

Brent's letters to her. Brennig had taken them! Hidden them from her. How could he do such a thing?

She went hot with anger. He could do such a thing because he was jealous of Brent, and he had to win her affection away from Brent in order to accomplish his mission.

Not wanting to be caught up here in case Brennig returned to the house unexpectedly, she grabbed the letters, closed the drawer softly and hurried back down the narrow stairs to her bedroom on the second floor.

She sat on the bed and ripped open the envelopes one by one. Brennig hadn't opened them, hadn't been concerned, evidently, with what was in the letters, only that Ellen didn't receive them and believed Brent hadn't written.

How dare he! And with all that insistence that her decision to come with him had to be *her* idea, because she wanted to. How could he ask her to make such a grave decision without having all the facts?

Tearfully she sorted them by date and read through Brent's letters. They were chatty, loving, with news about his activities and asking about hers, and certainly no hint that another woman was dancing on the fringes of his life. In the first letter he talked about their being together in Wales. The next two worried that he hadn't heard from her and ended with anxious anticipation of seeing her soon.

Brent's words of faith and love. Wiping tears from her eyes, Ellen opened the fourth letter, scolding herself that even if another woman *hadn't* found him, he wouldn't come now, because she hadn't written. What clearer message could he have had that she didn't want him to come? Ellen couldn't really fault him for not being faithful, when she herself hadn't been. Brent must have sensed she wasn't. Had this Laura person told him she'd phoned? Laura... Laura Davis. That name... Ellen scratched her head, trying to remember, and suddenly when it came to her, she couldn't hold back an involuntary yelp. Laura Davis was Brent's sister! Divorced, she lived in Atlanta and was constantly threatening to visit Arizona to see if she wanted to move to "the Wild West".

His sister. Oh, God, why hadn't she remembered his sister's name? Why hadn't she phoned him back? Brent had told her how sweet Laura was; she had been anything but sweet on the phone.

The thin airmail paper shook in her hands. Halfway through the letter, Brent had written,

> I finally convinced Laura that summer in Tucson was no worse than Atlanta, so she's on her merry way. I'm worried about you, Ellen, and I wish there were some way I could get hold of you by phone. Please let me know you're okay and that the Welsh gardener hasn't carried you off into the wild hills....

In the last letter, he didn't mention that he would come. How could he, when he hadn't heard from her? Ellen began crying. If she'd received those letters, she would have answered them, if only out of a sense of duty. If she'd read the letters, she'd have been reminded, even while under Brennig's spell, of Brent's love. If she'd received the letters, she wouldn't have been able to pull so far away from Brent for these short weeks.

And Brennig knew it.

It was only by chance that he hadn't gotten away with stealing her letters. That impulse to see what the loft floor looked like, and then to open a drawer because it seemed so strange to see a room unlived in, had been pure chance!

Ellen folded the letters back into their envelopes with a great sense of loss. Seething, she went down to the kitchen, opened the door and called him inside.

He came willingly. "You've been gone a long time, Elra. Where were you?"

"Talking with one of the village children. I got back some time ago, but I've been busy." Feeling weak, she sat down at the table and Brennig sat across from her.

"Something is wrong," he said. "You have such a strange look on your face. What is that look?"

"Anger," she answered.

"At me?"

"Yes." She paused. "I was taking pictures of the cottage, and I went upstairs to your loft to see what it was like. I happened to open a drawer and found my letters from Brent, the ones you'd taken."

He was frowning. As Ellen looked at him, Brennig's image faded for a second or two, and then returned. He said nothing.

She came a step nearer, her anger subduing her fear. "Why, Brennig?"

He looked down at her from what seemed a great height. "Where are the bracelets I wove for you?"

She took hold of her right wrist protectively, rubbing lightly. "They got too tight. I couldn't wear them anymore."

"I wanted you to wear them."

She glared. "I know. But I couldn't. You haven't answered my question. Why did you take my letters?"

His voice changed, lowered. Clearly he wasn't pleased about the bracelets being gone. He answered, "You know why. I don't like my wife receiving letters from another man who thinks he loves her."

"That's extremely unfair!"

"Not from my point of view."

Her voice grew louder. "You shouldn't have done it!"

He shrugged, as if he believed all was fair in love.

She shook her head in exasperation. "I'm surprised you didn't read them while you were at it."

"I can't read," he answered matter-of-factly. "I can make out a few words in Gaelic Welsh, but I can't read a word of English."

"Oh, I see! And otherwise you would have."

"Perhaps. I don't know."

She ground her teeth. "You've probably ruined my relationship! It was a mean—"

"There was no relationship," he interrupted impatiently. "The curse finished that, he just didn't know it. I did you a favor."

Aware that her lips were trembling, Ellen tried to look at him, and it was difficult because his image tended to blur. "You told me you couldn't make a difference to the fate of other people."

"It's different where my wife is concerned, because your fate and mine are intertwined."

She closed her eyes. "And what if you're wrong about my being your wife?"

"I'm not wrong. And you know I'm not." Brennig rose and began to pace. His movements were now too fluid to be human. "I'm sorry you're angry, Eira. I was only trying to help things along."

"Along *your* wishes. Not mine."

He turned his pale eyes on her. She felt a chill and braced herself. It was easier to build courage from anger than from fear.

He'd picked up on the foreboding intimation. His voice seemed to echo when he said harshly, "Your wishes are not mine?"

A silence filled in. Finally she cleared her throat and answered. "No... I've thought long and hard about this, Brennig, and I have decided I must stay. My life isn't finished yet. What I have left to do here is very important to me. I feel as though I'm supposed to stay."

Brennig didn't answer for a long time. The cottage felt so cold Ellen rubbed her arms and shivered. Then he said, "It's him, isn't it? The man in America."

"As you said, that relationship is probably ruined, but I would fix it if I could. I am convinced that Eira could not love another man."

"You love *me*."

"I do, in one way. But not..." She stopped. There was nothing to be gained by trying to describe to Brennig the solid, pure love she felt for Brent.

Brennig was angry. "It is only because you have forgotten what we had. I thought your heart remembered. You are only substituting that other man for me. He is no doubt like me and that's why you were drawn to him. Even his name is like mine."

"I've thought about that," she said, almost under her breath. "And I can't explain it...."

"I can!"

Brennig's pain wasn't easy to deal with. She felt herself absorbing it. It was the most miserable feeling in the world to hurt someone the way she was hurting him now—a way even she couldn't fully comprehend. Ellen felt the pain all through her. She couldn't hold back the tears.

"Brennig, all I know is that I am drawn very strongly to life, to earth. *Very strongly*. It's not just a fear of death, because you've dispelled much of that fear. It's a need to live out my life here as I was meant to. I want to have children, and run with them in fresh meadows, and feel the sun and the rain, and look for rainbows. All my intuitive senses tell me I am supposed to live...to live longer here on the earth."

He was still pacing. "Hang intuitive senses! It's only the human fear of death you're talking about. I remember it. Hell, I remember it well."

"You're still very bitter that Nesta cheated you out of so much of your earth life. You wanted to see your children grow—"

"I wanted most to stay with you," he said. The voice was no longer filled with affection. His anger and disappointment caused an odd echo when he spoke, as though he were putting out more emotional energy than his weakening body was able to cope with. *"And this is the thanks I get for my love."*

Ellen didn't answer. Her heart was pounding. Confronting a man with rejection was a horrible experience and bad enough, but Brennig wasn't a man. And in spite of his insistence to the contrary, she *didn't* know him.

She really didn't know him at all.

What she did know was that, from his point of view, she was condemning him to an eternity of loneliness. Ellen didn't believe it, though. Maybe, she thought, it *would* have made a difference if she believed this were true. But her love for Brent was too strong. She clung to this. Eira couldn't want Brent so much if she truly was with her husband again.

She muttered softly, head down, "I am not your wife."

In an ice-edged voice, he answered, "You are my wife and you'll not desert me!"

The room was turning as cold as a winter night. The dishes on the hutch began to shake. A plate fell to the floor and shattered. The window shutters slammed. Alarmed, Ellen looked around for Brennig and couldn't see him.

But he was there, all right.

Two more of the shaking dishes hit the floor. A chair slid across the room and crashed into the stone fireplace, knocking over a copper pot.

She wanted to scream, *Brennig, stop it!* But what good would it do? What right did she have to expect him not to be furious?

For the second time today, Ellen realized she might be in actual danger. Why didn't he show himself? Was it intentional? Or was it possible his physical form had left him for good?

Was it over?

The teapot on the stove began whistling, throwing out steam into the room, even though the stove hadn't been turned on a few minutes ago.

Please stop! she begged him silently. What the hell was he trying to do?

When a ceramic plaque hanging on the wall suddenly shot across the room, she let out a shriek, turned and ran. Not daring to look back or slow down, she rushed through the hall toward the dimly lit foyer, knocking over the wood-and-brass umbrella stand as she pushed open the front door.

Her rational mind thought, he's a ghost; he can follow me. Not logic, but panic prevailed. She had to get away from that cottage and from the restless, angry ghost who had haunted it for the past three and a half centuries.

The sunshine of the early afternoon had disappeared and the summer warmth with it. Clouds borne on cold air currents were moving down from the hills, dragging a thick bank of fog behind them.

Brennig's anger was out of hand. Had he chosen to act like that, or was he really out of control? Either way, it was terrifying. The thought of returning to the cottage was just as terrifying, but of course she would have to. There was no way to flee Wrenn's Oak without her handbag and her plane ticket home.

Not now, though, not yet. Damn, she had to find a way to communicate with him. Not just leave him and have the rest of her life to think about what she had done, and think of him in that peaceful place he lived, sentenced to an eternity of loneliness. Was there any way left to talk to him? Perhaps not; Brennig felt the only woman he had ever loved had betrayed him. The ultimate betrayal: she had not been willing to die for him.

To die—with no guarantee that her act of love would break Nesta's curse. Brennig only assumed it; he didn't know for sure.

Ellen wondered what Brennig, the person, was really like. Had he been so sweet only because he wanted something from her? There was no way of guessing about that.

Hurrying down the street, Ellen's thoughts assailed her like darting arrows, coming fast and furiously out of her mind's dark confusion. She felt the damp of the first fingers of fog moving over the village. There might soon be a fire in the fireplace at the little pub, but Ellen rejected the idea of taking refuge there with no money and no explanation for her weird behavior. Before long, she realized that she was wandering aimlessly, moving in the direction from which she first had come to Afan House—the direction of the churchyard and the bridge.

As before, she seemed to be drawn toward the bridge. It was puzzling, because for all its medieval beauty, Ellen had come to hate that bridge and the slow-flowing river that sang beneath it, reeking of evil in its secret depths. Today, for some reason, it beckoned her.

In utter despair, she plopped herself down on the low stone wall that surrounded the churchyard. Brennig's grave was behind her. She had glanced at the dark, ominous stone from the path, and then averted her eyes. It was heart wrenching to look at the cold, weathered gravestone now, one of the dark slabs forming shadows in the fog.

Damn. She *had* wanted to find that tombstone in Wrenn's Oak. The brimstone butterfly leading her to Afan House was no coincidence. She had sought out Brennig Cole's ancient grave, and found his ghost.

The fog-blurred shadows behind her seemed to be moving. It was eerie how the weather had changed so suddenly. The warmed earth shivered in the descending mist. Feeling lost and alone and frightened, Ellen tried to figure out why, having run from Brennig, she would return to the graveyard by the bridge. Perhaps to try to back up time and obliterate everything that had happened since she first walked here.

The sky darkened, shutting out the last bit of sun. A storm was forming behind the fog, she thought. Rain for Brennig's damn garden, where poisonous plants were carefully cultivated, hidden and waiting for her.

Brennig had told her he had twenty-eight days. It had been only twenty-six. In her heart she knew he would come after her. Maybe that was why she'd run to his grave. Out here where his body had been laid to rest centuries ago, she might confront him more safely than inside the cottage he haunted.

Could she? Or was it even more dangerous here? Was she too close to the river to be safe? Aching because of Brennig's awful pain, and trembling with fear of his unknown powers, Ellen looked up suddenly to see a figure forming through the fog.

CHAPTER TWENTY

It was the figure of a man on the bridge carrying a suitcase. He appeared to be walking over from England. At first Ellen admonished herself for being startled at so ordinary a sight as a lone pedestrian, then, slowly, her senses went on full alert and her heart began to beat faster. There was something familiar about the way the man carried himself, walking in long, even strides.

Could it be? *Brent?*

Or were her eyes and her mind playing tricks? Leaping to her feet, she stood by the low stone wall, trying to make sure she wasn't delusional with wishful thinking. Afraid to move for fear it wasn't Brent but only a stranger approaching in the fog, she stood immobile and silently prayed as he came closer. Then, heart thundering, she began to run toward the figure on the bridge, more certain with every footstep that it *was* Brent's walk.

And he was crossing from the English side. No! He mustn't cross that cursed bridge! She was close enough now to recognize one of Brent's favorite outfits—tan slacks and his brown leather jacket.

Ellen ran faster, waving an arm and yelling. "Don't cross, Brent! Don't come across!"

He halted abruptly. "Ellen?"

"Don't cross the bridge into Wales! I'll come over there! Just don't—"

But it was too late. He'd already reached the bridge's center before he stopped. Confused, he set down his bag and waited there until Ellen caught up with him. She ran into his arms breathlessly, overcome with the joy of seeing him again.

"Brent! Oh, Brent! You're really here! Oh, thank God! I didn't think you were coming!"

He planted a warm kiss squarely on her lips and pulled her tightly against him. "I said I'd come, didn't I?"

"I was afraid you'd changed your mind because I haven't written."

He held her close. His body was strong and warm and solid.

"What are you doing out here in the fog, Ellen? Surely not waiting for me?"

"Maybe I was and didn't know it. Something kept leading me to the bridge all day. I couldn't believe it when I saw you just…just walking toward me! Why are you on foot?"

"No sense in my renting a car when you had one. I took a bus from the Manchester airport to Wrenn's Oak, and it dropped me on the other side. Why were you yelling at me not to cross?"

Pressed against the warmth of him, grateful for him, Ellen had allowed herself to forget the dangers for a moment. "The bridge…it's haunted. The river, too. Let's get off here!"

He didn't move. "Wait a minute. What are you talking about? Honey, are you okay?"

She shook her head. "No, but I can't explain right now. We must find a place to talk." *And quickly,* she thought, because there was no telling how Brennig would react when he discovered Brent was here. How the devil she was going to explain everything, Ellen had no idea, but it had to be done, as fast as possible.

Brent paused at the railing, concern in his eyes. "I should have come with you in the first place. I knew it from the moment you left. Something's happened here. I should have come sooner."

She tugged at him frantically. "Come on! We'll walk to the corner pub. We can talk there."

Before he yielded to the pulling on his jacket sleeve, Brent glanced down at the river. Ellen saw him grip the rail. His jaw dropped open and his shoulders went tense.

"My God!"

She closed her eyes. *Oh, no!* she thought, *no, please...* But denial was futile. Terrified, she forced herself to look. It was as horrible as before—so frightening she could barely find her voice. "I hoped you wouldn't see it, Brent! It's... it's the face of an evil witch who jumped from this bridge and drowned in 1631."

Brent gave no indication of having heard a word. He stood staring down into the gray water at the shadow-eyes, the evil shape of the mouth, the hair flowing out on the ripples. "Is this thing some kind of... optical illusion?"

"No. The ghost—she's called Nesta—lives in the river. It's true, Brent, you'll have to believe me. Please don't look at her! She's horribly evil." Ellen was tugging at him, but he wouldn't budge.

"It's the most ghastly looking thing I've ever seen in my life!"

"You don't know how ghastly. Only descendants of Brennig and Eira Cole can see it, which means you are on that bloodline, too, as I suspected all along. The witch Nesta has put a curse on us all. *Please,* Brent! Please let's get off this damned bridge!"

She expected Brent to ask something like how many drinks she'd had that day or how long she'd been without sun, but he didn't. The sight of the face was too sobering for a skeptic like Brent. He couldn't stop staring at it even as it was slowly being swallowed by the thickening fog.

"It's a curse," she said softly, still urging him off the bridge. "Legend says that anyone related to the blacksmith Cole who crosses over the bridge will never find his or her true love."

"You don't believe stuff like that, do you?"

"I didn't believe a lot of things before I came here. But now, yes, I believe in curses...and jealous witches...and ghosts." She paused and looked up at him. "And I believe I love you more than I ever thought I could love anybody."

This last remark was powerful enough to pull Brent's attention away from the face in the water. "Do you mean it?"

"I never meant anything more. You don't know how overwhelmed I am to see you."

"Then that makes two happy people. Lovers shouldn't be apart. Never again." He turned his back on the river and slid an arm around Ellen. "I was getting a little worried when I didn't hear from you."

"But not worried enough to change your mind about coming, thank God."

"Actually, I thought about not coming, because I figured your silence was your way of letting me know you had changed your mind about our plans. I didn't want to think it, but it wasn't like you to be so silent."

"I'm dreadfully sorry. So many times I wanted to write or talk, but something stopped me...." At the edge of the bridge, she took his arm. "I will explain, Brent, but I can't just now...it will take a long time to explain."

Through the fog, they couldn't see the church spire, much less the tombstones in the churchyard, for which Ellen was grateful. She asked, "What did make you decide to come, then?"

They stepped onto the road leading past the churchyard. "It was the damnedest thing, honey. I don't think you'd believe me if I told you what—" Abruptly he stopped, because a man had appeared on the path and had stepped directly in front of them.

Brennig!

Ellen drew in her breath, releasing her grip on Brent's arm. Her heartbeat raced. Searching for words—any word—proved useless. Brennig had appeared out of the fog as if from nowhere and stood blocking their way.

"Brennig..." Ellen managed to say finally, before her voice failed. After the tantrum he'd thrown when she couldn't see him, she'd hoped desperately that he had lost his human form for good and couldn't appear again as a man. Wishful thinking and premature, he'd wanted to scare her by proving her worst fear—Brennig had an uncontrollable temper when things didn't go his way.

When she said Brennig's name, Brent looked curiously from Ellen to the stranger and then back again.

Desperate, feeling more awkward than she had ever felt in her life, Ellen muttered, "Brent, this is... this is Brennig Cole. Brennig...Brent Cole..." Her voice had dropped to a whisper before the sentence was out.

Brennig stood stone still, glaring. She was afraid to look at his eyes.

Brent took an annoyed step forward. "Is there something you want?" he asked.

Brennig's cold, transparent eyes focused only on Ellen. They showed no emotion whatsoever, only the coldness.

Beginning to shiver, she remembered what caused his eyes to go so icy cold: anger.

"You deceived me!" Brennig accused. His deep Welsh accent caught on the misty air like an echo. "You did not tell me he was coming, and then you came to the river to meet a man who knows nothing of who you really are."

Brent, absorbing the other man's hostility, took another step forward. "Hey! What are you babbling about?"

Brennig sneered. His lips were trembling with rage or hurt, or both. Ellen wanted to grab Brent's arm and pull him back from the danger, but she knew this gesture would only make Brennig more angry... and Brent, too. So she stood helplessly on legs that were becoming too weak to hold her weight, wanting to warn Brent that the person he faced wasn't a human being, and not knowing how to do so. Brent wouldn't believe her if she did tell him; how could she even expect him to?

They were standing on the churchyard path. Impatient, Brent quickened his step, wanting to be rid of the intruder. His reunion with the woman he loved was not open for any more interference. Taking Ellen's hand, he sidestepped the other man in an attempt to lead her away.

Infuriated, Brennig would have none of this. He blocked the path. Brent pushed him.

Ellen whispered. "Don't start anything."

"Me?" Brent's eyebrows shot up. "Look, I have only so much patience—"

"And *I* have only so much patience," Brennig responded, his voice slightly stronger than before, but with the same strange echo. "I will thank you to unhand my wife."

"Brennig, please," Ellen said in a shaking voice. "Stop referring to me as your wife."

"You are and you know you are," he replied.

She shook her head vehemently.

Brent's voice came loud and harsh, while the other two had been almost whispering. *"What the devil is going on?"*

She looked at him pleadingly, knowing he wouldn't miss the fear in her eyes. "I can explain. Brennig thinks I'm someone else."

"Obviously!"

Brennig's angry tone softened ominously. "You cannot leave me . . . not forever. You wouldn't do it."

The despair in his voice caused her heart to sink. Suddenly, she found herself thinking of his beautiful singing in the shower that first morning. She remembered the first time he'd given her flowers from his garden. Ellen hated herself for getting into this mess, hated herself for hurting Brennig so—as if there were a choice. She said in a strained voice, "Brennig, we've been over this . . ."

She looked up desperately at Brent. What must he be thinking? She'd be lucky if he didn't just turn his back on her in disgust; it was obvious his girlfriend was involved with this weird Welshman. Anger sparked and grew in Brent's voice and in his eyes, but confusion was there, too. This was somebody's nightmare, but whose? Tension crackled in the tepid summer air.

Suddenly Brennig was gone. Just gone. Brent looked about, stunned, while Ellen waited in dread for the repercussions. They weren't long in coming, but not from Brent.

A cold wisp of a breeze blew in from nowhere, over the flower beds and across the green lawn, pressing her skirt against her legs and blowing her hair about her face. A crow cawed shrilly from high branches.

"Let's get out of here," she said to Brent.

He had set down his bag. Now he picked it up again. "Get out of where? Where do you want to go, Ellen? I think you'd better explain what the hell is going on!" His hair curled in the damp air and fell over his forehead. Impatiently he brushed it back, looking down at her with an expression Ellen had never seen. "How did the guy just disappear into the fog like that?"

While her stomach twisted with panic, she tugged again at his sleeve. "Let's get away from the river. We're still too close to it. I don't know how Brennig disappeared, but I know he'll be back. You must understand, Brent, he's not... He's..." She trailed off. The word *dead* wasn't appropriate. Brennig obviously was very much alive, but in a way she couldn't understand, and neither would Brent.

The air around them was frosted with cold. A branch fell from a nearby tree with no apparent provocation. The side gate to the churchyard began banging.

Brennig's temper. Again. Ellen recoiled as Brent's arm came protectively around her.

"Is he crazy? He is, isn't he? You've been victimized by a crazy man who thinks you're his wife and won't leave you alone. Damn, honey, why didn't you tell me this was going on?"

"I didn't realize what *was* going on..." she muttered. Brent's anger had subsided in the shadow of his trust. He trusted her because he loved her.

"Well, I'm here now. We'll go get your things and leave this town as soon as possible. I don't like whatever's happening here. That guy is *not* your everyday scorned lover. What have you gotten yourself into?"

"Brennig is no ordinary man," she answered. "In fact, he's not a man at all. He's a ghost. Don't look at me like that, Brent. I swear it's true. He can disappear suddenly because he is a ghost. This cold wind and the fallen branch are manifestations of his anger."

Brent looked at her incredulously. "Oh, come on, Ellen!"

"It's true. He's Brennig Cole, who died over three hundred and fifty years ago. And he's an ancestor to us both. He is convinced I'm his wife who—"

She was cut off by the sight of Brennig, showing up in the fog again, this time near the bridge. He stood, legs apart in a challenging stance, and called to the other man in the hollow echo that had become his voice, "Are you afraid of ghosts?"

Ellen expected Brent to counter with a disgusted, "I don't believe in ghosts," for she was pretty sure he didn't. But to her surprise, he squinted at the dark figure in the mist and merely smiled.

"So you claim to be the living dead, do you?" he asked guardedly.

"Aye," sounded the deep echo. Even that one word sounded like a threat.

"If that's so, then you're in the wrong element here. This place is for the living."

Brennig snarled, "I came back to get what was mine."

Not to be intimidated, Brent took a step closer. "That would be Ellen, I take it."

Was this Brent talking to Brennig like this—talking to a ghost as though he actually believed that what was happening was...was really happening? Ellen reeled, too light-headed to think rationally. The nightmare was sweeping them all up into its horror! In the nightmare, Brennig had changed. He'd always talked about love before. Now he talked about possession. And Brent was challenging him.

Angry, Brent let his bag slide to the ground and moved closer to the ghost. Ellen tried, unsuccessfully, to pull him back, wildly apprehensive that Brennig was addressing her again.

"You cannot do this to me! I have searched the centuries for you. I will not surrender to Nesta. You must agree to come with me and break the curse. Don't leave me alone, Eira...."

Ellen, standing next to Brent, felt him jerk to full alert, then his body stiffened, quickly-frozen. The name formed on his lips and seemed to stick there. *"Eira?"*

The expression on Brent's face caused Ellen's mouth to drop open. He showed more shock at hearing the name Eira than he had on learning they were facing the wrath of an angry ghost!

Before she could explain who Eira was, Brent was moving in on Brennig. He walked straight toward him. Brennig stood in the thick, wet fog of the river shore. When Ellen tried to pull Brent back yet again, he shrugged off her efforts.

"Just what do you want from her?" he demanded of the ghost.

Brennig's eyes were as silver as the clouds behind the fog. "This has nothing to do with you, and you are interfering."

"It has plenty to do with me. Ellen is afraid of you, anyone could see that."

"Only because you have made her so." The echo of Brennig's voice did not carry well on the fog.

Ellen steeled herself against the spirit's anger. Trying to catch her breath as she came up behind Brent, she lifted her head and affirmed, "I have given you my answer, Brennig. I'm not going to change my mind. I'm sorry. I'm dreadfully sorry to make you so unhappy. But I've made my choice. I've chosen life."

"Chosen *him,*" Brennig snapped. It came like the sound of thunder.

She forced herself to look into Brennig's eyes, and nodded slowly.

While her heart ached for Brennig, it longed for Brent. Brent's happiness mattered, and their love deserved a chance, the same chance Brennig's and Eira's love had had once . . . long ago.

Brent was not about to let another man stand between him and the woman he loved—whether the man was human or not. He strode to the bank at a fast clip, but before he got there, Brennig disappeared again.

"Damn you!" Brent cursed. And then, "Okay, fine! It's settled, then."

No sooner had the words left his mouth than Brent ducked in alarm, holding the side of his head. A heavy branch, picked up by another freak gust of wind, had come swooping down, hitting him a hard blow.

Ellen cried out.

Brent turned back to the figure, again visible on the riverbank, as blood streaked down his temple. "You fight a coward's battle!" he raged. "If you think you can scare me off by behaving like a ghost, forget it. I don't scare. I won't leave Ellen's side until you go back to wherever it is you came from!"

Brennig didn't move. He answered threateningly, "No mortal may call me a coward without regretting he did so! Nor will any man take what belongs to me, I will not allow it!"

"It isn't your choice to make, I don't care what you are. This isn't your plane we're standing on, it's mine. You belong someplace else! Don't threaten me in my own element, Brennig. Mortality has the advantage here."

"I think not. Mortality is but a fleeting condition!"

"Fleeting, maybe, but strong." Furious, spurred by an adrenaline rush, Brent reached the edge where Brennig was standing, not more than three feet from the shallow bank. "I don't like to be threatened." As he said this, Brent reached out as if to push a warning at Brennig, and then drew back in shock. Ellen knew why. She knew the sensation was like grabbing at air; Brennig's body was little more than illusion now, like a light bulb that keeps glowing as it is burning out. He had little form left, and little physical strength in his body. His power was the life-force within him that could not die, and the life-energy was strong. Ellen dreaded the power manifested by his anger.

It didn't take long for her dread to turn to fright. Brent nearly lost his balance. A force he couldn't see was pushing him closer to the river.

Taken by surprise, he tripped on something unseen and slipped over into the slow-moving river.

Ellen's heart stopped. Too late she realized that Brennig had been trying to get Brent close to the river's edge from the very start—close enough to force him in. If Brennig hadn't the strength left to do away with his enemy, Nesta would be enraged enough to do it for him. She screamed frantically, "Get out of the water, Brent! It's too dangerous!"

Even as she said it, the water began to roil and toss; an angry storm seethed in its depths. Brent struggled against the tremulous currents.

"Brent!" she yelled.

"It's okay!" he yelled back with confidence to remind her that he was, indeed, a very strong swimmer. A champion swimmer. Water had never frightened him, and didn't frighten him now. But the water storm was becoming so violent, it was able to push Brent toward the middle, where the river was deepest. He began to struggle hard against it.

Ellen watched in horror. Brent had seen the face—witnessed for himself the evil that writhed in the ancient river. He would know it was more than a current he was battling.

Because the fog made it hard to see, she rushed to the bridge, all the while pleading with Brent to get out. From the railing, looking down, it was clear he was in even more trouble than she'd thought. The river storm raged with demonic vengeance. The harder Brent tried to swim to shore, the more the treacherous current pulled him toward its whirling vortex.

Brent sank. Ellen felt herself die a little. In a moment, he fought his way back to the surface, thrashing savagely at the enormous weight that pulled and pushed and tossed him. Then his head went under again.

Ellen screamed, "No!"

A strange shadow moved through the water, but it wasn't Nesta. It had to be Brennig!

"No!" she screamed again, against the treacherous storm. Against Nesta and Brennig both, Brent didn't have a chance!

CHAPTER TWENTY-ONE

Brent's head disappeared from the surface of the fog-blurred water for the third time. Even the trained endurance swimmer wasn't strong enough to save himself from the wrath of the river.

Ellen's heart sank with him and ceased to beat, then began thundering in her throat. This wasn't happening! It couldn't be! Brent was too strong to die!

But he was under. Ellen went ice-cold. Brent could not—*must* not drown because of Brennig's feud with Nesta! Or because she'd gotten herself involved in it! As she stood at the bridge rail looking down, the writhing water once again formed the evil face of the witch, to taunt her, flaunting impending victory.

To her horror, the outline of Brennig—a dark form that faded, got stronger and then faded again—kept appearing in the midst of the fray. No wonder the power of the river was so strong! Brennig—too weak now to conquer his human rival physically—was fortifying his own energy with Nesta's to overpower Brent in the water.

And it was working!

There was no longer any hope of communicating with Brennig or reasoning with him. She knew the desperation with which he wanted Brent dead. But why did Nesta? There was a reason, some reason, *had* to be some reason.

Ellen's heart was pounding against her chest. Her head was spinning and throbbing. Brent wasn't strong enough to fight both of them; he was losing the struggle against the power of the two raging spirits and he was going to drown because of her.

"Nesta!" Ellen yelled through the fog. "You can't do this! It isn't Brent you want! *I'm* the one you want!"

Her own voice echoed back to her through the dampness, telling her Brent must not die.

Her love for him was excruciating and blinding and all that mattered on earth. "I'm the one you want, you damned witch!" she screamed again. Her legs tangled in her full skirt as she lifted them over the low rail. Nesta's face had been just below the center; defiantly Ellen leaped into the river at that very spot. Brent *had* to survive, even if she didn't.

The second she hit the water, the evil energy focused itself not on Brent, but on her—as she knew it would. Grabbed by the pull of the voracious current, she could hear an echo—Brennig's voice—shouting, "No!" For a silvery split second in time, she heard his voice in her memory telling her that she must not die by Nesta's design or they would never be together.

It was too late for Brennig . . . but it mustn't be too late for Brent. He had a life to live, even without her. With both arms and legs, she fought to hold herself up, and couldn't. The weight of her clothes pulled her down, and the fevered turbulence of the water held her like a thousand grasping fingers.

"Ellen!" Brent yelled. Wrenching free, turning full circle and gasping for breath, he strained forward in her direction. Strong strokes. Strong arms pummeling the water savagely.

Sinking, she felt the shock to her lungs, accepting, knowing the only way to save Brent was to absorb all of Nesta's attention, all of her rage. She closed her eyes and prayed it wasn't too late. Prayed that Brent could make it out.

The squeezing of the river's hands got tighter. Struggling was futile. Ellen was somehow aware of Brennig's presence very near, helpless this time to save her, for his earth-body strength was all but finished. Still he hadn't left her.

The river's hands...no...they weren't the river's hands, nor Brennig's ... The slipping grasp she felt was Brent! Ellen recognized Brent's touch even here, even now.

He was still alive. Thank God! She had jumped in in time.

In the violent, roiling river storm, Brent lost hold and then found her again, communicating with his touch that he was trying to move in closer. She couldn't move at all against the current that was suffocating her even as it spun her away from him.

But Brent's strength in the water was indomitable, unmatched by most men, which the witch could not have known. Fury nourished by adrenaline made him stronger still; the woman he loved was drowning. Ellen felt his hands tighten around her shoulder and then her waist as he maneuvered into a solid grip.

At last she felt his body against hers. Nesta's rage battered them with the heavy weight of the river, but Brent wouldn't let go. He was pulling her toward the surface.

Kicking for buoyancy, she felt Brennig's presence near, but he wasn't interfering, wouldn't even if he could, for he couldn't bear to see Nesta kill her, even if Ellen *had* betrayed him.

Almost directly under the bridge now, Brent was tugging her toward the English shore. With each second, his grip seemed to get tighter, but Nesta was fighting tirelessly to pull them into the depths where death lurked. The witch's strength was hate powered. It weakened against the force of love—Ellen's and Brent's together. Holding her tightly, Brent slowly began to conquer the width of the river, one heavy stroke at a time. Ellen, a good swimmer herself, did what she could by hanging on to him and kicking hard against the water's convulsions. She fought for every breath.

Away from the center, as the water gradually became more shallow, the river seemed to gain strength. It kept trying to pull them back toward the middle. Brent was struggling against bruising fatigue, determined not to lose her. A desperate lightning-fast thought assailed Ellen—if she and Brent were to die together, would the curse hold so that they couldn't be together in death? Yes, it would hold, because Nesta would have drowned them. And where would that leave Brennig? Such frightening thoughts had no place right now. It was all she could do to concentrate on keeping her head up far enough to breathe. She could hear Brent gasping for air. He was dangerously depleted.

Suddenly Brent stopped tearing at the current. An unexplained lull, like a swell, came through the water.

"Eira!"

To her shock, it wasn't Brennig's voice who yelled Eira's name—it was Brent's!

Through the sustained lull, as if the river itself had been stunned, Ellen followed Brent's gaze toward the shore of England. There, hovering in the fog, was the ghostlike figure of a woman. In flowing white, she was moving like a cloud, from out of nowhere, closer and closer to the river's edge.

It had to be Eira! Brent had been the one who'd said her name! How could Brent know Eira? How could Brent possibly know Eira?

From the river center directly behind Ellen came Brennig's echo—like a gasp through tears.

"Eira!" he called. *"Eira..."*

The middle was as far as Brennig could go. With Nesta guarding her curse, he couldn't get across to reach his wife. The vibrations of his astonishment and his new, savage desperation to get across the river formed a vile electricity in the water, like shock waves. The white ghost floated out over the water, but not quite as far as the river's center; she, too, was blocked by the curse.

The river quivered, as if coming out of paralyzed shock, and began to writhe again, angrier than ever. The appearance of Eira triggered the most murderous rage yet. Ellen screamed. She felt Brent let go of one of her hands. He's losing hold, she thought, panicked.

Somehow, through the hellish turmoil, Brent reached up out of the water, into the air, toward the hovering ghost.

What is he doing? Ellen's heart was screaming.

Without any hesitation, Eira reached down and took Brent's hand. *As if she knew him...*

Her voice came like a small gust of wind, breathing out of a distant sky. "Brennig! Brennig! My love, come! Come back to me!"

It was Brent who answered at once, panting for air as the water churned maleficently around them. Holding Eira's extended hand with his right one, he grasped Ellen's hand tightly with his left. "Brennig, take Ellen's hand! Hurry!"

Suddenly she understood. And just as suddenly, so did Brennig. She felt the light pressure of Brennig's hand close on hers. A surge of warm, splendid energy passed through her.

Energy of blood bonds, reaching across the river. Ancient family bonds, reaching across the perimeters of a time-weakened curse.

Energy of love bonds, stronger than any hate.

Holding tight to Eira's hand and also to Ellen's, Brent yelled out, "Nesta! Your hate is no match for blood alliance! Drown your damned curse! We no longer acknowledge your power!"

Ellen whispered to the now-whimpering water. "Brennig and Eira are united through us. You've lost, Nesta...."

The river twitched and shivered, and the currents died.

Her joy choking out on a sob, Ellen breathed, "Brennig, Eira *has* been waiting for you!"

Brennig didn't loosen his hold, but moved with them effortlessly through the water to the shore. She wondered why he couldn't just rise up out of the water, but he evidently couldn't until they were out of the river and standing in the reedy shallows... on the soil of England.

Panting, Brent pulled Ellen close. Brennig stood next to them, his strange eyes shining with a light that looked like tears—eyes turned toward Eira.

But he couldn't release Ellen's hand without the farewell she deserved. He whispered, "Forgive me... I was mistaken. I might have..." His voice faded as the shimmering ghost floated in front of him. Hurriedly, distractedly, he muttered, "Thank you, Ellen. Thank you for your love...." He wasn't looking in her direction as he said this last goodbye, but she could feel his touch, like cobwebs, brushing against her face as he moved toward the gentle, white-clad spirit with flowing yellow hair.

Eira held out her arms. The moment they embraced, the river shuddered a terrible sigh of death. A ray of sunshine pierced the fog.

Brennig's human form gradually fell away as he and Eira began to walk hand in hand into the mysterious mist. When Ellen and Brent could no longer see Brennig, the form of Eira remained for some seconds before she, too, vanished.

Ellen felt her body leaning into Brent's for support. Breathing hard, they slid down onto the grassy shore, shivering, but strangely warmed by new sunshine cutting through the mist.

Had it all been a dream?

She turned to the man she loved. "Brent, you called Eira by name and reached for her!"

He held her tightly. "You nearly drowned! It was all I could do to hang on to you! Why on earth did you jump into the river, knowing how dangerous it was?"

"Because," she answered, feeling his heart beating against her chest, feeling the rise and fall of each living breath he took, "Nesta and Brennig were trying to kill you."

"You intended to save my life by sacrificing your own!"

"Yes." She hugged him tighter. "I guess that proves how much I love you, doesn't it?" I wasn't willing to die for Brennig, she thought. But to save Brent, I would have.

He nodded wistfully. "It proves how much you love me, all right. I think more than you knew yourself, until now."

"And you—you saved *my* life." She drew slightly away and looked up at him. "And you knew how to break Nesta's curse! How? You haven't answered me, Brent. How did you know?"

"I can't tell you, exactly. I think Eira was communicating with us, because you knew, too. Didn't you feel the incredible energy that flowed from Eira to Brennig, through us?"

"Yes, I felt it. But, Brent, when Eira appeared you called her name. Yet you couldn't have known her."

"I knew," he said, and smiled, "because I had met her."

"What?" For a split second Brent was a stranger and nothing in the world made sense. Eira had reached for him...knew him. *How?*

They sat on the riverbank, dripping wet and alone. Her voice squeaked, "Met Eira? What do you mean you'd *met* her?"

Brent brushed wet hair from his eyes and looked at her tenderly. "Yesterday, when I was at home working on my computer, I saw a strange reflection in the screen, as if someone were standing behind me, blocking the light from the window. When I turned around, no one was there at first, and then slowly the form and face of a woman appeared. You know me, Ellen, I don't believe in ghosts, but I hadn't been drinking and I wasn't sleepy, and I just knew that a ghost was standing in the room with me. She looked filmy, I could almost see through her, although I could see the facial features plainly. Except the eyes. Her eyes were clear."

As he talked, his arm went around Ellen, guiding her away from the spot on the shore where Brennig and Eira had disappeared.

Dazed, Ellen walked beside him, shivering and anxious to get back to the cottage and a fire and dry clothes, but far more anxious to hear the rest of this astounding account. *Eira had appeared in Tucson? She had found Brent?* "What...what did you do?"

"What *could* I do? I asked her why she was there, what she wanted."

They hurried over the bridge. The water below was calm, the river ran sweetly. Swans were swimming through the lifting fog as though nothing unusual had happened. Brent picked up his suitcase from the Wales side flagstone landing.

"What *did* she want?" Ellen asked anxiously.

"To tell me you needed me at once."

"Me?"

Brent nodded. "She said her name was Eira. 'I am not Ellen,' she said, which scared me. Her voice was deep and whispery, and then she repeated her name. She said I needed to go to you in Wrenn's Oak without delay because something was wrong. I tried to get more information, but that was all she would—or could—say. I was blown away, I don't mind telling you, Ellen. And scared something had happened to you. Hell, I never believed in ghosts. But I was looking at one, hearing one tell me that you were in trouble. I knew I'd better do as this apparition said and get over here. I was on the first flight I could get. Whatever the hell the thing was, her message was clear."

Ellen shook her head in wonder. "She knew Brennig had mistaken me for her because he wanted so desperately for me to be her. She wanted you to get me away from him."

They were passing the churchyard. With the fog thinning, the sun was shining on the old steeple and gleaming on the worn, damp stones. Ellen glanced at Brennig's grave—a lonely, cold stone, leaning with time, symbol of a man's life and untimely death. It looked so bleak, so forlorn. The stone had nothing anymore to do with Brennig Cole. He wouldn't come back again. At last his spirit was at peace.

Brent walked with his arm around Ellen as he allowed her to lead him toward Mrs. Jenkins's cottage. "Bizarre as it was, I knew it was an important message. I didn't know what to expect when I got here. Hon, I can't tell you how relieved I was to see you at the bridge."

"I was getting so scared. Scared of Brennig. Scared I'd lost you. The sight of you was the answer to my prayers."

"I saw how much fear was in your eyes when Brennig showed up. He was sinister as hell," Brent said seriously.

"Now I know why you didn't question my sanity when I told you Brennig was a ghost."

Brent grinned, only now showing signs of releasing the tension. "First the face in the water. Then a ghost wanting to fight me over you. With what you'd told me about a curse, I figured out what was going on after Eira appeared and I heard the way Brennig said her name."

"You figure things out in an awful hurry," she said.

"Eira was helping, I know. And there was no time to question the logic." He looked at her. "Thank God, you're all right. You *are* all right, aren't you, honey? You're shivering!"

"Post trauma jitters. Add the fact that we're both soaking wet."

They turned onto Pembroke Lane. Within minutes, they were in Afan House. Brent looked at her quizzically when he saw the overturned umbrella stand and dishes broken all over the floor.

"What happened here?"

"The ghost threw a tantrum because I wouldn't allow him to take me away with him."

His mouth dropped open. "*Take* you?"

"He wanted me to die to be with him because he thought I was his wife reincarnated."

"My God..." Brent raked his fingers through his wet hair and replied shakily, "Eira must have been terrified he would convince you."

"Terrified enough to go to you for help."

"You were in grave danger, Ellen."

"But it's over now. You're here and Brennig has found the love he came back for." She looked up at him and smiled. "Because of you."

"Because of *us*," he corrected.

In the parlor, Brent touched a match to a fire Brennig had already set up. The paper and logs took quickly, and moments later the flames were blazing. Ellen had promised on the walk to tell him Brennig's story, but the rest of it would come later, much later, and Brent was satisfied with that. Right now all that mattered was the fact they had survived a brush with death and the curse was broken, which meant they—like Eira and Brennig—could be together. They stood in front of the fire, feeling the warmth. Brent, holding her hand, said, "We've wasted too much time, Ellen, and spent too much time apart."

She nodded in agreement, heart soaring. "Just the sight of you today—when I wasn't sure you'd come..."

"I came because I love you," he said. "And now, for the first time, I know how much you love me."

"I do love you," she whispered. "Oh, how I love you!"

Their lips came together in a kiss Ellen would remember for as long as she lived; Brent's love burned like sweet fire on her lips.

"It's our time, my darling," he whispered. "For the rest of our lives, it's our time."

Our time... and far beyond that, she thought, for Brennig had taught her there are no earthly dimensions to deep and lasting love.

EPILOGUE

The slopes of the Santa Catalina Mountains shone pink in the Arizona sunset, the September evening holding heat from the day and carrying the scent of cactus flowers. Silhouettes of giant saguaros spread arms like sentinels over the tiny Chapel in the Desert. Ellen stood alone in the back room of the adobe chapel, adjusting her silver tiara in front of a full-length mirror. She wore an ice pink Mexican wedding dress, fitted in the bodice with a lace-tiered skirt. Just beyond the double doors, Brent waited.

Brent. The thought of his handsome face brought a smile to her lips and a flutter to her heart. "I'm the luckiest woman in the world," she said aloud to the pink-and-white image in the mirror.

One last adjustment to her hair. When she picked up her bouquet of white roses and turned toward the doorway, Ellen gasped. An apparition appeared suddenly, out of nowhere. It floated between her and the door.

"Eira!"

The image became clearer, so clear Ellen could see her features. Dressed in white, her blond hair flowing, Eira Cole carried a small bouquet of flowers—the same flowers Ellen had seen so often in Brennig's garden. They splashed so brightly against the white image as to shock the eyes.

She reeled. "Eira! I can't believe it!"

The ghost, smiling, drew nearer and reached out both hands to Ellen, offering the flowers.

"For me?"

Only a slight nod was her answer; the image began to fade. Trembling with excitement, Ellen dropped her roses onto a table and accepted the bright bouquet with a tearful smile. She sniffed them and closed her eyes, for she was holding the sweet scent of her memories of Wales and the garden Brennig Cole had tended so carefully for his wife.

"Thank you..." she muttered to a presence still lurking, but now unseen. "Thank you, Eira."

The flowers must be enchanted, she thought, for the moment she held them, Ellen felt a great surge of joy. Perhaps it was for Brennig and Eira, together at last. Perhaps it was for her and Brent, together forever.

Brent smiled and stepped out to meet Ellen as his bride moved down the narrow aisle. In those moments, she was unaware of the small group of family and friends who sat on the old wooden benches of the chapel. Her eyes were only for the man who waited for her, the man who was about to become her partner for life.

When the brief ceremony was over, they made their way down the aisle and out into the soft pink twilight. A crowd gathered around them. In the midst of laughter and good wishes, Ellen felt Brent squeeze her arm suddenly, tightly. She looked up at him, and he nodded in the direction of a tall palo verde tree.

There, among their guests, were Brennig and Eira. Of course he would be here, too!

The bride and groom exchanged secret glances. Ellen raised her arm and the flowers, in a small wave. Brent smiled and winked. Several guests, assuming the wave was for them, waved back. I won't toss this bouquet, she thought. Not a gift as special as this! With a wave in return, the images began to fade, and in moments, there was only the desert and the shadows of the evening where they had been standing.

Brent squeezed her hand tightly. She whispered, "They came to tell us something."

"I think they want us to know that love is forever."

Ellen nodded. "My darling, promise me we will never lose each other."

"I'll be beside you," he said, gazing at the shadows where their unexpected guests had disappeared. "I'll be beside you always."

* * * * *

He staked his claim…

HONOR BOUND

by
New York Times
Bestselling Author

previously published under the pseudonym Erin St. Claire

As Aislinn Andrews opened her mouth to scream, a hard
hand clamped over her face and she found herself face-
to-face with Lucas Greywolf, a lean, lethal-looking
Navajo and escaped convict who swore he wouldn't hurt
her— *if* she helped him.

Look for HONOR BOUND at your favorite
retail outlet this January.

Only from…

where passion lives. SBHB

Take 4 bestselling love stories FREE

Plus get a FREE surprise gift!

Special Limited-time Offer

Mail to Silhouette Reader Service™

3010 Walden Avenue
P.O. Box 1867
Buffalo, N.Y. 14269-1867

YES! Please send me 4 free Silhouette Shadows™ novels and my free surprise gift. Then send me 4 brand-new novels every other month, which I will receive months before they appear in bookstores. Bill me at the low price of $2.96 each plus applicable sales tax, if any.* That's the complete price and—compared to the cover prices of $3.50 each—quite a bargain! I understand that accepting the books and gift places me under no obligation ever to buy any books. I can always return a shipment and cancel at any time. Even if I never buy another book from Silhouette, the 4 free books and the surprise gift are mine to keep forever.

215 BPA AKZH

Name	(PLEASE PRINT)	
Address	Apt. No.	
City	State	Zip

This offer is limited to one order per household and not valid to present Silhouette Shadows™ subscribers.
*Terms and prices are subject to change without notice. Sales tax applicable in N.Y.
USHAD-93   ©1993 Harlequin Enterprises Limited

Relive the romance...
Harlequin and Silhouette
are proud to present

A program of collections of three complete novels by the most requested authors with the most requested themes. Be sure to look for one volume each month with three complete novels by top name authors.

In January:	**WESTERN LOVING**	Susan Fox
		JoAnn Ross
		Barbara Kaye

Loving a cowboy is easy—taming him isn't!

In February:	**LOVER, COME BACK!**	Diana Palmer
		Lisa Jackson
		Patricia Gardner Evans

It was over so long ago—yet now they're calling, "Lover, Come Back!"

In March:	**TEMPERATURE RISING**	JoAnn Ross
		Tess Gerritsen
		Jacqueline Diamond

Falling in love—just what the doctor ordered!

Available at your favorite retail outlet.

REQ-G3

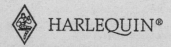

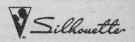

Share in the joys of finding happiness and exchanging the
ultimate gift—love—in full-length classic holiday
treasures by two bestselling authors

JOAN HOHL
EMILIE RICHARDS

Available in December at
your favorite retail outlet.

Only from  where passion lives.

**Silhouette Books
is proud to present
our best authors,
their best books . . .
and the best in
your reading pleasure!**

Throughout 1993, look for exciting
books by these top names in
contemporary romance:

DIANA PALMER—
The Australian in October

FERN MICHAELS—
Sea Gypsy in October

ELIZABETH LOWELL—
Chain Lightning in November

CATHERINE COULTER—
The Aristocrat in December

JOAN HOHL—
Texas Gold in December

LINDA HOWARD—
Tears of the Renegade in January '94

When it comes to passion,
we wrote the book.

BOBT3

**Fifty red-blooded, white-hot, true-blue hunks
from every State in the Union!**

Look for MEN MADE IN AMERICA! Written by some
of our most poplar authors, these stories feature fifty of
the strongest, sexiest men, each from a different state in
the union!

Two titles available every other month at your favorite
retail outlet.

In January, look for:

DREAM COME TRUE by Ann Major (Florida)
WAY OF THE WILLOW by Linda Shaw (Georgia)

In March, look for:

TANGLED LIES by Anne Stuart (Hawaii)
ROGUE'S VALLEY by Kathleen Creighton (Idaho)

You won't be able to resist MEN MADE IN AMERICA!

SILHOUETTE.... Where Passion Lives

Don't miss these Silhouette favorites by some of our most popular authors!
And now, you can receive a discount by ordering two or more titles!

Silhouette Desire®

#05751	THE MAN WITH THE MIDNIGHT EYES BJ James	$2.89	☐
#05763	THE COWBOY Cait London	$2.89	☐
#05774	TENNESSEE WALTZ Jackie Merritt	$2.89	☐
#05779	THE RANCHER AND THE RUNAWAY BRIDE Joan Johnston	$2.89	☐

Silhouette Intimate Moments®

#07417	WOLF AND THE ANGEL Kathleen Creighton	$3.29	☐
#07480	DIAMOND WILLOW Kathleen Eagle	$3.39	☐
#07486	MEMORIES OF LAURA Marilyn Pappano	$3.39	☐
#07493	QUINN EISLEY'S WAR Patricia Gardner Evans	$3.39	☐

Silhouette Shadows®

#27003	STRANGER IN THE MIST Lee Karr	$3.50	☐
#27007	FLASHBACK Terri Herrington	$3.50	☐
#27009	BREAK THE NIGHT Anne Stuart	$3.50	☐
#27012	DARK ENCHANTMENT Jane Toombs	$3.50	☐

Silhouette Special Edition®

#09754	THERE AND NOW Linda Lael Miller	$3.39	☐
#09770	FATHER: UNKNOWN Andrea Edwards	$3.39	☐
#09791	THE CAT THAT LIVED ON PARK AVENUE Tracy Sinclair	$3.39	☐
#09811	HE'S THE RICH BOY Lisa Jackson	$3.39	☐

Silhouette Romance®

#08893	LETTERS FROM HOME Toni Collins	$2.69	☐
#08915	NEW YEAR'S BABY Stella Bagwell	$2.69	☐
#08927	THE PURSUIT OF HAPPINESS Anne Peters	$2.69	☐
#08952	INSTANT FATHER Lucy Gordon	$2.75	☐

	AMOUNT	$ _____
DEDUCT:	**10% DISCOUNT FOR 2+ BOOKS**	$ _____
	POSTAGE & HANDLING	$ _____
	($1.00 for one book, 50¢ for each additional)	
	APPLICABLE TAXES*	$ _____
	TOTAL PAYABLE	$ _____
	(check or money order—please do not send cash)	

To order, complete this form and send it, along with a check or money order for the total above, payable to Silhouette Books, to: *In the U.S.*: 3010 Walden Avenue, P.O. Box 9077, Buffalo, NY 14269-9077; *In Canada*: P.O. Box 636, Fort Erie, Ontario, L2A 5X3.

Name: _____

Address:_____ City:_____

State/Prov.: _____ Zip/Postal Code:_____

*New York residents remit applicable sales taxes.
Canadian residents remit applicable GST and provincial taxes.

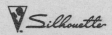